DAMAGED GOODS

Roland S. Jefferson

Distributed by:
Milligan Books
and imprint of Professional Business Consultants
1425 W. Manchester Blvd., Suite C
Los Angeles, California 90047
(323) 750-3592
(323) 750-2886 Fax

Book formatting by Chris Ebuehi/Graphic Options Los Angeles, CA

First Printing April 2003
10 9 8 7 6 5 4 3 2 1

ISBN # 1-881524-93-0

Publisher's note
This is a work of fiction. Names, characters, places, and incidents either are product of the author's imagination or are used fictitiously, and any resemblance to actual persons, living or dead, events or locales is entirely coincidental.

Dedication

For Pops—

Who turn them down on 'e' ...

ACKNOWLEDGMENTS

The author would like to thank Ms. Helen Bungert for her enthusiastic editorial input. Also Dr. Rosie Milligan for her continued support and encouragement over the years. A special note of thanks to Marc Gerald whose suggestions early in the manuscript's development proved invaluable in rounding out its definition and form.

PROLOGUE

Crane had planned the bank robbery for months. When he first saw Steve McQueen in the "Thomas Crown Affair" he was struck by the feasibility of it all. Five doors in. Five doors out. Smoke bombs to mask the action. Get-away car ready at the drop. Divide the loot in a cemetery. Instead of Switzerland, he'd fly to Rio with Marjorie and live like a king, dance in the streets at Carnival the way Orpheus and Eurydice did in "Black Orpheus." True, it was just a movie. But in Crane's mind, the story was real, authentic with possibility, and something inside his brain clicked, the way new spark plugs bring a dead engine to life. So he set about a slow methodical search of the L.A. basin for a bank where life could imitate art.

Nothing worked in L.A., but he found a small savings and loan in the all–white enclave of Calabasas in the west end of the valley. Middle of nowhere, as far as black folks were concerned, but freeway-close. It doesn't have five doors, but it has three—three will work. On the corner of a busy intersection with an entrance facing each one and a third one in the unguarded parking lot. He cases it for months. Photographs it. Videotapes it. Builds a perfect balsa wood model complete with tin doors and cellophane windows. Knows how many employees, their schedules, their days off, how many times they go to the bathroom, and what time they break for lunch. What company has the security contract, how often they rotate, when each takes lunch, where they eat, only one guard at a time inside.

Crane knows where the police station is. How many cops. How many cars. Knows their cruise schedules and routes, how long it would take one to get to the bank on a sunny day. Just under a minute if they were in the vicinity. Four if they were at the city line. He knows this from calling in a phony tip about a robbery in progress. Crane drives the city streets of Calabasas day and night until he knows every conceivable escape route. Attends funeral services of unknown people at every cemetery within ten miles of the city in every direction.

Silas is the muscle. Crane's dog since a childhood of streets, juvenile halls and city jails. They'd had each other's backs for as long as each could remember. Silas is a slim, muscular, rat-faced man with skin still blemished from childhood eczema. Beady eyes that didn't trust white folks or the police, and a sixth sense about danger that kept him alive on many occasions when he should've been dead. Crane wouldn't dare go into this operation if Silas said otherwise. But Silas likes it. He had always thought Crane was a little 'crazy,' said this Calabasas bank deal just confirmed it. Still, he likes it. Says he's in.

Henry T is the driver. Tall and fair-skinned with a crop of reddish brown hair he combs back in a Don King style. Crane never knew the source of Henry T's nickname. Neither did Henry T. But he likes to steal cars, tear them down, rebuild them, sell them, steal them again. Henry T can build an engine from scratch blindfolded, stick it in a bucket and challenge street racers all over L.A. He loves drag racing and young girls … too young, Crane thought.

Marcus, BoBo and Reese are the bagmen. Marcus is big and solid like a lineman for the L.A. Raiders. Coal black in color, he has African features of which he is justifiably proud. Crane often wondered why Marcus didn't stay in school and try for a football scholarship. Marcus said school didn't hold anything for him. They never taught him to read. So he became a strong-arm man. In and out of jail for robberies since his teens. Crane's Calabasas bank job is just another robbery as far as Marcus is concerned. And that's all right with Crane because he knows Marcus is reliable once he commits himself.

Bo Bo is the thief of the group. The booster. He can steal the watch off your wrist and you'd never know it, he's so smooth. Short, dark and with long thin arms that don't seem to fit the body on which they're attached. He was nicknamed Bo Bo as a child by a circus clown who resembled him. Bo Bo likes to drink ... too much, Crane thought. Still, Crane knows he can count on Bo Bo once he gives his word.

Reese is the con man of the group. They call him Pretty Boy because he has a sort of Denzel Washington profile, a flair for clothes and a meticulous obsession with his relatively good looks that draws women to him like flies to rotten meat. And he knows how to use his looks to live off women, to romance them, drain them dry of cash and move on to the next one. An all-around hustler, he'll lie, steal, cheat his own mother if he thinks it'll bring him a buck. And for this job Reese is perfect.

Worried the guard might be a little too curious about four black men in a bank in Calabasas, Marjorie is added at the last minute as a diversion. Tall, jet black and statuesque with firm thighs, well-defined calves and an enormous chest all her own, Marjorie should be the ideal diversion. But she's not. She's a basehead. She's gorgeous to look at but that's as far as it goes. The team wanted someone else. But she was Crane's girl and he'd let his pussy-whipped mentality override good judgement. Big mistake.

January. Thursday. Raining. Tom Bradley is Mayor. Police chief

Darryl Gates chasing black folks all over L.A. like the great white hunter on safari in Africa. "Sex, Lies and Videotape" is still playing in the theaters, and "F' The Police" by NWA is headed platinum. The men all wearing three-piece suits, wigs and false moustaches. Crane is in the vault on the pretext of checking his safety deposit box. Marcus at New Accounts. Bo Bo applying for a loan. Reese standing at the desk, fumbling with deposit slips. Silas in line. Marjorie is a knockout in a see-through raincoat, short tight skirt, blouse showing lots of cleavage, and a wig of Shirley Temple curls. She's entertaining the fat white guard with stupid questions like what time the bank closes for lunch ... dropping things from her purse on the floor and getting lots of help from the guard and other men standing in line. Everyone's waiting for the smoke bombs to go off. Everything going like a charm until the guard starts walking toward the desk.

Marjorie is strung out, paranoid, thinks the guard is onto them. She suddenly flips out, jumping on his back, knocking him down, struggling for his gun. Teller hits the security button before the smoke bombs go off. Nobody moves for ten seconds, waiting for them to explode. Cops and helicopter on their way. Four minutes suddenly become two ... maybe less. Silas handles the patrons, puts them on the floor. Children laugh and giggle, think it's a game. Some women scream, start to cry. A man pees in his pants. Everybody goes over the counter, grabs what cash they can, runs for the station wagon. Marjorie still struggling with the guard, his gun firing wildly in the air, somehow shoots himself in the thigh, drops the gun but manages to hold onto Marjorie. Crane rushes to her rescue, frees her, but the guard grabs Crane, pulls his weight on top. Only thing that saves them is the rain. Cop car collides with a truck on the way, delays them by a minute. Marjorie makes the get-a-way car in a dead run, the station wagon turning into the rain-slickened street at normal speed just as cops pass them coming the other way. In the end, it was the rehearsals and Crane's constant military-like discipline that saved them. It was close, but he gets them all out. Unidentified.

Crane isn't so lucky.

The surveillance camera shows lots of smoke but no faces. They get away with only forty-eight grand. State case will only be seven to ten but the Feds want it because of the elaborate scheme, thoroughness of the planning, wounding of the guard. No bail for bank robbers. Crane sits in County jail two years while they decide. Watches Rodney King make history, L.A. burn like Kuwaiti oil fires.

At his trial, prosecutors dub Crane the "Motion Picture Bank Robber," show the jury clips from "The Thomas Crown Affair," the meticulous hand-crafted balsa wood model. They offer him a deal to plea down if he'll name his accomplices. Crane refuses, gets twenty-five years to life on "Special Circumstances" because the guard shot himself. No credit for time served.

The press brands the guard a hero. He gets a book deal and takes a meeting at Paramount.

First six months are the hardest for Crane. After that, time doesn't matter.

Twenty-five years to life.

TEN YEARS LATER ...

Chapter 1

I T ALL STARTED AFTER DINNER FOR THE THIRD-TIER CONS. He'd settled
in the rec room to watch Training Day starring Denzel Washington.
There were mostly blacks and a few Mexicans in the audience. The
film didn't appeal to many white cons. Talbot Needham, a big, burly
white guard with flat feet, premature gray hair and rotten teeth tapped
Crane on the shoulder with his baton just as the lights dimmed, motioned
with his finger for him to follow.

"Warden wants to see you, Crane," he said when they were on the
ramp and motioned for Crane to hold out his hand and right foot.

Crane asked, "What's Warden Moffett want with me?" He held up his right foot for chains. Needham snapped shackles on first one foot then the other. "What the hell I do, Needham?"

"You know better than to ask that, Crane. You been here a while. If the warden wants to see you, he wants to see you. Move." Needham placed his baton between Crane's shoulders, pushed him forward against the weighted inertia of noisy chains.

They walked the length of third-tier, entered the atrium, walked down three flights of stairs and out across the yard to the administration building. Once admitted, they climbed two flights of green steel spiral stairs that opened to a long wood-paneled corridor. A slow five minute walk brought them to the warden's office. The massive teak door was flanked by two white guards Crane didn't know. The tall one ... young, crewcut hair, polished shoes and Marine Corps discipline, patted him down. The short one ... older, heavier, experienced, G. Gordon Liddy square jaw and deepset malicious eyes, knocked on the door three times. A deep booming voice Crane recognized as Moffett thundered permission to enter and when they did, it was into an office whose atmosphere was saturated with corruption.

Cranford Moffett had been warden of Marion Federal Penitentiary for as long as Crane had been an inmate. And before that he had run Leavenworth and a host of others. In his late fifties, tall and powerfully built, his deep resonating baritone voice had earned him the nickname of 'The Speaker' among prison inmates.

Flanked on either side of a massive mahogany desk by two more white guards whose corrupt faces paled in comparison to the warden's and who could have been Olympic wrestlers, Moffett motioned for Crane to sit down next to three other inmates similarly shackled. Surprised by their presence, Crane shuffled to an empty seat, chains rattling.

Collectively known as the 'Committee,' these men headed up the three gangs that ran the prisons of America.

A white boy in his thirties with a massive upper torso that supported a neck wider than his skull, P.J. was head of the Aryan Brotherhood. He hated anything that wasn't white. Underneath his uniform Crane had seen the massive tattoo across his chest that said WHITE POWER along with the Nazi insignia. A skinhead, his shaved, pale skull also sported tattoos of hatred.

Jimmy 'José' Garcia was head of Marion's Mexican Mafia. A small, slightly built man in his fifties, his jet-black hair was pulled back into a long ponytail that hung to his waist. He too carried authority in numerous tattoos under his uniform, the largest one reading LA FAMILIA, numerous smaller ones on his arms and neck, and a teardrop tattoo below his left eye.

The black inmate was Lee 'The Bear' Douglas and ran the Black Gorilla Family. A large man with a massive tattoo of a black bear on both chest and back, Bear fronted a gold tooth over his incisor, while a diamond-studded earring pierced his right lobe. His head was shaved bald. Younger than the others by at least a decade, Bear had made Crane his dog shortly after his arrival at Marion.

A guard stood behind each of the chairs, and as Crane reached his, Needham took up his position. Knowing the protocol required, he accorded each inmate respect before acknowledging the warden, but slapping Bear's hand to show where his allegiance lay. When he finally looked over to the warden, Moffett said, "Glad you could join us, Crane."

Crane asked, "What am I supposed to have done?" still suspicious.

"Nothing, dog," Bear said. "Speaker got a proposition for you."

"Warden Moffett, Douglas," said Needham, threatening.

Bear turned around, looked silently at Needham with raised eyebrows of contempt.

"A proposition? What kind of proposition? What's this all about, anyway?"

"We have a problem, Crane," Moffett began, "and we think you might be able to help us. We need," he said cautiously, "to get our hands on something that will benefit everyone." He sat back in his chair, eyes taking in the entire room. "It belongs," he went on, gray eyes moving across the faces of the gang members in turn, taking them in, "to these gentlemen here AND to me."

Thinking he was being accused of theft, Crane blurted out defensively, "I haven't taken nothin' from them or you," and his eyes, still suspicious, now fearful, darted from the faces of the convicts to Moffett. He started to stand but the powerful meaty hand of Needham slammed down on his left shoulder, pushed him back in his seat, chains rattling.

"Nigga," said Bear impatiently, "ain't nobody said you did. What? You got a guilty conscience or somethin'?"

"I'm just saying I ain't ripped nobody off. That's all."

"We know that, you muthafucka," said P.J. "Why don't you do us all a favor and shut the fuck up and let him finish?"

"As I was saying, Crane," Warden Moffett went on, "we need some way to get our hands on this item and figure you just might be the one who could help us do that." The warden looked Crane levelly in the eyes, drawing him in.

"Well," said Crane, "what is it?"

"A trunk," said Bear. "A big-ass muthafuckin' trunk—like the kind you seen on the Titanic. 'Member them old-time steamer-type trunks they showed them rich white folks loadin' up?" Crane remembered the movie

… remembered every Titanic movie Hollywood made. He shook his head.

Crane said, "Steamer trunk. Alright. What's in it?"

"That's not important, homes," said José softly behind steely black eyes, lilting latin accent. "Not for you. We just need you to get it for us. That's all."

"Alright," said Crane, confused. "*Where* is it?"

"Here," said Moffett, sitting up, handing Crane a photograph across the wide expanse of the desk. Crane looked at the photograph and laughed, but stopped when he noticed the others were silent. He looked at the photograph again.

"It's in this building, you say?" he asked, still fishing.

Warden Moffett leaned across the top of his desk and with a long steel ruler pointed to a spot on the photograph. "In a room on the top floor. That's where it is."

"And this building is where?"

"Los Angeles," said the warden.

"What do you want from me?"

P.J. was restless. Impatient. "Jesus, Crane. We gotta spell shit out for you? We need you to tell us how to get the trunk from point A there," and he pointed to the photograph with his fingers from across the space, "to point B here!" and he slammed both hands on the armrests of his seat, chains rattling.

"Well, who's got it now?" Crane asked.

"*We've* got it, you dumb muthafucka," cried P.J. "At least our people have it."

Crane said, "I don't understand. Just have them bring it here, why don't you? Seems simple enough."

"But it's not," said Moffett. "The building is under surveillance.

DOJ has been on the trunk since it arrived."

The fog was beginning to clear. Department of Justice. A trunk full of drugs. Crooked inmates. Crooked warden. Crooked guards.

"I see," said Crane. "You want me to devise some kind of plan your people can use to get the trunk out the building without the Feds knowing. Right?"

P.J. slumped in his chair, long thick arms dangling between his legs, chains scraping the floor. "Finally," he said.

Crane bristled. He said to P.J., "Well, if you'd said that in the beginning instead of all this double talk ..."

"Fuck you, nigga," P.J. said.

"No, fuck you, you punk-ass faggot white boy!" Crane snapped. He tried to stand but Needham shoved him down hard, his chains rattling in his lap. "I'll tell you who you can fuck. You can fuck your mama first. And then your sista and ..."

"Shut up. Both of you," Moffett boomed loudly, his voice deafening, filling the room. "We're here for mutual interests. Let's remember that." He looked at Crane. "We had to be sure, Crane. You can understand that. Right?" he said, voice returning to its normal but still slightly thunderous pitch.

"We don't usually bring cons in on Committee business, dog," Bear said.

"Why me?" Crane asked, still fingering the photograph, eyes spitting hostile glances at P.J.

"Because you the famous bank robber, homes," José said, genuine admiration behind the words. "You're a legend. Your shit is poetry in motion. If the girl hadn't broke, even you would've got out of dodge. You got a bad break. But it was beautiful to watch, homes. Smooth, like in the movies."

Crane stifled the urge to smile, thought of The Thomas Crown Affair.

It took great effort for Crane to conceal his pride. He kept his eyes on the photograph until the moment passed, then looked up at Moffett. "I guess I can give you a couple of ideas to pass on to your people in L.A." he said, placing the photo on the desk.

The room exploded in laughter. Guards. Moffett. Gang leaders.

"The dumb shit still doesn't understand," grunted P.J. bending over, head hanging down as if straining on a toilet.

"Just a couple of ideas, homes?" José managed to say, laughing softly with the others.

"Yeah," said Crane, not reading behind the humor. "A couple of ideas. What more do you want? L.A. is two thousand miles away and I'm here twenty-five to life."

Moffett's laughter stopped as abruptly as it had begun. "That could be changed," he said as the laughter died.

Crane wasn't sure he'd heard Moffett correctly. He said, "What did you say, Mister Moffett?"

"I said it could be changed," the warden repeated.

"That's the proposition, dog," said Bear, bringing manacled hands to Crane's shoulder. "Warden gonna spring you from here. Send you to L.A. to get our shit."

"Go to L.A.? Serious?"

"As a heart attack, homes."

Crane was in shock. He looked at Moffett as if seeing him for the first time.

"You figure out a way to get our trunk from under the noses of the

Feds, your twenty-five to life is history," Moffett declared from across the desk. "No DOJ record. No Federal Bureau of Prison record. Nothing. Nada. Everything about Alonzo Crane is deleted from DOJ's computer. You'll be a free man, Crane. Probably have to change your name. Get a new social security number. New identity and all. Can't see that being a problem for you."

"You down for this, dog?" asked Bear, envious.

"The fuck you think!" Crane said, "But let me make sure I understand what Mister Moffett is saying. If I can come up with a plan to get your trunk and deliver it here—?"

"Not here, Crane," the warden interrupted quickly. "You won't deliver it here. Pick a safe place. Our people will take it from there."

"Alright," said Crane. "And if I do that you'll fix it so I won't do anymore time? Have I heard you correctly?"

Warden Moffett leaned heavily back in his chair, crossed his legs. "You have," he said. "Of course, if you don't want to do this," Moffett went on, "then no hard feelings." Suddenly Moffett sat up and leaned back across the desk, eyes burning into Crane's, "And this meeting never took place. Understand?"

"It's a new chance at life, homes," said José, looking at the warden but speaking to Crane. "A chance to be free. And how often does that happen to someone here? You'd better take it while you can, homes."

What Crane understood was no hard feelings meant he wouldn't live another twenty-four hours. He knew what happened to inmates who refused the Committee. Not even his friendship with Bear could protect him. More importantly, he had always benefited from providence—when he recognized it. No one with another fifteen years in prison would refuse an offer of freedom regardless of the danger. And since it would be his plan, he felt he could control the danger to a large degree. Still, something about the offer troubled him.

"What guarantee do I have you won't change your mind when it's all over?" he asked, addressing himself more to Moffett than the others. "How do I know you'll keep your word—won't roll over on me, play me for a chump?"

P.J. said, "Warden Moffett doesn't want a prison riot on his hands, Crane. Especially one that starts in his joint and spreads across the country. Which is exactly what'll happen if he rolls over on you. Isn't that right, Mister Moffett?" P.J. was anything but subtle with his threat.

Moffett yawned. "Who wants that?" he said, agreeing.

"And, homes," José added, leaning forward to look around Bear and catch Crane's eyes, "If you're thinking of running out on us—don't! There's no place in America you can hide. Nowhere in the world you can go we won't find you. Remember that. For the moment, your freedom is ours to give—or take away. You remember that, homes. This is not a game."

Crane said, "I'm no fool," gratitude and reproof in his voice. "I'll hold up my end."

"That's why we chose you, homes. Because you're smart. And you're no fool."

"Word," said Bear, touching manacled fists with José.

"Alright then," Crane said, picking up the photograph, studying it once again. "I'll need some time to work things out. A week. Maybe two. How long will the trunk be there?"

Bear said, "Until you come for it, bro." Crane nodded, satisfied.

Crane said, "I'll need more pictures. Maps. Anything else you can get on the building will help."

Warden Moffett pushed himself back from the desk, opened a drawer, withdrew a large brown envelope and handed it to Crane. "We anticipated that," he said smiling, gray eyes pleased with himself.

Crane took the envelope, leafed through its contents without removing them, sealed it back up. "Good," he said. "Now. I'll need some front money. About ten grand should do."

"What for, dog?" Bear asked.

"Planning. Equipment. Supplies. I'll need to pull a team together. Six. Maybe seven men. That costs money."

"You could use some of our people," P.J. suggested. "Save money."

"Thanks but no thanks," Crane said, shaking his head. "I choose my own team. It's not negotiable." The balance of power had shifted in Crane's favor. He was taking control now.

Bear said, "Everything's negotiable, bro."

"Not this."

"You been here ten years," said P.J., "How you gonna pull any team together?"

"People owe me."

"*IF* they're still around. What do you do if they're not?" José wanted to know.

"Like Scarlet O'Hara in *Gone With The Wind*, I'll worry about that tomorrow."

"You'll worry about it today, Crane," Moffett thundered across the desk. "We'll arrange a place for you to stay in L.A. and a contact man," Moffett went on, scribbling on a yellow pad. "The money will be there before you."

"When can we see your plan?" P.J. wanted to know.

"You don't," Crane said, growing bolder.

"Muthafuck if we don't," cried P.J. "You think we just gonna let you take chances with our shit and not know what you up to? In your dreams, muthafucka!"

Crane said, "That's how I work."

"Not this time," P.J. said, agitated, trying to stand, being pushed back down by his guard, chains rattling in his lap.

Crane tossed the envelope back at Moffett, sat back in his seat, relaxed.

"Fine," he said. "Get someone else. I go tell you the plan … may as well put it on *CNN* … start selling tickets. I don't work that way. You said I was poetry," and Crane turned to look at José. "If you believe that, it was because of good planning. I never let my right hand know what the left is doing until the last possible minute. I don't intend to change that. So if I can't do it my way, you get someone else. I'm out," said Crane, playing poker, bluffing.

José was silent. He looked at Crane for a long time, studying his face for truth. He brought his manacled hands first to P.J.'s shoulder, then to Bear's. "We have a lot to lose, homes, if you fail."

Crane said, "And if I fail, what? I come back to the joint? Lose my freedom?"

José said, "Maybe your life, homes. I can green-light you in less than a second."

Crane turned to Moffett. "So that's the way it is? No margin for error. That what you're telling me, Mister Moffett?"

The gray eyes blinked hard before the booming voice escaped. "Failure," he said, "has never been in my vocabulary, Crane."

Crane now understood fully. The offer was conditioned on success only.

"Then you'd better let me do it my way if that's the case. 'Cause for what you want I'm the closest thing to a guarantee you'll ever get."

The room was silent for what seemed like a long time. Each looked at the other, weighing the odds. Finally José nodded to Moffett. It was barely perceptible, but Moffett saw it and took his cue. He picked up the envelope and handed it back across the desk to Crane.

"Alright, Crane," he said reluctantly, "your way. I hope for all our sakes, but especially yours, Crane, that what you come up with will deliver the goods."

Crane didn't smile. He wanted to. But now was not the time. He would smile when he was really free. He studied the envelope. A long forgotten movie popped in his head, followed by a second. Soon there were others, a myriad of heist films that spanned a century began flooding his brain. And then it suddenly came to him, the entire plan. Beginning to end and he knew then he could pull it off and he knew how.

"Mister Moffett," he said, relishing control again, "I'll get your trunk for you. Trust me. The Feds'll never see it coming. Because what I have in mind," and with this he began to laugh, more to himself than the others, "you only see in the movies."

Chapter 2

A N UNSEASONABLE SEPTEMBER FOG had stolen across the sweltering L.A. basin and settled for a day-long stay in the hills just below the Hollywood sign, temporarily shielding the eyesore of cheap unpainted duplexes and chipped graffiti-marred two-story stucco apartment houses that lined the decaying back streets of a Hollywood long gone. On Whitley Avenue, just north of Hollywood Boulevard, a five-story transient hotel, the Royalty—converted from its grandeur days during Hollywood's golden age—dominated the street. Now serving as a beacon for the dispossessed, it was a crowded ant colony housing an ethnic assortment of addicts, prostitutes, runaways, dope dealers, thieves, gangbangers, parolees and other lowlifes. Two of them lived on the fourth floor in a cramped single facing the alley. Loud music signaled they were home.

The soft hissing of the shower was barely audible over the desperate wailing of Nirvana on the boombox. A girl sat naked, on a bed whose size turned the dusty room into a matchbox. Her back curved slightly to support a head covered with a forest of wild blonde hair. Her attractive face was a web of freckles that trapped a pair of soft blue eyes, slightly crooked nose sporting a gold ring in the left nostril and a mouth whose full, pouty lips, when not smiling, guarded a fortress of perfectly straight teeth and an experienced tongue with a gold stud in the center. Firm, sexy legs crossed over and under one another as they balanced a lap tray covered with ever-decreasing lines of cocaine disappearing into the 7-Eleven straw married to her nose. Well-conditioned and muscled, the smooth inside of her right thigh bore a tattoo that read ENTER HERE with a long arrow creeping up to and stopping just short of her neatly manicured crotch. Large pink ring-pierced nipples dominated the tight, rounded contours of melon-sized breasts that moved with every short, jerky rhythm of her breathing. SUCK HARD was tattooed on her left breast and fed a short arrow that pointed to her nipple. Through her navel protruded a gold stud on the end of which was attached a large–faceted Zirconium that matched the six smaller ones decorating the rim of her right ear.

The shower stopped. A tall, strikingly dark, well developed black man strode into the room behind frantic movements of a towel over limbs still dripping wet. His color was that of coal. Nose broad and crooked as if he'd been in one too many fights. His mouth was not unduly large, but the scar that crossed and distorted his lower lip gave him the appearance of a perpetual smile. His head was small and pointed but the massive crown of Rasta braids gave the impression it was larger and he much older than his twenty-eight years of hard living.

He hammered a tight black fist onto the switch of the boombox, plunging the room into a silence that matched the approaching twilight. Trixie looked up, jerked her head in his direction. Stuporous slow–motion eyes caught up, squinted, bringing him into focus. "Cut that shit off," he snapped. "Muthafucka's dead. You play the same shit over and over and over again twenty-four-seven. Play Snoop, or Busta Rhymes or Jay-Z if you in a funk bag. But not that Nirvana shit. Fuck that."

"Nirvana is life, Duffy."

"You mean death, Trixie. Can you understand dead, like six feet below where we livin'?"

"Nirvana is God."

"Nirvana is a dead white boy. A dead, wacked–out white boy who couldn't hang in his own world. He ain't no God."

"Nirvana is life itself," she said, seeming not to hear him.

"Maybe to cokeheads like you and all them other wacked–out white boys. He don't mean shit to niggas."

"Stop calling me a cokehead, Duffy. I just use it now and then for special occasions like today."

Duffy said, "Alright, so you're a special occasion cokehead. What're you celebrating today?"

Trixie said, "My birthday. I'm twenty-one."

Duffy's expression told her he'd forgotten. He winced.

"No shit. Happy birthday baby." He leaned over, kissed her lightly on the cheek, apologizing.

Trixie said, "You didn't remember?" She couldn't believe he'd forgotten, wondered just how much she really meant to him. "Said you'd get me a card and take me some place special."

Duffy straightened, shook his braids violently, splashing out remnants of water. "I'm sorry, baby," he said. "Had a lot on my mind this week what with Crane gettin' out and all the runnin' around I had to do for him."

"You didn't even fuck me last night," she went on, face of freckles twisted in genuine hurt. "You could've at least fucked me, Duffy. That would've been something." Trixie pushed the tray to the side, lay back on the bed, legs open, inviting.

Duffy tried to look away. "Haven't got time for this right now, Trixie. We gotta meet his train at ten."

"Then make time, Duffy. It's my birthday. Fuck me." She moved her legs back and forth, the studded tongue wetting pouty lips, her slow–moving eyelids speaking silently.

Duffy's resistance nearly faltered. He said, "Crane is business, Trixie. Money. Lots of Benjamins. I'm not gonna blow it. Not behind pussy!"

"*I'm* your business, Duffy. I bring in money, so you take care of me like you would any business investment."

Business investment. She had been at first. Nothing more. Just another white girl he picked up in a Payless Shoe Store looking for a place to stay and a daddy. It was easy to pimp her the same as it was Camilla and Laquita. But something happened between he and Trixie that didn't happen with the others. It wasn't the pussy. He couldn't really say it was because she was white—he'd had white girls long before Trixie. And it wasn't her looks although she was certainly a knockout. He couldn't real-ly explain it and it bothered him that he couldn't. Her loyalty maybe. He really didn't know. But he was strung out behind Trixie the way she was strung out behind cocaine. His nose was so wide open for her a Mack truck would fit inside. He denied it to others, of course. He wouldn't dare let his homies know he was actually strung out behind one of his whores. They'd laugh him off Crenshaw. Him, Duffy the player ... got his nose open behind one of his whores? Naw, not Duffy. But it was true. God, how it was true.

"Yeah, you bring in money," he heard himself saying. "But not the kind of bank he's talking about. He's gonna make us rich, baby. I'm talking Michael Jordan rich. I mean we gettin' ready to blow up bigtime. Understand?"

Again Trixie seemed not to hear. Her legs continued to move, demanding attention. She said, "It's my birthday and I want you to fuck me."

"Trixie—"

"My birthday, Duffy—"

Duffy's eyes caught the flash of the Zirconium and the slow subtle movements of her limbs. He knew there were times he couldn't resist her. But this shouldn't be one of them. Not now. Crane was more important. Still—God, she was so beautiful, the way she looked at him, her powder-blue eyes flashing, full lips so inviting. Damn, he hated giving in to her like this. He just hated it. But he knew he would.

He didn't notice the towel fall from his fingers. Was hardly aware of his moving toward her, on top of her, his tongue caressing the stud in hers, hands massaging her breasts. His teeth jerking first one nipple then the other, sending soft tight screams of painful pleasure into his ear. His tongue caressing the naval Zirconium, then finding the sweet moistness between her legs where it probed until she begged him inside. Trixie was a crescendo of screams as he found his rhythm, her legs wrapped around his waist, heels drumming his butt like a rider spurring a horse to gallop. When she felt him stiffen, knew he was about to come, she thrust herself violently up, forcing him even deeper inside as her legs locked around him, preventing escape.

"MOTHERFUCKER!" she screamed as her moment joined his in the paralysis of rapture that consumed them, their breathing deep and rapid, bodies drenched in sweat.

When it was over they lay together a long time in silence, her leg between his, fingers stroking his chest, lips nibbling his ear in gratitude. Duffy nodded when she said, "Thank you."

Duffy said, "Happy birthday."

Finally he opened his eyes, seeing curled flecks of dead paint hanging from the ceiling. He reached over, fingered his Rolex.

"Time to go, baby." He sat up, pulled her up beside him. "Birthday party's over."

"Tell me about Crane," Trixie asked when they had showered and were drying. Duffy brought the towel to his waist, fastened it tightly and pulled out clothes from the lone battered chest of drawers that supported an aging black and white TV with a clothes hanger antenna.

"Met him in the joint when I caught my last case," he said, not looking at her.

Trixie said, "Where was that?"

Duffy said, "Marion. Federal joint in Illinois. Did three years there before they transferred me out here to Lompoc my last six months. Crane's a genius. I idolize the nigga. Everybody knows he does."

Trixie said, "You idolize a con?"

"Like I said, Crane's a genius. Smart nigga from the old school. I learned a lot from him."

"Smart? The motherfucker wound up in the joint. What does that tell you?"

"You wouldn't understand," Duffy said. "Crane said he got a plan gonna make us rich. Michael Jackson rich. Know what I'm sayin'?"

Trixie said, "Yeah, right. What was he in for?"

Duffy said, "Bank robbery. He caught twenty-five years to life."

"Twenty five years? He must be old as dirt?"

"Not really. He only did a dime."

Trixie said, "Ten years? He caught a federal case for bank robbery and just did a dime? No way. With the Feds you have to do ninety percent of your time. The man would have to do twenty-two-and-a-half before they'd even look at him. How'd he get away with only ten years?"

Duffy didn't know and said so. But he'd asked Crane the same question when he'd first got word he was getting out and wanted to hook up with him. Crane had told him his conviction got overturned on a technicality.

"Cool," said Trixie, slipping on Guess jean cutoffs. "But why business with a con?" she asked, betraying concern.

"I told you—'cause he's smart. That's why. Let's face it—nigga got hisself out of a twenty-five year stretch. That's a hell of a lot smarter than the niggas still there. Why not him? Shit!" Duffy put on tan Tommy Hilfiger pants, a green Tommy Hilfiger T-shirt and a pair of brown polished Florsheim pull-ons. He fastened a one-inch gold-link chain around his neck and slipped a matching gold bracelet over his right wrist.

Trixie said, "Alright. So what's this Crane got planned? He gonna sucker you into another bank robbery or something like that?" Displeasure for Crane was already growing by the moment.

Duffy said, "Ain't no bank robbery, Trixie. And if it was, I wouldn't be down for nothin' like that. I'm taking penitentiary chances as it is, right? But I ain't no North Hollywood bank robber, baby. Know what I'm saying?"

"Glad to hear that, at least," she said, relieved. "So what kind of scheme you figure'll make you rich and all if it isn't a bank robbery?"

"You sure ask a lotta questions for a white girl."

"Why is everything so racial with you, Duffy? You always throw that in my face—'You're a white girl'—I know I'm a white girl. I don't have to be reminded. And besides, what's wrong with being a white girl? You sure as hell enjoy fucking me every chance you get!"

She was right, of course. He did. But it wasn't because she was white. There was just something about his attraction to her he couldn't explain. Maybe because he trusted her. Yeah. Maybe that was it. Because he sure as hell didn't trust any other woman ... black or white. Didn't really trust any man. Except Crane. He trusted Crane. He'd trust Crane with his life if he had to.

Duffy said, "Damn, baby. Ease up. Don't get your little flat white ass all in a funk bag."

"There you go again," Trixie said, spitting out her annoyance. "That's what I'm talking about, Duffy. How'd you like it if I went around calling you nigger this and nigger that all the time?"

"Trixie," he said, latent menace in his voice, "you'd only say that once 'cause I'd smash my muthafuckin' fist in your mouth and knock your little vanilla ass through that window, you cokehead!"

Enraged, Trixie balled up her fist, swung at his face. "You fucker, you—" Duffy caught her wrist in mid-air, forced it down and behind her back, pulling her to him, holding her tightly.

"Don't make me hurt you, Trixie."

"Yeah, right. I'm shaking all over, you motherfucker." She tried to wrench free but Duffy pressed her even closer, bending her arm up behind just enough to cause a wince of pain.

"Duffy, my arm—"

"Just chill. Alright? Ain't no thing but an expression. S'all it is. It's just you be askin' me questions about Crane I can't answer." He continued to hold her until he felt the anger drain from her arm, then released his grip. She pushed away, freeing her arm. Hostile eyes avoided his as she brushed past him, snatched a halter from off the bureau. Slipping it on, she struggled to adjust it sufficiently to cover the puffed-out bulk of her breasts to make it legal, but not so far down as to obscure her bare midriff and naval Zirconium. She dropped on the bed to fasten Banana Republic platforms.

"Can't answer?" she asked cynically, eyes looking past him. "Or won't?"

"The answer is I don't know, baby. Crane can't say nothin' about nothin' till he gets out. Alright? He just asked me to look up some niggas for him. That's all I know. But I'll get the four-one-one tonight when we pick him up, know what I'm saying?"

He bent down to kiss her cheek. She turned away, avoiding his eyes, hurt not yet melted away. "That's all you had to say, Duffy," she said, her voice softening. "You didn't have to hurt my arm."

He tried to sound apologetic. "I'm sorry, baby. But you know better 'n to get all up in my face. Know what I mean?"

Trixie said, "You called me a cokehead after I asked you not to."

"I said I was sorry, didn't I. Don't go pushin' your luck, alright?"

Trixie accepted his apology for what it was, but it was the first time she'd seen this side of him, this dark, violent side and it made her uneasy. She realized too for the first time how little Duffy knew about her, how little *she* really knew about him and now, not really sure she wanted to know any more. She said, "And leave the white girl shit out of it from now on." She stood, still not looking at him, walked to a half-broken mirror attached to the door. She swiped a large comb through her hair, put on Channel's Vamp blue-black lipstick, finished it with gloss and put a swipe of Fendi behind her ear. She slipped a dozen rings on ten fingers, gave herself the once-over at the mirror.

"I'm ready. You?"

Duffy looked at his Rolex. "We only got half an hour."

"We'll make it."

"Got any cash?"

"How much you need?"

"How much you got, Trixie?"

"Enough," she said, a trace of bad feeling still in her voice. She'd remember this, Duffy nearly breaking her arm over bullshit. If this was going to be the future she'd better start thinking about getting out. "C'mon, let's go."

Duffy checked himself in the mirror, sprayed on too much Polo cologne. He wedged a small diamond-and-ruby ring on the middle finger of his left hand. "Hold up a minute," he said, rushed. "My piece—"

Trixie looked at him sharply. "You need that just to pick up a friend?"

Duffy ignored her. He reached behind the bureau, withdrew a plastic bag, unwrapped it, pulled out a 9mm pistol. He ejected the clip, counted 16 rounds, slammed it back in, cocked the action. He reached behind and wedged it in his waistband, covering it with his shirt. He said, "Now we ready to get Crane."

Trixie opened the door and they walked into a corridor of music.

"Whatever. Let's go get your con business partner," she said, as if having to do an unwelcome chore.

"You need to check that cocaine attitude, girlie."

"Motherfucker, I told you I'm not a basehead. Why don't you get the fuck off my back!"

"God don't like ugly, Trixie."

Trixie's hand slashed through the air in an exaggerated sign of the cross.

She said, "Bless me, Father, for I have sinned. It has been twenty-one years since my last confession—"

Duffy pounded the button on the wall. "Nice little Catholic girl, huh?"

"I was, until the priest stuck his hand between my legs. After that I didn't believe in shit."

The doors opened with strained effort. They stepped into the elevator from hell. Antiquated graffiti-covered iron doors practiced snail-paced maneuvers in closing, noisy like special effects in an old Lon Chaney movie. The smell of fresh urine covered one wall.

"You'll like Crane," said Duffy as they descended. "He's a down O.G."

"O.G.?"

Duffy said, "Original gangster. Old school. Older guy, you know."

Trixie said, "Right. I'll try to remember how smart he is."

They reached ground level, walked into and through a lobby masquerading as a day-care center. Noisier than any boombox, it was a crowded kennel of unattended children playing with movie tie-in toys on stained and frayed carpeting that reeked with an odor of raw sewage.

Outside they headed for the corner. The warm September night and light sensuous breeze seemed to whisk away the last of Trixie's anger. She hooked Duffy's arm with hers, walked in his stride.

Trixie said, "By the way, I dance tonight."

"Say what?"

"Yeah. Patrick called. One of the girls is sick. He wants me to fill in. I gotta be there by eleven, so don't let the family reunion with jailbird make me late. Okay?"

"Word. Just picking him up from the station, Trixie. Ain't goin' to no party. I'll get you there. Maybe Crane'll catch your show?"

Trixie said, "Right. I'll send him a printed invitation. Just don't make me late."

Duffy's car was a 1993 two door Buick Regal. Painted a two-tone iridescent green, it sported expensive Dayton wire rims, even more expensive Vogue white wall tires, a Nardi steering wheel, a Pioneer stereo sound system with oversized speakers that filled the trunk, and a customized Alpine alarm system with a pre-recorded amplified warning that blared: *GET YOUR ASS AWAY FROM MY CAR!*

Duffy beeped off the alarm as they approached and climbed in. He removed the 9mm from his belt and stuck it in a hidden pocket deep under his seat where he knew the cops weren't likely to find it in case he was stopped and searched. He put Busta Rhymes's *It Ain't Safe No More* ... into the CD player. Four switches brought the Regal up from the curb, quickly drove the short distance to Hollywood Boulevard and headed east toward the Hollywood Freeway. Traffic was light. Windows down, warm dry air filling the car. Trixie put her seat back, adjusted her seatbelt, propped bare shapely legs on the dash, fingers snapping, lips in sync to

Busta's rap.

They arrived at Union Station precisely at ten. Duffy brought the Regal to a screeching halt in the red, jumped out. Trixie didn't move, still grooving to Busta's lyrics.

"You coming?" Duffy yelled, walking away fast.

She shook her head. "Naw. Go get your jailbird friend. I'm gonna smoke me a joint." She unrolled a handkerchief that covered a dime bag of weed. She pulled out Zig-Zag's, rolled a joint, flicked on her lighter, took quick deep breaths, held it, exhaled slowly, waited for the buzz.

When she finally looked up, eyes wide and slow moving, brain luxuriating in the mellow numbness of *chronic*, Duffy was gone. She saw blurred images of people with suitcases coming and going, friends bidding farewell, others embraced with the excitement of welcome. She half-laughed, half-grunted deep in her throat, remembering her own arrival in L.A. and the nightmare circumstances that brought her here.

On the outskirts of Boise, Idaho Trisha Jean Tyler had lived the trailer park existence of poor white trash. As a child, pronouncing Trisha came out sounding like Trixie and the nickname stuck. Her mother drank and drew welfare to support Frank, her sometimes-employed husband and Trixie's stepfather. Frank had been molesting Trixie since she was ten. Stealing to her bedside when her mother was in a drunken stupor, and sometimes when she wasn't, he would feel and caress her, talking dirty in her ear with threats of harm if she told. When her body arrived at twelve the caresses turned to rape. The third time she called his bluff and told her mother. Her mother's response was numbing: "It's alright he wants you," her mother had said without the slightest trace of surprise or outrage. "No blood kin to you. Keeps a roof over our heads, feeds us right well. So he wants a little fun. He's a man. What do you expect? You're pretty. You have what men want. When you're older they'll even pay you for it."

Well then, that was it, wasn't it. She knew where she stood. The price of her mother's love was to become a whore. So she did. By the time she was fourteen she'd had two abortions. By seventeen her promiscuity was legend. Three more abortions despite a prescription for birth control pills she never filled. There wasn't a boy in the senior class she hadn't fucked. Even Anthony Jones, the school's only black student. A football player. From childhood she knew her mother hated blacks, riddled her youth with lies, myths and misguided reasons to avoid any association with them. But provocative statements without explanation generates a curiosity that demands satisfaction. And Trixie, if she was nothing else, was always curious. She didn't tell anyone about Anthony Jones. But she told about the others and wore her reputation as the school slut like a badge of honor.

Through it all she'd kept up her grades. On a dare she tried out for the Drama Club. She was a natural. Especially to play a whore. She would play Sadie Thompson in Somerset Maughm's *Rain*. On the night before the play's presentation she came home from dress rehearsal to an empty lot. The trailer was gone. No forwarding address, the trailer park manager had said. No note. Nothing.

Her sole possessions that night were a pair of high heel shoes and the provocative Sadie Thompson outfit she carried in a bag. With no money, no reliable friends she could turn to, she walked three miles to the business district in a driving rainstorm. Her mother had said she had what men wanted, that they would pay her for it. Trixie put on the Sadie Thompson dress and high heels. She stepped to the curb and waited.

Her mother had been right. They paid for her soaking wet. By the morning she had seventy dollars and the next, nearly a hundred and fifty.

Three days after her mother's abandonment she spent a hundred and thirty-one dollars for a one-way bus ticket to Los Angeles. The trailer park was a dead memory. But Sadie Thompson was alive and well.

Chapter 3

D UFFY SPOTTED CRANE IN THE MIDST OF A PACK OF NUNS midway down the platform. Wearing an ill-fitting, plain gray, single-breasted suit issued by the prison, he walked slowly, mechanically towards the gate, his left arm only slightly weighted by a black garment bag. He didn't look the same as Duffy had remembered when they were cellmates. The change in his appearance was unbelievable. Crane had aged terribly. Where he once sported a full head of woolly brown hair it was now a thinning cover of salt and pepper. The wide mouth whose bright smile Duffy remembered showcasing two rows of gleaming straight teeth was now a darkened cave guarded by fragments

of some, the complete absence of others. Most startling of all was the
presence of a tic on the left side of his face that jerked ferociously at the
corner of his wide mouth and flat nose, turning his grimace into the kind
of contorted gargoyle one would see in a carnival sideshow.

They greeted one another silently as Crane reached the gate—a
brief, tight hug of recognition and bonding. Duffy grabbed his bag.

"It's been a while, Crane," Duffy said, taking the lead through noisy
hurried crowds. "Been lookin' forward to seeing you again."

Crane allowed himself the first smile of freedom. "You look good,
dog," he said to Duffy's shoulder. "I see you wearing all the right shit,
Hilfiger and all."

Duffy turned and smiled, surprised at the compliment. Crane added,
"*Vibe. Source.* I keep up."

"Hell, Crane," Duffy said, reading his meaning, "you young still."

"Maybe. But I feel my age, dog. Know what I mean? See, you've
only done short stretches that don't let you feel your age. Young brothers
always feel they can do time sittin' on a pin-head. You don't notice
getting older. But get my age, dog. Get forty-five and do time. My kind
of time. Hard time. You feel it. Feel it all over. Feel youth gradually slipping away."

Forty-five. Crane looked sixty if he looked a day.

Duffy slowed, waited for Crane, then matched his stride. "I ain't
plannin' on doing no more jail time if I can help it, and neither should
you, homie. We out now. And we gonna stay out, know what I'm sayin'?
Get us some big money. Benjamins. Some Grants. Some Jacksons. Live
large. What do you say to that?"

Crane smiled a second time, stuck out his palm. "I say it's time to
get paid, dog." Duffy slapped his palm, held the door as they entered the

cavernous high-domed lobby seen in a thousand movies.

When they reached the street, there was no Regal, no Trixie. Then she suddenly bounded around the corner in a full gallop, platform shoes clattering.

"Sorry, Duffy," Trixie said breathlessly, eyeing Crane through a marijuana haze. "Cop was giving out tickets so I had to park two streets over." She extended her hand, grabbed Crane's before he'd raised it, held it a moment longer than expected and gave him a warm, inviting smile Duffy didn't catch. She said, "You must be Crane. I'm Trixie."

"Trixie—?"

"Duffy's girlfriend." She continued to pump his arm, rattling on like a telemarketer reading a rehearsed pitch. "Duffy's told me all about you. About how smart you are and how much he learned from you when he got sent up. Told me all about some plan you got to make us some money, too."

Crane shot Duffy a look. He said, "Us?"

"Sure hope it works," she said, "cause we can really use it."

Crane said, "Duffy talks too much." He was speaking to them both, but he was staring at Duffy with cold, impassive eyes.

Trixie noticed the tic for the first time, and the missing teeth. She stopped the mile-a-minute handshake but didn't let go of Crane's hand. She said, "Jesus. What happened to your face? It's jumping all over the place." And she brought her free hand to his cheek, let her soft gentle fingers glide over the spasm for an instant. "Prison do that? You poor baby. And your teeth?" she went on, "Duffy, you gotta get Crane here some teeth. He'd be a nice looking guy if he had some teeth. Jesus!"

Crane instantly withdrew his hand from hers, brought it to his mouth in embarrassment, shooting Trixie an incredulous look but softening at the recollection of her compliment, " ... he'd be a nice looking guy ..."

Duffy said, "Chill, Trixie." He played off his embarrassment with a laugh. "Don't pay her no mind, Crane. She's like that—Energizer bunny."

Trixie, loose and uninhibited from the weed, seemed not to appreciate Crane's frost. She turned, galloping away. "C'mon. Show you where I parked," she called over her shoulder.

When she was some distance ahead Crane grabbed Duffy's arm, slowed him to a near standstill. "You didn't tell me you had a white girl, dog." He said it as if Duffy had committed a mortal sin.

"Just a girl, homie," Duffy said casually, missing the subtle hostility in Crane's voice. "Ain't no big deal. You want one? Trixie's got friends."

"I don't trust nobody white, dog. And definitely no white girl. So don't go blabbing my business to her. Understand?"

Duffy said, "You been in the joint too long, Crane. When it comes to pussy, ain't no color at all. It's just pussy. You'll see. Now when it comes to money, that's different. All that black and white drama back in the joint translates to green out here in the real world. That's the only color that really counts. After all, we're still in America and there's only money. Know what I'm sayin'?"

"Sorry, dog," Crane said, realizing he'd been too hard, falling back into stride beside Duffy. "Still living in the joint. I guess things have changed."

"Some things, homie. But not everything. Heard about Rampart?" Crane said he had. Duffy went on, "Daryl Gates may be gone, but his Five-0 thugs still on the streets, still just as ruthless. So watch your back, know what I'm sayin'?"

Despite his protestations about Trixie, Crane's eyes took her in as she pranced ahead. "She's a thick white girl, dog," he said after a while. "Got big legs. And ass like a sista. Them titties real?"

"They real enough, Crane," Duffy said. "Don't go gettin any ideas, homie," he went on, first sense of distrust creeping into his voice. "We'll get you some pussy in short order. But this one is *mine*. You remember that." He played his insecurity off with a laugh and quickened their pace and said, "She dance up in Hollywood. Place called the Baby Doll Club. Titties pay the rent."

Crane said, "I'm sure they do."

Trixie had had to park nearly four blocks away. It was ten thirty when they reached the car. Crane fumbled through his pockets and gave Duffy a scrap of paper with an address. Duffy squinted in the glow of a streetlight and said, "Figueroa Street. Damn, homie. You smack dab in the middle of the hood. Sure you wanna stay here?"

Crane said, "It'll do for now."

Trixie sat in the back, Crane's garment bag beside her. Duffy started-ed the Regal and headed for the freeway. He put on Ja Rule's *The Last Temptation* CD as he made the transition from the Hollywood Freeway to the Harbor.

"Is Crane your first name or last name?" Trixie asked leaning forward.

"Just Crane."

Duffy said, "I'm known as the Pharaoh, dog," sense of pride fluff-ing the words.

"The Pharaoh." Crane laughed, thought it was funny and said so.

"Means King," Duffy said.

"I may have been stupid … never dumb," Crane said. "Pharaoh …" Crane thought about it for a second. He said, "Didn't call you that in the joint?"

"They do on the street."

Crane said, "What I got in mind has nothing to do with the streets, dog. I know you as Duffy." No negotiation in his voice. End of discussion.

Duffy thought about forcing the issue, conceded instead. He said, "Guess it's all right for you, Trixie here. Anybody else call me that likely to get hurt."

Trixie pulled something out of her handkerchief. "Care for a joint, Crane?" She took one herself, gave one to Duffy, offered one to Crane.

Without appreciation or comment Crane took one, lit it, inhaled it, closed his eyes as the buzz came. He said to Trixie, "This some good shit, white girl."

Trixie exhaled angrily. "First Duffy, now you. O.J. fucked everything up, didn't he? The name's Trixie, not white girl. You don't know me well enough to call me white girl. Isn't that right, Duffy?"

Duffy looked at Crane and laughed. "She got a mouth on her, Crane. Got attitude too. White girl attitude."

Crane was feeling too mellow to argue. He nodded his head, smiled but said nothing. He took another drag on the joint. Trixie settled back into the leather seat, exhaling slowly.

"You check out those names I gave you?" Crane asked after a while.

"Yeah, they around. All but this dude named Silas ... something or other."

"Silas Bingham."

"Yeah, Silas Bingham. He's dead. Four years ago. Some woman shot him."

Crane seemed bothered at the news. "Damn," he said. "Silas was my dog ten years ago. Always had a lotta women."

From the back seat Trixie said, "Guess he had one too many, huh?" Crane ignored her.

"What about the others?" he asked Duffy.

"Marcus Jones in jail. Caught a DUI on an expired license. Be out in a month."

Crane chuckled at fond memories. "Old Marcus—but a month's too long ...? What about Henry T?"

Trixie grunted, "One dead, the second in jail. Who's on third?"

"Henry T figure he some kind of celebrity. Got himself a gig driving a limo for rock stars and shit. Said he drove Michael Jackson to the Grammys once."

Crane shook his head, remembering. "Yeah. Henry T was always good with cars. What about Morgan Reese? You find him?"

"Reese? Yeah, I found him. Man, that nigga's crazy. He's insane. Muthafucka thinks he's a preacher. Standin' on Crenshaw every day dressed like some space alien. Be wearing his hair all long and preaching 'bout how he from some tribe in Israel or some shit like that."

Crane came out of his buzz for a moment, frowning. "Preaching, you say?"

"Do I look like a parrot? The nigga's preaching. On Crenshaw. Least he was when I found him."

Crane grunted to himself, shaking his head. He took one last drag on the joint, eyes closed. "What about Bo Bo?"

"Who?"

"Leon. Leon Davis. We always called him Bo Bo."

"Oh, him. Yeah, Leon. Nigga in rehab, Crane. Guess he's an alcoholic. Said he's been in every program they got. Said he's been clean and sober for six months now. But he's got to live in rehab to stay that way."

Crane said, "I can't imagine Bo Bo an alcoholic," disappointment edging his words.

Duffy took his last drag on the joint, tossed it out of the window.

"You've been gone ten years, Crane. People change."

"Whatever."

"Don't none of these niggas believe you out."

"Seeing is believing."

Trixie tossed the last of her joint away, sat up between them.

"Speaking of that," Trixie began slowly, "just how did you get out of a twenty five to life after only ten years?"

Crane turned, shot Duffy another look. "Damn, dog. What the fuck else you tell this bitch?"

Trixie's half-open eyes fluttered closed then opened again in slow motion. She said, "That's another thing you don't call me—bitch. You don't call me white girl or bitch. My name's Trixie. Call me that or don't call me nothin'! You understand?"

Looking at Duffy, Crane laughed and said, "Got a mouth on her, dog. You right about that. Most strawberrys do."

At this Trixie's eyes flew open like a windowshade with a broken spring. *"STRAWBERRY?"* she shouted indignantly. "Who are you calling a strawberry, you fucker, you? You don't know me. You don't know anything about me, you ex-con faggot! I'm no goddamn strawberry. I may have sold some pussy to buy food, but I never sold it to buy drugs. Who in the hell you think you talking to?" Crane's accusation hurt because she liked him. She liked him the moment she saw him, gray hair, missing teeth, tic and all.

Crane turned, looked at her with surprising calm. He said, "I know a strawberry when I see one."

"You don't know shit, you fucker!" Trixie screamed, angry words ripping the warm night air, drowning out Ja Rule. "You been in the joint for ten fucking years. You don't know shit!"

"She's right, Crane," Duffy said, interrupting. "Me and Trixie been together ever since I got out. We a team. Anything I got going with you gonna include her 'cause she got my back. I didn't spend all this time away from my hustle trackin' down these niggas just so you could dis my lady. That's fucked up, brother."

Crane couldn't believe what he was hearing. He couldn't believe Duffy's nose was that wide open for a common street whore, even one as fine as Trixie—he had to admit she was fine. But then he remembered Marjorie … big, fine, jet black Marjorie … remembered he thought the sun rose and fell on everything she touched. He also remembered she cost him ten years in the joint and her memory suddenly turned sour. He said, "Hustle? What do you do, Duffy—you sell dope?"

"Yeah."

"Jack cars? Gangbang?"

"Now and then."

"Shoplift? Steal? Forge? Did three and a half on stolen money orders—?"

"So?"

"Pimp this girl here?"

"She ain't on the street no more."

"So you pimpin' her titties at the … what was it you said, the Baby Doll Club? You still pimpin' her … "

"I do what I gotta do. So fuckin' what?"

Crane said, "How much cash you got on you, Duffy?" Duffy's eyes caught Trixie's in the rear-view mirror. She held up one finger. Then another.

Duffy said, "A grand. Maybe two."

Crane said, "Chump change. Just enough to keep you taking penitentiary chances. I'm talking about a deal gonna make us seven figure niggas, dog. I need people I can trust. That's why I had you look up my dogs. You want me to believe Miss Trixie here—whose got you so pussy-whipped you can't see straight—you want me to believe she's got your back ... and you know she's a coke freak? Shit! Nigga, you're a fool!"

"No," spat Trixie, enraged. "You're the fool, Crane. Sure, I snort every now and then. So does Duffy. So do you. But I ain't no addict." She knew she was lying on this account, hated the fact Crane could see right through her, but admired him because he could. Something about him intrigued her. Still, it pissed her off and she went on, "And I sure as hell ain't never been a strawberry. And another thing, Crane," she ranted on angrily, her words streaming out unchecked like the rush of water from a broken pipe, "whatever you think of me ... like I really care—" She knew she was lying about this too. She did care what Crane thought. She wanted him to like her, sensed he wasn't like Duffy at all. He had a thing about white people he'd have to get over first. She could change that, she was sure, once he respected her—and he'd have to respect her. They'd have nothing together if he didn't. "—but whatever you think of me I never had my ass poked unless I wanted it," she went on. "Even money you can't say the same!"

Her torrent broke Crane's composure. "Bitch, I ought to—"

He turned completely around to face her, his hand going for her throat. But Trixie had anticipated him. Crane never heard the snap of the blade or caught its glint in the flash of passing headlights. But he felt its cold deadly point against his pulsing carotid. He knew the pale white hand that held it was capable of taking his life with the slightest provocation.

Trixie said, "Do what—"

Crane froze, his hand barely at his shoulder. He didn't dare turn or even shift his eyes from her face, her jaws tight with rage. Her blue eyes, their pupils dilated, unmoving and focused, spoke to him in terms he understood. The slightest rise and fall of the Regal over freeway concrete produced pinpricks of pain on his neck.

"Get her off me, dog," he commanded, still defiant but slowly, carefully lowering his hand.

Again Duffy eyed Trixie in the rear-view mirror.

"Chill out, baby—" He spoke as if to a pet dog expected to obey its master. But it was a long, silent interval before Trixie's death grip on the switchblade relaxed. She folded it with one hand, never taking her eyes away from Crane's face, wet with fear and perspiration.

She fell absently back into the leather seat, mumbling hurt to no one in particular. "Stupid ex-con fucker. Calling me a strawberry—" Maybe her feeling for Crane was a mistake. Maybe she'd misjudged him. Maybe he *was* like Duffy. Maybe it was to be her lot—men like Duffy and Crane … angry, brutal, self-centered men who respected no one but the streets and the damaged goods it produced. She was damaged goods. They all were and the thought was depressing.

Even with the blade off his neck Crane couldn't turn away from Trixie, not knowing if he was out of danger. His hand fished through pockets for a handkerchief, finding nothing.

Duffy said, "I think you owe her some props, Crane." He turned off Ja Rule. Only then did Crane turn back around, resettling himself.

"Nigga, please—"

Suddenly Duffy turned the wheel violently, swerving the Regal dangerously through traffic across three lanes, braking to a sliding halt on the shoulder just short of the Florence Boulevard exit. He reached across Crane and opened the passenger door.

"Get out," he said.

Crane was slow on the uptake, gave Duffy an incredulous look. "Say what?"

Duffy spoke to Trixie in the rear-view mirror. "Baby, give this dumb-ass nigga his bag."

Despite her brooding Trixie was reluctant to see Crane go. She grabbed his bag with a hesitancy Duffy didn't notice, pushed it over the seat into Crane's lap.

Duffy said, "I said get the fuck out. That's what, nigga!"

Crane looked at Duffy in disbelief. He said, "You gonna throw away the chance to make millions," and he stole a quick glance back at Trixie, "for her, dog? You that pussy-whipped?"

"Trixie ain't your problem," Duffy said over the roar of passing traffic. "Your problem is them old tired-ass niggas you had me track down."

Crane frowned. He said, "What are you talking about?"

"Them niggas say they don't want no part of you. Say they don't owe you shit. Say it was the sista's fault things got fucked up. Now, I don't know what went down ten years ago, no more than what you told me, and personally I don't give a shit. But them niggas be saying the debt is paid—whatever that means."

Every vein in Crane's face and neck seemed to pop out in anger.

Crane said, "That's what they say. I say different. I did *their* time. Everybody's time. They owe me." He said it as would a judge pronouncing a sentence prescribed by law.

"Ain't the way they see it," said Duffy, still open to partnership. "You got a problem if you figure on using them again. Serious. But I can get around that. Get you some real niggas that ain't about some bullshit. Niggas I know we can trust. Know what I'm sayin'? And as far as me and Trixie go, we in or we out. Either way, we go together. So it's on you, homie. If we in, give us the four-one-one. If not—get the fuck out my car!"

Crane leaned back in the seat, tired eyes focused on bleeding taillights in the distance, the muted silence broken only by the hiss of passing cars, horns blaring angry warnings. Crane had seized the only opportunity there was to free himself. He'd taken the deal knowing there were strings and needing former partners to cut them. But Duffy's suggestion they might be uncooperative unnerved him. Not once during his ten years in prison had he considered the possibility they'd take their freedom for granted and, in the end, be ungrateful. Maybe the girl was right—after ten years locked up maybe he didn't know shit. Maybe he'd misjudged her. With this thought he conceded that an uneasy alliance with Trixie might be his only option— for the moment, at least. He remembered how he felt about Marjorie, what he had said to the group when they didn't want Marjorie in on the bank robbery. "'Marjorie's with me. She don't go, I don't go!'" And remembering that, hearing the same familiar echo from Duffy ten years later, he realized finally he would have to concede on this point.

His tic subsided as he weighed the compromise. When he was sure of his decision he grabbed the door handle and pulled it shut, then pushed his bag back over the seat without looking. Trixie slapped it to one side, cursing, but not too long and not too loudly. Crane turned and met Duffy's gaze, but his words, harsh and measured, spoke to the girl at his shoulder.

He said, "There's only one leader—me. Understand that. You do what I say, when I say, without question. Is that clear?"

"Word," said Duffy making a fist, touching Crane's. Trixie saluted, bringing a hostile middle finger to her brow.

"You fuck this up," Crane went on, "I'll hunt you down like a dog in the street and kill you myself. Both of you."

At this Trixie burst into mocking laughter. "I can't tell you how afraid I am," she said, thrashing about in the seat as if a child cowering before the shadow of a puppet projected on the wall. "I'm shaking all over, Crane. In fact, I'm so afraid I think I'll have a joint. You want one? Yes?"

Crane said to his shoulder, "Just so we understand each other," then turned back around as Duffy brought the Regal off the shoulder and into the flow of traffic.

Trixie opened her handkerchief, Zig-Zags, rolled a joint, lit it and leaned forward between Crane and the door, sticking the joint between his lips. Out of Duffy's vision in the rear-view mirror, she stuck her tongue deep in Crane's ear just before sitting back in the seat. It was so unexpected and exciting, it sent shock waves through his body. Marjorie used to do that, stick her tongue in his ear. He'd forgotten how good it felt. So this girl wanted to play, thought Crane. What was it Duffy had said ...? *This one is mine—you remember that!* If he decided to play he'd have to be careful. The girl was scandalous and Duffy was possessive. That combination was dangerous. And right now he needed Duffy's help more than he needed pussy. But the girl *was* fine—God, was she ever, basehead or not, white girl or not—and it had been so long since Marjorie, since any woman. Still, now was not the time. He didn't flinch or move a muscle, just drew deep on the joint and maintained his cool, barely.

But Trixie knew what it had done and she began laughing and said, "Oh, we understand each other alright." It was a sweet victory. She'd gotten his respect. Tentative as it was, she knew now the possibilities with Crane were endless. He wasn't aware of it yet. But he would be. They'd be working together and time was on her side. She looked at the rear-view mirror to see if Duffy had picked up on her flirtation. But he wasn't looking at her, preoccupied with changing CDs.

"Yo, Crane," Duffy said, breaking for the south central exit at Manchester Boulevard, turning west and adjusting the volume on Mary J. Blige all in one motion. He took the joint from Crane, inhaled, passed it back. "What happened to the girl? One they said fucked everything up, got you sent to the joint?"

Marjorie.

Memories hurt. Marjorie had been his rib since they were teenagers. Grew up together on the same block. Next door neighbors who played together as kids. She was a skinny-legged, ebony-complexioned girl whose skin was so dark other kids nicknamed her charcoal. At thirteen her grandmother got sick, sent Marjorie to live with a relative in South Carolina. When she returned a year later, Crane hardly recognized her. She was a gorgeous, statuesque, fully-grown fourteen year old woman. A week after her return she offered Crane her virginity. From that point on he never looked at another woman. There was only Marjorie. Only time they were apart was when he was in the joint. And without direction, without someone to stand up for her, Marjorie was lost. That's how the dope man got to her. She was sixteen. When Crane got out, he pulled her off the Figueroa 'stroll,' put her in rehab, went looking for the dope dealer who'd turned her out. Caught another case before he could find him—In the company of known felons—His P.O.

Violated him. Another eighteen-month stretch. Marjorie didn't stay in rehab a week after Crane left. Still, when he got out he knew where to find her. Her brain may have belonged to the dope man, but Marjorie belonged to him. Four years into the bank robbery stretch he got Uncle Joe's letter. They found Marjorie dead in an abandoned car, needle still in her arm. It was the one and only time in his life he cried. Promised himself if he ever got out he'd find her grave, pay his respects.

"Dead," Crane said after a moment, hint of sadness in his voice. "She was twenty-four."

Duffy said, "That's fucked up, homie ... your woman dying young like that."

Trixie sat up, took the joint from Crane and inhaled deeply.

"Right," she said, dropping back into leather comfort and the buzz of *chronic*, the last of her anger slipping away, buried in the lyrics of Mary J. Blige. She made a half-hearted sign of the cross and said sarcastically, "I'll say the Rosary for her next time I go to church."

Duffy said, "You don't go to church."

Trixie let Duffy's comment pass. She said, "Whatever," took a deep drag on the joint and sat up between them, exhaling. "What say we get back to the present," she went on impatiently. "What I want to know about, Crane, is this plan you got suppose to make us rich?"

Crane waited until they'd passed the joint around again, until its buzz had bled the last of the tension and animosity from between them. He wouldn't tell them everything. Not about the trunk. But he'd tell them enough. Enough so they'd know he was serious, that he was professional. Just enough to test their loyalty. And at the mere thought of what he was planning, Crane smiled.

He said, "Ever heard of the Duchess?"

Chapter 4

DUFFY PULLED THE REGAL TO A STOP at the Figueroa Street address scribbled on the paper. When Crane stepped out he was immediately surrounded by a circus of perfumed black and Mexican *Figueroa girls*, the hookers whose domain he'd just invaded, all talking at once, sticking out bloated over-sized chests, hiking tissue-thin, skin-tight dresses and burrowing firm muscled hips into his own. Trixie came out of the back seat with Crane's bag and replaced him as Duffy's shotgun passenger. She closed the door, leaned her body halfway out the window for Crane to get a good look at her cleavage hanging loose in the halter. None of the Figueroa girls, busty as they might be, could hold a candle to Trixie and she knew it. So did Crane. With her back to Duffy so he couldn't see, she licked her lips, winked and shouted goodbye over *MC Lyte,* waving as the Regal sped away.

The *Hardcore* Motel was in the middle of the block on Figueroa Street between Florence and Manchester at the low end of south central L.A.'s *'strawberry'* district. Running all the way to and beyond Century Boulevard, Figueroa was a cesspool of misery teeming with the black and brown refuse of L.A.'s dispossessed. Populated its entire length by hookers, pimps, strawberrys, addicts, dope dealers, crack houses and liquor stores, it was anchored by a network of one and two-story stucco and plaster motels with names like *All Night Long*, the *Quickie*, the *Love Dollar*. The *Hardcore* would have to be considered a cut above the rest, but just barely. Its single neon sign flashing *Rooms By The Hour Or The Minute* bathed a worn, battle-scarred concrete zone of spiked heels, short dresses and artificial dreams that seldom went further than a ten dollar trick and a five dollar rock, not necessarily in that order. The front office was through a driveway that fed a poorly lit parking lot hidden largely from the street. Once inside Crane knew the *Hardcore* would live up to its name. He'd be shit staying in an unflushed toilet.

It was just after eleven when Crane entered the deserted matchbox that passed for an office. Dimly lit by a single unshaded bulb from a broken lamp in one corner, it had a smell that reminded Crane of the urinals at Marion. He dropped his bag on the floor, rapped his knuckles on the splintered wooden counter that served as combination check-in desk and stain-spattered kitchen table. A sleepy-eyed, half-stoned Mexican in his early 30s stumbled lazily behind the counter, his putrid breath reeking of marijuana. He wore a cap of jet black hair pulled into a ponytail and a stained and torn under-sized white T-shirt that covered a muscular upper torso of familiar tattoos Crane had seen on Mexican Mafia inmates during his ten years at Marion.

"Yeah?" he said, flipping to a blank page in a registry book, turning it for Crane to sign. "How many hours you want it for?"

"Name is Crane. I'm suppose to have a reservation."

"Reservation?" The Mexican said it as if the word was alien to the English language. He withdrew another ledger, flipped through pages, his thumb running down the margin of each page. Stopping suddenly, he looked up, eyes level with Crane's and said, "Crane. Yeah, it's here, homes."

"How much a night, esé?" Crane asked, going in his pocket for cash.

"Nothing, homes. You got friends in high places. Paid your room in advance. Thirty days. Said you wouldn't need it after that."

Thirty days? That was all they were giving him? Crane couldn't believe it. On a job like this he'd need at least two months, maybe three to set it up. Hadn't they been listening? He guessed not. Thirty days. Jesus. He'd have to move more quickly than anticipated. He hated being rushed.

The Mexican closed the ledger, pushed the registration book back in front of Crane and said, "Gotta have a name, homes. You say it's Crane, it's Crane." He handed Crane a broken pen, watched him scribble on the last blank space of the page. The Mexican turned the book around to read Crane's signature. He said, "Doc McCoy. Guess Crane's your nickname. Got any luggage?"

Crane said, "None I can't carry."

At that moment a chorus of stoned laughter ushered in a gorgeous black hooker on the arm of her *trick,* a gray haired white man in his 50s whose toothy, mile-wide Richard Nixon smile seemed to say he was expecting heaven between the legs of a black goddess. Smelling of yesterday's cheap perfume and wearing a flimsy show-all, the hooker wore a tight-fitting dress that hit her sexy thighs just below her crotch. She had big shapely calves accentuated by cheap stiletto heels, a tattoo of the word *Princess* surrounded by a coiled snake emblazoned across the top of a full heaving chest Crane guessed was her own. On her head was an outlandish blonde wig whose long curls moved stiffly about narrow shoulders when she flipped ring-covered fingers through artificial strands. She tossed her head to either side with the effected haughty self-centered air patterned after white girls she'd seen in Clairol commercials, thinking she was Farrah Fawcett. Her flat nose, ringed in one nostril, and her beady brown eyes trapped a heavily caked strata of makeup on a face dominated by a gold incisor whose sparkle was marred by streaks of excessive lipstick applied to full African lips.

"Give us the penthouse, Antonio," the hooker said interrupting, ignoring Crane and not really caring. "How long you wanna play, baby— hour? No? Two? Yeah? Two hours, Antonio. Pay the man, honey. Twenty-five dollars. Andrew Jackson and old honest Abe Lincoln. I'm gonna rock yo' world tonight, sugah." The trick pulled out a wallet fat with cash, started counting out bills.

Antonio said, "Penthouse booked, Princess. Whole month. Give you 210 or 212?"

Princess got an attitude and frowned. She said, "What 'chu mean booked for a month? What kinda shit you pullin, *AN-TONIO?* Ain't no regulars got a right to tie up the penthouse for no muthafuckin' month!"

"Is if they payin' cash in advance, Princess. Ain't no regular neither."

Princess said indignantly, "Who then?"

Antonio looked at Princess and her trick. He said, "You want 210 or 212? Make up your mind. I got a customer waiting." Antonio looked at Crane, shrugged his shoulders in apology.

Princess looked at Crane for the first time and said, "You the mutha-fucka got the penthouse?" Crane said he was.

Princess cut cold, dilated eyes at Crane but her words were for Antonio. "Well this nigga can just wait, shit. I want the muthafuckin' pent-house!" Then she said to Crane, "Me and daddy here got business. You can wait two hours, can't you?" demanding, not asking his permission.

"Not really," Crane said, matching her cold stare with his.

The trick said, "No big deal. Give us 212. How much?"

"Fifteen," said Antonio.

"Aw hell no, muthafucka," Princess shouted in protest, more to Crane than to Antonio. But Antonio was already putting the cash in the register.

The trick pulled out a fifty, slapped it in Princess's hand to avoid a scene. He said, "This make up for the penthouse, baby? You said the penthouse was extra?"

It's amazing how money dissolves anger. The frown lines on Princess's face melted behind the blonde curls and her snarling angry lips turned into the prettiest smile Crane had ever seen. With a smile like that she could've been a model on the ramp of an Ebony Fashion Show—except for the gold incisor and blonde wig. She'd have to lose those and Crane guessed it wasn't in her plans to do so. Princess gave Crane a 'fuck you' look and swished out the door ahead of her trick, laughing.

Antonio turned his attention back to Crane. He said, "You got a package, homes. Message too." He disappeared through a door and returned a few seconds later holding a shoebox-size package wrapped in brown paper and secured by string and rubberbands. Crane shook it, felt its weight. It made no sound. Antonio handed Crane a folded slip of paper with the word *Crane* scrawled on one side. He opened it to see a phone number printed in heavy black ink.

"You suppose to call soon as you check in," Antonio said curiously.

"Call *who*?" Crane said, turning the paper over, looking for more information. Crane's bewildered stare caught Antonio's blank face, the shrug of his shoulders.

Antonio said, "He didn't say, homes. Just for you to call soon as you checked in." Antonio reached behind him, withdrew a key from the board. He said, "Penthouse on the second floor, all the way to the end. Hope you enjoy your stay, homes."

Crane yawned, grabbed his bag and slipped the package inside. He said, "Right," and headed for the door.

The moment Crane stepped out of the office the blunted tip of cold steel jammed hard into his rib cage stopped him dead in his tracks. Experience told him it was probably a Colt .45. Behind him, a vaguely familiar voice, hoarse and coughing and black, said, "Just keep walking, Crane." Still carrying his bag, trying to put a face to the voice Crane moved forward, stumbling and nearly losing his balance when a meaty hand pushed him hard between his shoulder blades. He started to turn around but the hand caught him again, shoving him forward into the parking lot. "Don't turn around, muthafucka. Keep on across the parking lot to the white Impala over there."

"What's this shit all about?" Crane was more curious than fearful, trying desperately to put a face behind the voice. "How do you know my name?"

"Everybody knows you, Crane. Just keep walking," the voice said, slipping into a spasmodic cough Crane thought would never end.

Crane said, "How's anybody know I'm out?"

The vaguely familiar voice said, "I ain't just anybody," and pushed Crane forward across the lot, the meaty hand repeatedly jabbing into Crane's back. "What I am, see, is your worse nightmare come back to haunt you. Told you I would, didn't I, nigga. Said if it took the rest of your twenty five I'd be waitin' for your black ass. 'Course back then I was just talkin', see. Didn't never figure on seein' you again. Not really. Imagine my surprise hearing you got sprung fifteen years early. What you do, nigga, pay somebody off? Fuck ole Moffett in the ass? Suck Needham's dick three times a week?" Still trying to put a face on the voice, Crane said he didn't know what he was talking about, that he didn't remember anyone telling him they'd be waiting when he got out. "Well, don't make no difference nohow," the voice with the cough went on, still jabbing Crane in the back, forcing him across the darkened lot. "Yo' ass mine now, muthafucka."

As they reached the Impala a large black figure with a clean-shaven peanut-sized head stepped out from behind the wheel. At first he thought it was Marcus, realized it wasn't when he opened the back door, motioned for Crane to enter, closing it behind his capture. The giant got back behind the wheel, started the engine and drove the Impala out of the lot and onto Figueroa headed south without saying a word.

The flickering streetlights of Figueroa broke up shadows in the back seat, allowed Crane his first glimpse of the face that belonged to the voice. It was barely recognizable, bloated and covered with a scrubby uncombed beard, bushy eyebrows and gold fronts. But it *was* recognizable. Leroy Jones.

"Leroy Jones," Crane said finally, his face flush with distant memory of the man, knowing now why he was there and suddenly growing cold with apprehension.

Leroy smashed the barrel of the Colt .45 hard across Crane's face and said viciously, "That's right, nigga—*LE-ROY.* You remember me, don't you." It wasn't a question. It was a command. "And you know why I'm here, don't you, you black punk-ass muthafucka."

Crane knew but didn't say so. It all came back to him now ... so many years ago, one incident out of hundreds in a rat trap where only the strongest survive. Leroy Jones survived because he got out after doing only three years of a five-to-ten-year beef for simple assault. He'd come to Marion in Crane's fifth year, a loudmouth wannabe with a knack for gambling, squeezing cons for interest on money they owed him when he won. The cash to play coming from what the cons had on the books, what they earned at chump-change prison jobs making license plates or what their families sent them each month. What a con had on the books dictated his status and influence with the others, including greedy guards like Needham. Leroy always had cash on the books from his brother, a real estate developer who'd always bailed Leroy out of trouble since they were kids.

It was a poker game. Leroy, Crane, Bear, Midnight and a few other cons on second tier's usual Tuesday night game. Needham got ten percent of every pot for looking the other way, no matter who won. And Leroy always seemed to win, could read another con's face, knew when he was bluffing and when he wasn't.

It was Crane who picked up that Leroy was cheating, dealing from the bottom of the deck, or could shuffle the cards with such speed and finesse you couldn't really tell he wasn't shuffling them at all.

The pot was close to a thousand when Crane accused Leroy of cheating, showed the others how he did it. From that moment on until his release nearly three years later Leroy's time at Marion was pure hell. Branded a cheat, all games were closed to him. He spent unjustified time in the hole for even minor infractions, was given the worse jobs to do and his money on the books drained as soon as it came in, divided between the cons who ran the poker games and Needham. Leroy never forgave Crane, vowed to kill him before he got out. He tried too, but he had no alliances and no money to form any. And those few he could get, loners, misfits or mental cases, backed down when they discovered Crane was Bear's dog, so nothing ever happened. The night before Leroy was released he told Crane he'd be waiting for him no matter how long it took. Crane had never been afraid of Leroy and dismissed his threats as easily as he dismissed Leroy himself.

Not now. He couldn't dismiss him now with a Colt .45 stuck in his ribs and vengeance glued to Leroy's eyes. Despite everything Crane was curious. He said, "Who told you I was getting out?"

"You ain't the only nigga with connections in the joint."

"Then you know why I'm out?"

"I don't care how you got out or why you out."

"You'd better," said Crane, not bluffing, assessing his chances against two gangsters in a moving car, realizing they weren't good any way he looked at it, sweat beginning to break out on his forehead. "If I could get out like I did must be a reason. You interfere with it, gonna be a lotta drama come down on your head. You don't wanna get mixed up in any M & M business. You'd better recognize."

Leroy hadn't changed. He laughed facetiously and looked around with exaggerated neck movements that reminded Crane of an ostrich and said, "M & M business. Yeah, right. I'm suppose to believe the M & M got you out the joint. Give me a muthafuckin' break, nigga. What could you do for the mob? I'll tell you what. Nothin', that's what! What I *recognize* is you don't have shit. I don't see no calvary, no John Wayne ridin' to the rescue, know what I'm saying, nigga?" Leroy continued laughing and coughing, calling Crane's bluff. "So if you got a better hand than me, let's see it."

Crane didn't have John Wayne but he had Duffy, though at the time he didn't know it. Duffy and Trixie had stopped at a liquor store on the corner of Figueroa and Century Boulevard after they'd dropped Crane at the *Hardcore*. Carrying a fifth of VSOP and a bag of pretzels in each hand, they walked out just in time to see the white Impala do a rolling stop right in front of them, turn onto Century headed west toward LAX. Duffy was sure he recognized Crane. The Impala passed so close he could see Crane hadn't changed clothes, wondered how he could've checked in the motel so quickly, didn't remember him saying anything about meeting anyone. Unless someone was waiting for him and he was sure Crane would've mentioned that.

Streets smarts and instinct are gifts from God.

"Get in the car, Trixie," Duffy said, running for the Regal, pulling Trixie along behind by the arm.

"What's the rush?"

Duffy jumped in the Regal, peeled away from the curb before fastening his seatbelt. He said, "Saw Crane in a car up ahead. Something about it don't look right."

Trixie said, "Crane? We just dropped him off!" She fastened her seatbelt, started to put on a CD by *MYSTIKAL* but Duffy's hand knocked hers away.

He said to Trixie, "Not now." Duffy moved quickly through thin traffic until he was four car lengths behind the Impala, following it on across Crenshaw Boulevard, past Hollywood Park racetrack, under the 405 freeway to La Cienega Boulevard where the Impala turned left and headed south past long blocks of warehouses that shook under the deafening noise of an L1011 on its final approach down the glidescope, its bloated underbelly glistening in the seizure of flashing strobe lights.

Suddenly the Impala slowed and made a quick right turn into an alley between two darkened and abandoned warehouses. Duffy slowed cautiously, turned off his lights before turning into the alley, catching a final red glimmer of the Impala's taillights as it disappeared behind a building. At the corner of the building he pulled the Regal to a silent stop in the dead shadows of flashing amber strobe lights and shut off the engine. He withdrew the 9mm from under the seat and checked the slide.

"Stay in the car," he said to Trixie as he slid silently out from behind the wheel.

"Don't let anything happen to him," Trixie said, catching herself too late, realizing her concern was more for Crane than Duffy, hoping Duffy didn't pick up on it and knowing if she tried damage control, it might draw Duffy's attention to her real feelings.

She needn't have worried. Duffy's razor sharp mind wasn't on Trixie. It was on calculating the odds as he inched closer to the Impala, his back flat against the rusted corrugated wall, his 9mm cocked and ready.

The Impala had pulled to a stop beside a large unlit steel warehouse with large faded letters on its side that read, *AMERICAN CONTAINER SHIPPING AND STORAGE* and whose massive floor-to-ceiling sliding aluminum doors hung loosely at odd angles to the building, peppered with the target practice indentations and perforations of a thousand pistol and rifle rounds.

The driver with the peanut-sized head undid his seatbelt, turned around facing Crane and Leroy, brought a massive .357 into Crane's face. Over the hum of the air-conditioning he said to Leroy, "Want me to take this nigga out for you now, dog?"

Looking at the .357 but talking to Leroy, Crane, sweating and nauseous with fear, aware now that he was urinating on himself, his voice choking on his words, said desperately, "You don't have to do this, Leroy. I'm tellin' you, man, you're making a big mistake!"

Leroy laughed. He said, "You right about that, Crane. My big mistake was not taking care of you when I had the chance. I—" The noise of an approaching 747 down the glidescope drowned out the rest of what Leroy was saying. Suddenly the man holding the .357 jerked up violently, eyes wide open, tongue protruding spasmodically from a mouth suddenly filled with blood, and keeled over on the steering wheel, dead amid a rain of shattered windshield glass. By the time both Crane and Leroy realized what had happened and before Leroy could mount a defense with his .45 it was too late. The orange muzzle blasts from Duffy's 9mm flickered through the window as it took off the right side of Leroy's head, bathing Crane in a shower of blood as the decapitated body fell limply forward on the seatback and slid to the floor at Crane's feet in a crumpled bloody heap.

When the 747 had passed the only noise was the Impala's horn. Duffy reached through a window of broken glass and pulled the big man's head off the steering wheel, plunging the car into silence. He looked into the back seat, saw Crane's shaken form and said, "You alright, homie?"

Crane nodded gratefully in the darkness, stumbled numbly out of the Impala in a daze, his clothes drenched in blood. Duffy opened the driver's door, watched the big man's lifeless form slump half-out of his seat, the peanut-sized head with the protruding tongue, scream still caught in its throat resting upside down on the ground like Warren Beatty in Bonnie And Clyde.

"Looks like I gotta babysit yo' ass too," Duffy said replacing a clip in the 9mm, slipping it back in his waistband. "What was that all about?"

Crane said, "Con I knew at Marion, before your time there ... claimed I caused him some drama."

"Did you?"

"He brought it on himself."

"Almost brought it on you. Would have too, if I hadn't been on my *J-O-B*, know what I'm sayin', homie?"

Crane looked at his clothes, wiped blood from his face and followed Duffy back to the Regal hidden in the shadows. Duffy seemed calm and unmoved by what had just happened. His face betrayed no emotion one way or another. He was neither pumped up nor overly cautious. Just cool and calm like it had all been just a day's work. Crane liked that about Duffy. From the very beginning at Marion when he asked Bear to intercede on Duffy's behalf because he kept getting into hassles with Needham and the other guards, he was impressed with his seeming calmness in the face of danger and never backing down, even when he was wrong. He said to Duffy, "Owe you one, dog."

Duffy said, "S'all right, Godfather. Anyone else gunning for you?"

Crane said, "Beats me. But I know who to call to find out."

Chapter 5

CRANE STUMBLED INTO HIS ROOM at the *Hardcore* Motel close to two in the morning, still shaking from his close call with death. Duffy had insisted on following him to his room to insure his safety. And given what had just happened Crane couldn't refuse. He absently discarded the bloody clothes, showered, and only then came to realize the penthouse was nothing more than a tiny room with a thimble-sized kitchenette. Crane wondered what Princess did in the kitchen that was worth fifty bucks.

The room smelled like a cathouse at war with a room deodorizer. It was thinly furnished with a queen-size bed, a single chair somehow bolted to the floor and badly in need of reupholstering, a 25-inch color TV bolted to the floor, a single lamp bolted to one of two nightstands, a clock radio and telephone bolted to the other. The carpet was worn so thin in spots Crane could see the mat underneath, the walls thinning under worn layers of paint and cheap peeling wallpaper. He dropped onto the bed wrapped in a towel and found it surprisingly comfortable, then remembered if nothing else the bed *had* to be comfortable.

He withdrew the package from his bag and began tearing at the paper. It was a shoe box tightly packed with neatly wrapped stacks of money in various denominations. Dirty money, literally. Bills worn and frayed. Dog-eared. Bills with coffee and juice stains. Bills smudged with grease and oil and marker pens. Bills with phone numbers written on the edges. Bills torn, taped together haphazardly. But it was money. Good money. A cursory look told him it was the ten grand he'd requested. He covered the box, secured it with rubberbands and dialed the number as his eyes took in the room's cheap furniture and faded wallpaper. It rang seven times.

"Romero." The lilting Hispanic accent was east L.A. Young. Maybe twenty-five. Arrogant. A soldier in the Mexican Mafia.

"This is Crane."

"I know who you are."

Crane said, "Who are you?" A long dead pause of silence told Crane his job was to listen. So he did.

Romero said, "You count your money?"

Crane said, "I'll take your word it's all there, esé."

"Call me back when you've counted it," and before Crane could answer, the phone went dead. There it was. The Committee wasn't taking any chances. Not even with their own soldiers. Crane unwrapped the box again, counted each stack, noted their denominations. It took him ten minutes. He dialed the number. It rang seven times. "Romero."

"I have twenty hundreds. Forty fifties. A hundred twenties. Two hundred tens. Four hundred fives. Total of ten thousand."

Romero said, "Alright. From this point on you need anything, you talk to me. You speak *ONLY* to me. If someone else answers this number, a voice you don't recognize, you hang up, go to a secure phone, dial the number on the inside wrapper of the hundreds. You see it?"

Crane pulled the wrapper off the stack of hundreds, saw the number scribbled in ink, copied it down.

"That's a pager," Romero went on. "You can trust anyone who calls back."

Crane appreciated the Committee's caution.

"When you get the merchandise in hand," continued Romero, "call me with the location. I'll arrange the pick up."

Crane said, "How will I know it's you, not someone pretending to be you?"

Romero said, "I'll be with someone you know."

"Who?"

"Don't worry about that now, homes. What do you need?"

"I need a ride," Crane began slowly. "Nothing flashy. Just dependable." Crane could hear faint scratching of ink against paper in the background. "I'll need a driver's license too," he added. More silence. Just continued scratching.

"What else?" Romero asked after a moment.

Crane said, "I'll need one of those portable telephones, kind you see people using walking down the street."

"You mean a cell phone," Romero said. "Good as done."

"Alright," said Crane, drawing a line through the first item on his mental laundry list. "I need a heater."

The scratching stopped. Romero covered the phone with his hand. Crane could hear distant muffled conversation in rapid Spanish, heated, intense, argumentative.

"What kind?" Romero asked, back on the phone.

"A three fifty seven," Crane said.

"Three fifty seven is heavy. Why not something light? Maybe a nine ...?"

"I prefer a three fifty seven. Is that a problem?"

"Nothing's a problem, homes."

"Good. Let's move on then," said Crane. "A friend of mine caught a case on a DUI. He's due out in a month. I can't wait that long."

"Name and booking number?"

Crane said, "Marcus Jones. Have the booking number tomorrow."

Romero said, "Alright. What else?"

"I'll need a case of C-4 plastic explosive and detonators."

"C-4?" Romero exploded through the phone. "You did ten years in the joint. What do you know about C-4?"

Crane said, "Is that a problem, esé?"

The Mexican went silent again and Crane could hear agitation in the scratching and heavy nasal breathing that filtered through the receiver.

"Take some time to get that. Maybe a week," Romero said after another intense muffled conversation with confederates.

Crane said, "A week is fine. I need some balsa wood, Exacto knife and model airplane glue."

Romero laughed for the first time. "I'm not budgeted for toys," he said. "What's this for?"

Crane said, "Don't worry about it. I need it. You just get it."

Crane could hear Romero's breathing deepen, could hear him mutter familiar Spanish profanities to himself as he wrote. "Go on," he said, knowing Crane had more.

"I need a dentist," said Crane. "Someone who can turn out a bridge for me in twenty-four, forty-eight hours."

Romero laughed for the second time. He said sarcastically, "Would you like a barber and manicurist too?"

When Romero's laughter subsided Crane continued on. He said, "What room is the merchandise in?"

"Fifteen seventeen," Romero said, levity gone from his voice.

"Is the room occupied?"

"Twenty-four-seven, homes."

"How many?"

"It varies. Anywhere from three to five. Why?"

Three to five heavily armed soldiers of the Mexican Mafia. It was a problem Crane had struggled with the entire train ride home. He knew Moffett and the Committee would have the trunk under heavy guard. But if his plan was to succeed, the soldiers would have to know about it, and if they did, the element of surprise would be lost. Bloodshed might result, dooming the plan to failure.

"That could be a problem," Crane said. "I'm planning a surprise. I wouldn't want anybody hurt. Tell your people to cooperate."

Romero sounded confused. He said, "Cooperate? Cooperate with who?"

Crane said, "My people. Do whatever they tell 'em. I don't want anyone to panic, start killing people when it's on, know what I'm saying."

"And how they suppose to know you ain't the Feds, homes?"

Crane laughed, but not too long. "Feds be wearin' body armor, carrying AK-47's and shit," Crane said.

Romero said, "So? What'll you be wearing?"

Crane said, "Won't be that."

Romero said, "Better know what you're doing, homes—"

Crane said, "Trust me."

"Alright." Romero didn't sound convinced or relieved.

"What can you tell me about the surveillance?" Crane went on.

Romero said, "We think the Feds are in fifteen fourteen or fifteen fifteen."

"You think?" Crane snapped derisively, pushing his power on the Mexican, trying to make him sound incompetent and genuinely surprised he had nothing to offer on so critical a point. "When will you know for sure?"

Romero said, "You'll get it when we do. Anything else?"

Crane said, "Yeah. Some muthafucka tried to kill me tonight … someone who knew I was getting out."

Romero seemed unconcerned. He said, "You sound alive to me."

Crane said, "Barely. Who else knows I'm out?"

"I'll check on it," Romero said.

"You do that, esé," Crane said angrily. "Cause I got the feeling people were selling tickets. You want your shit delivered, I don't need no outside drama. Know what I'm saying, esé?" Romero's answer was a dial tone.

Crane lay back on the bed, relishing his first night of freedom in ten long years. He would often lie awake nights in the joint wondering what would be the first thing he'd do when he got out. Get himself a woman was always first on the list. But now, with his freedom a tenuous reality, he was surprised to find a woman wasn't the most important thing on his mind. Neither was Moffett's trunk. It was just being free. No more clanging steel doors. No more uniforms or regimented work details under brutal guards or watching his back day and night for the shiv he never saw but knew was just a cell block away. Freedom. It was a narcotic as addicting as any drug he'd ever seen, heard of or tried.

He clasped his hands behind his head, eyes following the busy flight of a moth drawn irresistibly to the fatal danger of the light. Outside, a liquor bottle shattered against the ground. A woman's voice screamed. A man's voice was cursing. The sound of a door opening letting Alicia Keys escape for an instant into the night air, then slamming shut, angry fists pounding, demanding it be opened and when it was, soft cooing voices singing along with Alicia Keys until it closed, then draining away into drunken muted laughter. Crane's eyes closed effortlessly. He wondered if the moth ever got the courage to avoid the light or was it a victim of circumstances. But he fell asleep before seeing the answer.

Chapter 6

B Y THE END OF CRANE'S FIRST WEEK OF FREEDOM much had been accomplished. Romero had delivered everything on Crane's shopping list except the C-4. A Mexican dentist in Boyle Heights fashioned Crane's bridge almost overnight, and the car, flashier than he wanted, was a beige 1995 Lexus registered to the dentist. As per Crane's request, Duffy had located a base of operations for them, a storage hangar near LAX. Directly under the flight path on a fenced-in portion of isolated land, he said it was large enough to conceal a Mack truck if necessary. Crane wondered if Duffy was reading his mind.

One of the first things Crane did was to buy himself a funeral crypt complete with casket in the mausoleum of Compton's notorious Washington Memorial Cemetery. It cost nearly half his bankroll, but it was insurance and he was hedging his bets against betrayal. Death insurance he liked to call it. He bought some new clothes, had fake business cards printed up and drove around L.A. for a day to familiarize himself with ten years worth of changes: Metrorail. Staples Center. West Angeles Cathedral. Magic Theaters. TGI Fridays. The Bridge.

He went looking for Uncle Joe. Uncle Joe was Crane's only living relative. He'd gone to live with him instead of a foster home after his mother's death from cancer. He was ten. Uncle Joe was kind but he drank and ran women. He left the boy to raise himself, supplying the house and cable ... which was how Crane came to like movies. And since Uncle Joe drank up the food stamps and blew the clothes money on whores, Crane had to hustle. Everything from pop-bottle rebates and recyclable tin cans to stealing. He was especially good at stealing because he always planned things. Even as a child he planned things because he knew he couldn't count on Uncle Joe to feed him. No matter. Uncle Joe was always there—there the one and only time he ever saw his father. They shook hands, his father saying he could see the resemblance, promising to stay in touch. But he never did. Uncle Joe was there when Crane got out of juvenile hall ... youth authority ... county jail. And during the first five years at Marion it was Uncle Joe's disjointed, printed letters that gave him hope. But the letters became fewer and briefer in later years and never had the same address because Uncle Joe moved around so much. After a while they stopped coming altogether.

Crane managed to track him down through some of his drinking buddies at the south central poolhall he was known to frequent on Avalon Boulevard. He finally located him in a two bedroom frame house on East

70th Street. Crane hardly recognized the withered and drawn stick figure Uncle Joe had become. But Uncle Joe recognized his nephew the moment he opened the door, held him in a long, warm embrace neither was in a rush to break. Crane lied about his release. He and Uncle Joe spent the afternoon in the company of Chevas Regal rehashing mistakes they'd both made, learning about Uncle Joe's ailments. Crane wanted to know where Marjorie was buried. Uncle Joe said he understood her grandmother had buried her at Holy Cross Cemetery off of Slauson, then moved back south.

Crane found Marjorie's grave that same day, covered it with twelve long-stemmed red roses, told her spirit he was sorry he couldn't have been there to protect her. Afterwards, he went back to the motel and cried, drowning his sorrow in the elaborate model he was fashioning out of balsa wood.

But if he was bothered by Marjorie's death, it was his first meeting with former partners in Chinatown that was even more troubling. On the fringe of L.A.'s downtown business district he'd chosen Chinatown because Reese lived close by with an older woman he claimed was his girlfriend, Marcus was being released from nearby Twin Towers, and Bo Bo's clean and sober rehab center was just over the hill in Pasadena.

He, Duffy and Trixie had arrived early in the afternoon and played tourists. The two men had strolled along behind Trixie who, alone among them, was in sightseer's heaven. The main square housed tiny, cramped shops that sold porcelain curios from Taiwan, silk robes from Hong Kong, ornate wooden furniture from Macao, and illegal ivory carvings of elephant tusks from India. If you knew someone and spoke the language you could buy firecrackers from Jimmy Foy's Candy Shop. Trixie had been excited by silk dresses from Cathay, satin blouses from Manchuria, even more by the sequined Asian designs that adorned them and seemed fascinated by the mysterious lilting singsong nuances of the language. Crane recalled being surprised by her knowledge of Chinese history, the breadth and scope of her understanding of Chinese culture.

Bathed in the fragrance of burning incense, crisscrossed by the glow of delicate, softly lit paper lanterns and the never-ending tinkle of chimes strung across narrow darkened alleyways separating pagoda-like buildings that housed tourist traps and restaurants, the square took on an exotic and forbidden life of its own as the twilight dinner hour approached and tourists swelled its population.

Housed on the second floor of a turn of the century faded brick building, Madame Fu's Mandarin Restaurant overlooked the square crowded with tourists. Its interior design was dark and mysterious and lit only by the glow of flickering shaded table candles. Booths were scattered about at various levels, separated from one another by ornately decorated folding reed screens. The waitresses were all young Chinese girls who wore sexy form-fitting, ankle-length sequined dresses with slits up to mid-thigh and brocaded high neck collars. They all attended Los Angeles City College and spoke better English than most native born Americans.

From the moment they laid eyes on Crane it was obvious they resented him, had eyed Trixie's presence with even greater suspicion. Crane had made introductions, then warned them Trixie didn't like being called white girl or bitch. Reese was the only one who hadn't aged, though he looked odd wearing a preacher's frock with a chain and cross dangling around his neck. Still obsessed with his looks and his game, he'd come onto Trixie non-stop ... until Duffy had gotten up and whispered something in his ear. Then his eyes had opened wide with fright and he'd spent the balance of the evening hitting on every waitress who came near the table, pretending Trixie didn't exist. Crane had wondered how he did it because Trixie had been irresistibly luminous with beauty.

Marcus had seemed heavier and slower. He was missing front teeth and his head of cornrows had grown loose and frayed from neglect in the Twin Towers. He was now living in a Santa Monica trailer park with a young Mexican girl who'd just had his baby. Henry T was the only one employed, driving a limousine for Elite Limousine Service in Beverly Hills. His hair had turned completely white but he still wore it Don King style. Bo Bo had changed the most. Toothless and nearly bald, he'd grown so thin from years of hard drinking that his pants barely held up at the last notch of his belt.

No one had believed Crane was out on appeal and didn't really care. Crane had said he was calling in the debt, to a man they had said they didn't care. They felt they owed him nothing. After all, it had been *his* plan and Marjorie had been *his* choice. They reasoned he *should've* taken the heat. It was a crazy idea … robbing a bank based on a movie. If they'd known that they wouldn't have gone along.

Crane had told them no more than he'd told Duffy and Trixie—he needed them to help rob the Duchess, said they'd each come out million-aires. He'd reminded them again they owed him, but they had all laughed, said he was still crazy, asked what movie it was based on. That's when Crane had threatened them … told Marcus he'd drop his name to the Mexican Mafia about the cocaine shipment he'd intercepted out on Pigeon Pass Road in Moreno Valley. The M & M's had killed the Mexican girl they felt was the leak but she never rolled over on him, so Crane figured the girl must have really loved him. If he didn't feel he owed Crane, at the very least he owed her. She died for him and that ought to mean something. Marcus got mad and loud, had started to go for bad until Duffy stuck his 9mm in Marcus' crotch under the table, chilling him out.

Henry T still believed he was the world's greatest lover, had forgotten all about the video camera he'd hidden in his apartment to tape the girls he had sex with, until Crane threatened him with the tape of a strawberry, twelve if she was a day, giving him head. Crane said he'd hidden the tape before he went to the joint, along with the gun and bloody shirt he'd gotten from Bo Bo after a botched jewelry store robbery the two of them had committed that left both the owner and Bo Bo wounded before they escaped. Humiliated and resentful, Henry T remained quiet and sullen throughout the meeting. It wasn't his style to speak right up when confronted. But Crane knew he would. It was just a matter of time.

Bo Bo, on the other hand, had become incensed and jumped up, nearly knocking over the table. He'd said Crane was his dog back then, was suppose to get rid of the gun and shirt and wanted to know why he hadn't. Crane had said he just had a hunch, that was all. He had said they shouldn't overestimate their past friendships—he'd use what he had against them if they didn't cooperate.

Marcus had spoken for them all, but it was not without bitterness and rancor and hostile reluctance. They didn't like being blackmailed but they'd come on board and do their part. In exchange the debt was paid, and Crane would have to turn over any evidence he had. Crane had agreed, said that was all he asked. But Marcus had reminded him in no uncertain terms that if Crane ever changed his mind he'd kill him himself no matter how long it took, he didn't care how many dogs like Duffy he had.

Bo Bo had wanted to know the risks. Crane had lied, said they wouldn't need any weapons for a job like this. Marcus had laughed, said he wasn't going into any robbery without weapons. Even Duffy had agreed, touched Marcus' fist and eased the bad feeling between them.

Crane had asked Bo Bo if he knew a fence who could handle a million dollar deal. Bo Bo had said he wasn't stealing anymore, but he thought Willie Nance might still have a pawnshop somewhere in Watts. The only time Henry T spoke was to ask what his part was. Crane had said transportation, that he'd explain everything later. Marcus had said he had a van if it would help. Crane had said they could use it to transport tables and others things to the storage hangar. Reese had wanted to know his role. Crane had said he'd let him know when the time came. Reese had insisted on blessing the food and when they'd finished eating, made everyone hold hands while he prayed for the venture to be profitable. When the meeting at Madame Fu's had ended, angry conscripted partners had drifted hurridly away, losing themselves in the shadows of Chinatown's pagodas. Before leaving Madame Fu's Crane opened his fortune cookie. It read: *Be careful what you wish for, it may just come true.*

Duffy had said he needed a drink and Trixie wanted to go dancing, so they'd left Chinatown for the ten minute ride to Los Angeles Street and Little Tokyo's New Otani Hotel. There was no dance floor in the Rendezvous Lounge, only a piano bar. But that had been good enough for Trixie who made her own dance floor next to the piano, continued to bring Crane to his feet as her cautious partner while Duffy, Crane himself not far behind, was getting drunk on Johnny Walker Red. Crane couldn't remember what the piano player was playing, but he remembered holding Trixie close, remembered how incredibly soft she felt in his arms, the sweet smell of her perfume in his nostrils, the nonsense she kept whispering in his ear when Duffy wasn't looking about the two of them getting together. The last thing he'd remembered was seeing Duffy's two heads passed out on the bar and feeling Trixie's tongue deep in his throat.

Crane went through his well organized list of priorities with methodical precision, decided it was time to address the issue of transportation and Henry T's attitude. With Crane driving, Duffy riding shotgun, they paid an unannounced visit to the limousine company, picked up a very reluctant Henry T and headed for the Ventura Freeway East to the 405 South and LAX.

"Need a truck, Henry T," Crane said, once on the freeway. "Got to look legit, like a vendor making regular deliveries."

Henry T could barely conceal his contempt for Crane.

"No shit," Henry T spit out from the back seat. Half-expecting it, Crane ignored the attitude, talked to Henry T's reflection in the mirror.

"Got to be large enough to haul away twenty rooms of merchandise," Crane said, one eye on Henry T, the other on the road ahead.

"Go rent a truck why don't you," Henry T said, pulling a comb through Don King hair. "It's called U-Haul," he added derisively.

Duffy turned around, half-faced Henry T over his shoulder and said, "Be a lot easier on all of us, brother, if you'd drop some of that attitude, know what I'm sayin'?"

Henry T frowned and said, "Fuck you, nigga. Wasn't nobody talking to you?"

Big mistake.

Because he was driving Crane didn't really see what happened next. But Henry T did. Still half-turned in his seat Duffy, suddenly leaned up and over the headrest grabbing the back of Henry T's neck with his left hand in the same lightening motion his right brought the barrel of his 9mm into Henry T's left nostril.

Hissing angrily through a mouth of spit Duffy said, "You high yella muthafucka, I got a good mind to cap your ass here and now, throw you right out the door on the freeway!" Eyes still glued to Henry T but throwing words over his shoulder to Crane he said, "Your call, Godfather. Sure we need this little punk bitch? I know someone get us transportation in a heartbeat if that's all he's good for. 'Cause I'm not in the mood to be puttin' up with no attitude. What do you say?"

Henry T didn't take a breath, didn't swallow, didn't utter a sound, didn't even blink he was so frightened. The veins on his forehead were bulging out like special effects in a horror movie, beads of sweat suddenly popping up, running down the side of his face.

Crane didn't speak at first. He brought the Lexus onto the transition to the 405 South and headed for the run to LAX.

"Henry T and me go way back," he said finally. "Don't we, Henry T?"

Henry T felt it safe to swallow, managed to find his tongue and said, "Yeah, Crane. Sure. Way back. We go way back. I didn't mean nothin'. No disrespect to your dog. I'll give him his props, alright?" Henry T's voice squeaked like that of a child explaining his way out of a lie.

"I can't hear you, muthafucka," said Duffy, jamming the barrel of the 9mm even harder into Henry T's nostril, distorting his face.

Henry stammered, saying, "S ... s ... sorry. No disrespect intended."

Duffy said, "Nigga, you better recognize."

"I think he does," Crane said, anxious to get on with the business at hand. "I think Henry T gonna be one of the team now. That right, Henry T?"

Henry T shook his head as much as he could in the vice grip of Duffy's hand.

"I ain't so sure," said Duffy, his face only inches away from Henry T, relishing the moment, not wanting to give it up but knowing he had to.

Crane said, "Duffy ..." in a way and tone that said it was over and Duffy suddenly released Henry T's neck, brought the 9mm out of his nostril. Henry T fell back in the seat, coughing to clear his throat, grateful eyes staring at Duffy.

Duffy said, "Now the man asked you a simple question—?"

Henry T swallowed several times to bring moisture to his throat.

"Big rig probably what you want, Crane. Ten wheeler."

"All right," said Crane, more relaxed, back on tract. "You get us one."

"When you need it?"

"Soon as you can steal it."

"Where I'm gonna put it?"

"Going there now," Crane said. He added, "Need a limousine too. Not right now. But soon. I'll let you know day ahead of time. That work?"

Henry T said it did, wanted to know if he had to drive them both.

"No," said Crane, slowing for the Century Boulevard exit. "Just the limousine. Get Reese to drive the truck."

"Suppose he can't drive?"

"Then you teach him."

Duffy looked at Crane, began to chuckle and said, "Damn, Crane—we goin' to the Duchess in a limo? Now that's what I call mobbin' in style." Duffy thought it was funny ... him, a gentleman thief and said so.

"No. Just Henry T in the limo," Crane said without further explanation, deflating the mood.

Duffy frowned. So did Henry T.

"I don't understand?" Duffy said for the two of them.
"You will."

The LAX storage facility Duffy had arranged was perfect but they'd need earplugs. Directly under the glide path of screaming jets sliding down to the runway, it was one of many cavernous structures on a fenced-in portion of abandoned land that had at one time been a residential neighborhood before the City bought the property. Beyond the boundaries of the fence you could still see remnants of foundations where houses once stood. Resembling small airplane hangars, the walls were made of concrete blocks that supported high vaulted aluminum ceilings in the middle of which hung a single row of fluorescent lights. Entry was through two large side-by-side rollup aluminum doors and a metal hinged door on the side.

Henry T took some measurements, said a ten wheeler would be a tight fit but he'd have to separate the box from the cab. Crane wanted to know how long it would take him to get the truck. Henry T said about a week or less, depending on whether or not he got caught. Crane reminded Henry T he never once got caught stealing cars. Henry T said those were cars. This was a truck. Crane said he had bail money if that worried him. Henry T said the only thing that worried him was losing his job. He liked driving celebrities around. Duffy said when they were done he'd have enough money to buy the limousine company.

Crane felt bad about Duffy having to strong-arm Henry T, remembered fondly they had once been good friends back in the day. So on the way back he stopped at a bar, bought everyone drinks, started talking about old times. Talked about when he and Henry T used to gangsterize together ... Henry T stealing cars ... the whole group ripping off warehouses, liquor stores, jewelry stores and private homes. Talked about Henry T's penchant for young girls. Henry T letting the booze chill his seething hostility toward Crane for the moment, enjoy the memory of good times past, a long-ago friendship now gone sour. Henry T asked Crane about Marjorie. Said she was one of the finest black women he'd ever seen. Said Crane had to be pussy-whipped to let her in on the bank job. Crane said he was and laughed. Henry T laughed. And Duffy.

They stayed at the bar all day. It was dark when they left. Crane knew he shouldn't drive. He was drunk. They were all drunk. They climbed in the Lexus together, good buddies for the moment. Crane couldn't find the ignition. When he did, he couldn't find his keys. So they all got out and crawled around on the ground looking like elephants groveling aimlessly in the mud. One by one they began to laugh hysterically, cursing each other with the unintelligible thickness of words slurred by stupor. When they couldn't find the keys they staggered back to the bar blurry-eyed and ordered more drinks. Henry T and Duffy ordered beer. Crane ordered Chevas Regal. The bartender brought coffee. Crane sobered up enough with three cups to find his keys in the cuffs of his pants. Five cups let him drive. Knew when Henry T sobered up he'd go back to his old sullen self. He'd hate Duffy even more for putting a gun in his face, Crane for letting him. No matter. For a day it was like old times. But only for a day.

Tomorrow he'd have to watch his back.

Chapter 7

CRANE BOLTED UPRIGHT WITH THE FIRST HANGOVER of his freedom, dripping wet, breathing hard and a splitting headache. Shafts of bright sunlight poured in from around edges of broken and bent window blinds. The clanging steel door of his recurrent nightmare was in fact the clock radio, the sportscaster droning on about how good the Raiders looked in pre-season play, predicting they could very well make the Superbowl ... wondered if surgery on Shaq's big toe would hold up enough for the Lakers to win four straight championships.

9:00 am. Crane drug himself to the shower, let the water finish his wakeup call.

The doorbell rang. Crane opened it with a towel and a frown. They were early.

"Wazzup, homie?" Duffy said, sliding past Crane, Trixie following close in his wake, even closer to Crane, her breasts brushing across his bare chest, her powder-blue eyes and full puckered lips flashing silent conversations she knew Crane was reading. And now, having seen him more frequently in daylight ... rested, clean shaven, new teeth, he was even more appealing. It was all she could do to keep her feelings in check and out of the watchful eyes of Duffy. So in the tight space between them she gave Crane a wink and a quick kiss on the lips behind Duffy's back before he could stop her.

She was dressed in red leather thigh-high boots and matching hot pants that separated the cheeks of her butt. Her white, too-small, too-tight sleeveless blouse functioned more like a Victoria Secret's bra struggling to stay buttoned at the hands of a persistent lover, her cleavage magnified with each breath she took. Her hair was bleached platinum blonde, sprinkled with sequins and swirled wildly about her head in an uncombed tangle of matted strands like a dry mop.

Crane was disturbed by her outfit and said so. She was over-exposed for what they were about to do. Trixie didn't see anything wrong with the way she was dressed. She was an entertainer. "This is the way entertainers dress," she said to Crane, reminded him he was in the real world now. She made it clear she wasn't about to change so he left it alone.

Crane envied Duffy, but didn't quite know how to handle Trixie's flirtation ... whether it was just that, flirtation as a part of her nature, or a real come-on. But he knew his attraction to Trixie was building, becoming more difficult to deny, more difficult to suppress. Yet the fresh image of Marjorie's grave and the raw memory of their life together evoked the first twinges of guilt, as if he were betraying her. These would help control any feelings he might develop for Trixie—up to a point. Still, he had to admit if she persisted in her come-ons he wasn't entirely sure he could resist her. But he had to. Somehow. There were more important things to attend to than romance with a white girl, especially this white girl, Duffy's white girl. Crane knew his limits, realized now was not the time to risk Duffy's loyalty and trust, not over a woman. For now he'd tread very lightly. He owed Duffy his life as Duffy had owed him in the joint. That made them even in a way. It also welded them together with mutual respect and trust, like a father and son the way Crane saw it. Betrayal of that trust by either one would be catastrophic.

Duffy sat down at the table, helped himself to Crane's orange juice. Trixie paced nervously about the room, turned off by everything in it except Crane. She pulled out a joint, lit it and said, "This place is the pits, Crane. Can't you do better?"

Crane said, "In time. We finish our deal, gonna build me a house like you've never seen."

Trixie noticed the half-finished model on the table. She was genuinely impressed. She said, "That's what you're building now, a toy house?"

Crane hadn't meant for her to see it, for anyone to see it. He grabbed a dishtowel, gently covered it. He said, "It's anything but a toy house."

But Trixie rolled the towel back, exposing the model, recognizing the raw talent behind the model's early and still indefinable shape for what it was, what it could be.

She said, "Is this part of what we're all doing or is it a hobby?"

"Little of both," Crane said, irritated, snatching the towel from her hands, replacing it back over the unfinished model with a delicacy only

Trixie noticed.

"Still think you could find a better place to live than here," Trixie said, casting critical eyes in a face of frowns about the room as if it were unsafe to breath the air. "You should move up to Hollywood where we are," she went on. "They may be old but they're a lot cleaner than this. Safer too. You won't have to go through bullshit like what happened the other night. It stinks in here. Phew!"

"Word," Duffy said. "But I've lived in worse. Know what I'm sayin'?" And indeed he had. His mother had been a beautiful girl when she got hooked on crack by the time she was thirteen. Harold D. Andrews was born when she was sixteen and by then she'd become a strawberry. She told him his father was one of her tricks, she didn't know which one, added the D as a middle initial on his birth certificate at the last minute because it sounded proper. It took her six months to decide on a name, chose Duffy from a cartoon she was watching during a cocaine binge and never called him anything else.

For as long as he could remember Duffy had been shuffled from one group home to another, one foster home to another, spending occasional periods of time with his mother whenever she cleaned up. And even then she had so little money from welfare it barely fed them. And so she'd return to hooking, leaving him home alone days on end without enough food while she fed her crack habit—coming back to the apartment with Burger King or MacDonald's just long enough to see if he was all right, and get the color TV to settle a crack debt. Duffy couldn't remember how many times the lights were cut off for non-payment, how many eviction notices he'd seen tacked to the front door. She knew he wasn't going to school like he should, begged him to attend and graduate, knowing he wouldn't. Her pleas fell on deaf ears. Duffy hated school, except for the girls and the fights. It was a tough choice between girls and gangbanging. He got a high out of both and became an expert at both. He was suspended time and again for one thing or another, dropping out altogether in the eleventh grade.

Back to the foster homes, back to crack-addicted mother. Through it all his mother never lost affection for Duffy. She never beat him. She loved him the best she knew how. She never blamed him for her habit, often apologized at not being able to do more for him, implored him not to follow her path. One time she asked her sister to keep him for a while. She was married and well off with a house in Baldwin Hills. But her husband didn't like Duffy and used to beat him, so he'd run away.

When he was eleven they placed him in the first of many group homes. Duffy learned the streets in group homes, how to fight, how to survive, how to fuck, how to hustle ... how to become a man. And he was good at it. Very good. But the harshness of life made him callous ... and brutal when necessary.

He was seventeen and in his seventh group home when he got the word his mother had been shot to death in an alley by gang members who'd raped her first. He didn't cry or show any emotion. But he spent the next year methodically tracking them down, killing them one by one execution style, emptying entire 9mm clips into their bodies. He felt no particular joy nor did he feel remorse when it was over. He felt nothing. He did what he had to do. That's all there was to it. He was never suspected and never caught. He was living in a group home when he turned eighteen and the system let him go. He left with a garment bag of clothes and fifty dollars. He was not frightened or intimidated by being on his own. He knew how to survive in the streets. He was fiercely loyal to those he respected, absolutely lethal if crossed or betrayed.

Moving in and out of the bathroom pulling on pants, socks, shirt, tying shoes, spraying on cologne all in one motion, Crane waited for Duffy to finish his orange juice, Trixie to finish the joint. He looked at his watch and said, "Let's go, people," and ushered them out of the room, locking the door behind. "Let's not keep the Duchess waiting."

Chapter 8

THE DUCHESS HOTEL RISES FIFTEEN STORIES above Sunset Boulevard and commands the most majestic, panoramic view of the L.A. basin of any hotel in the city. Shaped like a smaller version of Miami's curved Fontainebleu, it has always been the hotel of choice for the rich and famous. With its salmon paint job, it doesn't really look like a hotel at all, but rather like an exclusive high-rise apartment building without the fanfare. And that had always been its appeal—a nondescript, subtle, laid-back sort of home away from home whose curved height blended seamlessly with its business and social surroundings. Crane hadn't appreciated that from the photos he'd been given in prison. But as

he made the sharp right turn off Sunset and into the narrow patched driveway that disappeared into a storm of bushes and trees, he could see the
wisdom of the Committee's decision. And as he approached the entrance,
came face to face with its commanding physical reality, he also knew it
would not be the easy task he'd anticipated.

The parking attendants looked like models from esquire with their
matching salmon-colored Georgio Armani linen suits, white turtleneck
sweaters, white Georgio Brutini shoes, sans socks. They were at the doors
before Crane braked to a stop, falling all over themselves with service
when Trixie stepped out smiling, playing to her audience.

"Cool," she said, eyes sweeping the hotel, taking in the caravan of
limousines, people checking in and out. Crane had been wrong about
Trixie's attire. Dead wrong. This *was* entertainment. She slipped on red
Versace sunglasses and pranced through swinging gold-lettered glass
doors into the lobby, centerstage. It was showtime and she was on.

Crane also played the role. From a tightly rolled wad of bills he
peeled off a C-note for the attendant, followed Duffy through the door,
both racing to catch up with Trixie.

The lobby was more like the ground floor of a high-rise office
building but without the desk and security guard, so deceptive was the
emptiness of its dead open space. The floor was a wide mosaic of
Mexican pavers that disappeared into walls of splashy art deco. There
were no chairs. No end tables with vases of flowers or lamps. No maga-
zine racks with tourist brochures of Disneyland, Magic Mountain or the
Universal Studios Tour. The elevator console dominated center space, its
three walls also a splash of matching art deco, its entrance hidden from
patrons standing next to mountains of luggage in tiny clusters of twos,
threes and fours. You knew they were rich because they were relaxed,

unhurried and white—familiar faces of passing celebrities, politicians and movie stars … occasional recording artists and a few NBA players to add color—just enough to prevent an NAACP lawsuit for discrimination.

Crane said, "May I speak to the manager, please?" flashing his card at the barely thirty-something Donnie Osmond clone with shoulder-length blond hair behind the small recessed booth at the far end of the pavers.

"Worldwide Music Entertainment Management," the man said, eyes moving from the card to the trio of faces, falling more frequently on Trixie's cleavage. "Mr. Rawlston …?"

Crane extended his arm across the desk. "I'm Rawlston," he said. "And you are …?"

"Stickle," the man said, shaking Crane's hand with his right, pushing out his name tag with the thumb of his left, trying hard not to look at Trixie, ignoring Duffy altogether. "Leonard Stickle," he went on proudly. "I'm daytime manager of the Duchess. Can I help you?"

Crane waved his arm at Duffy, taking in Trixie. He said, "These are my associates, Mark Crannis and Ms. Ida Vann. We're part of the team putting together the itinerary for Cold Hard Cash's first American tour and …"

"Cold Hard Cash?" Stickle interrupted, frowning.

"Rap group out of the big apple," Trixie chimed in, sensing his interest and breathing deeply, catching his eyes, buying time for Crane.

Stickle said weakly, "Don't believe I know them," and looking at Trixie with silent wishes, trying not to be obvious, his breathing starting to match hers.

"You will after March," Crane said, back on cue, pulling Stickle's eyes back to his own. "They'll have quite an entourage. We'd like to put as many as we can on the same floor, wouldn't you think, Crannis?"

Duffy was slow on the uptake. He said rather lazily, "Huh? Oh, yeah. 'Course."

"Suites?" Stickle asked.

"Well, of course suites," cried Trixie, feigning insult. "You act as if the Duchess is too good for Rap groups?" she went on, getting into the act, enjoying it, bristling with sensual attitude that was all part of the con.

"Oh, no, Miss Vann. Not at all. Sorry if I gave you that impression," he blustered apologetically. "We get Rap groups all the time—RUN DMC ... MC Lyte ... MASTER P—"

"Really," Trixie said, removing her sunglasses, her sparkling powder-blue eyes suggesting forgiveness.

"I only meant," Stickle went on in damage-control mode, "if you wanted suites just for the musicians or ... everyone?"

"Everyone, of course. Arthur ...?" Trixie said, taking control.

"Create havoc if we had to split them up," Crane said, playing along, suddenly realizing he'd misjudged Trixie. She was a natural. Spontaneous. Her timing was perfect. She seemed to know just what to say and how to say it. They should give her an Oscar. Crane realized now that he and Trixie would work the Duchess as a team. He didn't have to tell her that. It was already happening and she understood, perhaps even better than he, the art of the ruse and how to use it. Duffy was an appendage. Useless. The less he said the better. For that matter he could've stayed at home.

Stickle went to his computer. "Our suites are all on the fifteenth floor. Most are two, three and four bedroom townhouse suites. They run five thousand a night—?"

Five grand a night. Crane did the math. The trunk had been here at least a month, maybe more. Hundred and fifty grand already. No wonder the Committee was pressuring him to act quickly. Still, thirty days …

Trixie raised her eyebrows dismissively and said, "Not a problem. Any chance we can take a look at one … get an idea of its layout? I know you have brochures and all, but seeing it firsthand is so much better. You can understand that, can't you, Mr. Stickle?" and Trixie took an especially deep breath as the manager's eyes jumped back and forth between her chest and the computer.

"Of course," Stickle said. He grabbed a folder and a small ring of plastic cards from off the desk, retreated through the door, emerged into the lobby through another door nearly invisible in the art deco wall and headed across the pavers, beckoning. "If you'll follow me, Mr. Rawlston," he said to the trio but looking at Trixie, waiting for her to put on sunglasses, catch up, walk beside him. She did even better, taking his arm, making sure his elbow was pressed tight against the soft rounded incline of her breast as they walked. The smile that crossed Stickle's face would have done any sucker proud. Crane smiled too. And Duffy. Nothing else to do in the company of genius.

"We offer a rather unique setup," Stickle said proudly as they approached the elevator console. "Everything is private. No rooms face the windows of surrounding office buildings or high-rise apartments. No one can see us, except from the air, of course," he said almost apologetically.

"Of course," Trixie breathed.

"But," Stickle went on eagerly, his elbow married to the side of Trixie's chest, "we can see the entire city. Every suite has a view as you'll soon see."

"Make a note of that, would you, Ms. Vann?" Crane said pointedly. "Complete privacy except from the air."

Trixie smiled at Stickle, a silent apology for having to disengage her arm. She took off her sunglasses and scribbled efficiently on a yellow pad as she walked.

The elevator console contained four elevators. Two indicated floors L through 14. The other two had no floor numbers, but the letters PHS painted in yellow and outlined in black so as to stand out from the art deco walls. Crane asked what the letters stood for.

Stickle said, "Penthouse Suites."

Crane said, "I thought it might have to do with parking."

Stickle smiled and said, "There's absolutely no access to the parking structure except by the freight elevator or fire exits. We don't permit our guests in the garage. Only parking attendants and vendors."

"Suppose you need something from your car?" Crane asked.

Stickle said, "Parking attendants will bring the car up at no charge, then return it back to a pre-assigned spot for the duration of their stay."

Duffy said, "Kinda inconvenient, ain't it?"

Stickle said, "The price of security is always inconvenience, Mr. Crannis."

"Word," said Duffy.

"All the elevators are tied to our guests' room keys," Stickle went on, holding up a credit-card size plastic key for them to look at. "I'm sure you've used these before at other hotels. But the Duchess has gone one better, linking the elevator to the room key. When a guest checks out, we automatically change the room code to match a new code for the elevator. And in the case of an emergency such as a computer failure," he continued, inserting a steel key into the panel and turning it, "we can always operate the elevators manually."

"Ms. Vann?" Crane said.

"Right, Arthur. Excellent security on elevators and in the garage," Trixie replied dutifully, writing diligently on the pad.

A PHS elevator arrived, discharged guests, bellboys and luggage racks. The quartet entered, Trixie and Crane first, Stickle and Duffy following. As the elevator made its rapid ascent Trixie, eyes facing forward and out of the field of vision of the others standing in front, slid her free hand over Crane's crotch and squeezed. It caught him by surprise and he grunted, louder than he'd of liked, flinging her hand away and taking a step to the side. Trixie giggled, still looking straight ahead, smiling, saying something about her ears popping. Stickle and Duffy both turned around, curious, Stickle lingering a second longer than Duffy and catching Trixie's inviting wink.

The elevator doors opened in a console that faced dead center of an uncrowded crescent-shaped corridor whose unbroken wall of salmon-colored marble and gilded smoked glass mirrors swept its entire length to either side. The room numbers facing the console read 1500 - 1510 on the left; 1511 - 1520 on the right. Crane noticed from the elevators he couldn't see the end of the corridor in either direction because of its arc. As they stepped off the elevator Trixie's chest rejoined Stickle's arm, following his lead to the right, maneuvering around occasional housekeeping carts, infrequent comings and goings of hotel guests and familiar squeaking wheels of luggage carts. Crane surveyed the obstacles. He counted sprinklers in the ceiling, noting placement and number of fire extinguishers on the wall. He made a special note when they passed 1517, a Do-Not-Disturb sign hung on its handle, the room that held the key to Crane's future. And Trixie's. And Duffy's.

Stickle stopped at the last door. Some thirty or forty feet beyond, the corridor ended at the firedoor to the stairwell. There was no freight elevator in sight. Stickle pulled out a plastic card, opened the door to 1520.

Stickle conducted the tour. Trixie wrote as she walked, jotting down comments from Crane and observations of her own. Duffy tagged along in awed silence, mesmerized by oversized, thick-pile carpeted bedrooms that filled the upstairs and drained down a spiral staircase to a mansion-size first floor. The floor was flooded by the view of massive floor-to-ceiling windows and evenly divided by a huge center-console kitchen, living room, dining room, bar and recreation room complete with pool table and an eighty-inch Mitsubishi giant screen TV that hung from the ceiling.

They finished the tour back on the first level, seated in deep cushioned chairs that looked out over L.A.

Duffy said to Stickle, "Dope crib."

Stickle must have been a closet fan of hip-hop. He smiled and said, "Off the hook, isn't it? Nothing else like it in L.A."

"Word," said Duffy, held out his fist for the white boy to touch.

"Any questions?" Stickle asked. Trixie finished scribbling, turned to a blank page and waited.

"Each bedroom has its own safe, I see," said Crane.

"Sixty of them," said Stickle pointedly. "All digital. Guests make up their own combination. Works like an ATM machine."

Crane did the math. Sixty safes … sixty rooms. It wasn't a matter of how. It was a matter of how long. And a matter of who. He'd need a safecracker, reminded himself to see if Duffy knew one.

"What happens if there's a power failure?" Trixie asked.

"Auxillary power comes on in sixty seconds," Stickle said.

Duffy said, "And if that goes out?"

Stickle laughed. "Then we call a locksmith," he said.

"Word," said Duffy.

"I'm worried about fire," Crane said, irritated at Duffy's less-than-stellar performance.

Stickle jumped up smiling, walked over to the wall near the spiral staircase, pointed to a round plastic container attached to the ceiling. He said, "See that smoke detector? It's not like the kind you and I have at home. Anytime smoke of a certain density comes in contact with it, the sprinkler system is triggered. Same in the corridor. Most sprinklers are triggered by heat, and we have that kind, too. But we had this special system installed just as an added measure of precaution. If there's any suggestion of smoke or heat in any one of the rooms, there's a collector panel out in the corridor facing the elevator that receives all the sensors for smoke and water flow from every room on the floor. It's tied directly to the fire department."

"What about cigarettes?" Trixie asked.

"Smoke from a match or cigarette just isn't dense enough to set off the sprinklers," Stickle said.

Duffy said, "What about smoke from *stress*, or a Blunt?"

Again the white boy knew more than he let on. He shook his head and grunted. He said, "Not even from *chronic*."

Crane stood and said, "Well, I'm pretty much satisfied. How 'bout you, Ms. Vann?"

"Roof and garage, Arthur," Trixie said.

Crane snapped his fingers, grateful. "Right. Almost forgot." He was impressed. White girl was way ahead of him. He reminded himself to give her props later.

Stickle stood, hit the button that closed the drapes, shutting out sunlight. He said, "Like I said earlier, we don't permit hotel guests in the garage."

"We understand," Trixie said standing, moving past Stickle to the door, bumping her chest lightly against his, stealing a telling glance at Crane when sure Duffy wasn't looking. "But we're dealing with artists who are so peculiar I wouldn't want to leave anything to chance. You can see our point, can't you … Leonard? May I call you Leonard?"

Stickle's face exploded in smile lines. "Of course," he said, closing the door after Duffy, joining the trio in the corridor, his waiting arm once more pressed firmly against Trixie's breast, the bulge in his cheeks matching the one in his pants. "We'll access the roof by the stairwell at the other end of the corridor. It's next to the service elevator," Stickle said, eager to prolong this impromptu tour as long as Trixie stuck to him. Trixie smiled coyly, pulled herself closer, the firm nipple bulging through her sweater rubbing against the sucker's arm.

Stickle shut off the fire door alarm with a metal key and led them up to a roof of blistering tar paper, crushed rock and pigeon droppings. They may all have thought the short climb a waste, but it gave Crane another solution to a critical problem.

Back on the fifteenth floor Stickle opened the doors of the service elevator with his plastic key, ushering them into a padded cell buffeted by loud hissing noises. He said, "Air conditioning ducts." Crane's eyes followed Stickle's finger pointing to the roof. "Seems everything goes through the elevator shafts … power cables, phone lines. You name it." He pushed the 'P' button on the panel dropping them to the garage, picking up housekeeping personnel and vendors on the trek down.

They walked out into the stuffy dry heat and suffocating fumes of a noisy underground parking structure that was, for all intents and purposes, a well-lit showroom for BMW, Mercedes, and Rolls Royce vehicles. In one distant corner a steel cage housed what Stickle said was the emergency generators. Closer to the service elevator they had just exited, were a number of trucks from various vendors. Drivers were unloading their vehicles onto dollies, dashing quickly to the elevator, punching in codes on the ATM-type pad, waiting for the doors to open. And it was here that Stickle explained what the vendors were doing, Crane paying special attention to the lecture.

"Any vendor who services the Duchess has to call the desk from here," and he pointed to a speaker in the panel next to the elevator, "and get his or her code for that day. He or she notifies us when they've finished and the code is disabled. If the vendor leaves without notifying us, the codes are automatically changed every eight hours and *that* vendor no longer services the Duchess." It was the only time Stickle's voice seemed harsh and uncompromising. "Are there any questions?"

Trixie closed her pad, took Stickle's arm, rubbing it affectionately and said, "I think Cold Hard Cash will really like it here. Arthur?"

Crane said, "Absolutely."

They finished the tour back at the registration desk. Crane assured Stickle they'd be in touch to book the rooms just as soon as they'd gotten clearance. Stickle shook each of their hands in turn, Trixie's last. She gave him a kiss on the cheek and a brief tight hug that brought the full cushion of her chest against his. He smiled and quickly disappeared through a hidden door to take care of his erection.

Chapter 9

THEY CAME TOGETHER ... DUFFY CRYING OUT, falling helplessly back on the bed—Trixie screaming, collapsing on his chest in a shroud of blonde hair, their breathing heavy and rapid in the wake of pleasure.

Trixie moved first, rolled off Duffy, grabbed a joint from the night-stand, lit it, took a deep drag, passed it to Duffy. She wondered why she was still with Duffy. The answer was simple, she told herself. It was Crane. He just hadn't responded the way she'd anticipated. She'd been throwing him signals since they first met ... and nothing. Zero. No response. And earlier in the day, when they'd cased the Duchess and fell

into sync together, when it was obvious … she assumed it was obvious—
maybe it wasn't obvious to him—he still didn't respond, not even subtly,
not even when Duffy wasn't looking and it would've been safe for him to
signal … a smile, a wink—something, anything. But there was nothing.
She knew he wasn't afraid of Duffy. Cautious, maybe. But not afraid. He
wasn't gay, she knew that too. Yet Crane had remained stone-faced and
indifferent to her overtures, except this afternoon when he'd compli-
mented her on her performance at the Duchess and she chalked that up to
basic courtesy. Maybe she'd misjudged him. Maybe he wasn't for her
after all. She was just bored with Duffy. Maybe that was the whole thing.
She thought she saw excitement in Crane—an older man with unusual
ideas was quite exciting—but realizing now perhaps he was just as
boring. And if that was the case she may as well stay with Duffy. What
a letdown. She took another drag on the joint, suddenly sat up, folded her
legs over one another, cleared hair from her face and said, "Duff, what'll
we do when this is all over, when we have some money?"

Duffy said thickly, "What do you mean 'what'll we do'—? We
spend it. That's what we do. Gonna be livin' large, baby, that's what."

Trixie turned, swung her legs across his stomach and clasped her
knees. She said to Duffy, "Yeah, I know all that. But what else? What
about getting out of the life?"

Duffy half-sat up, propped on elbows. He said, "Gettin' out the life?
Who wants to get out the life? I'm gonna be the biggest dope dealin' nigga
on Crenshaw." Suddenly he began to laugh. He said to Trixie, "Remember
that nigga in Superfly," assuming she'd seen the film. She hadn't but let
him go on. "One who said he didn't wanna go to no Europe? Said he was
gonna stay right there in Harlem and get richer? Said he was gonna
become a black Prince?" Duffy laughed even louder and harder at the

very thought. "Well," Duffy said as his laughter eased, "that's gonna be me, baby. Only I ain't gonna be no Prince—I'm gonna be the Pharaoh of Crenshaw. The King."

Trixie's face fell. She said, "Nothing else?"

Duffy lay back down, hands clasped behind his head, eyes slowly closing. He said to Trixie, "That's all, baby. I ain't never gettin' out the life."

Trixie stayed silent for a long time, thinking. She hadn't realized Duffy was so limited ... that he had no vision beyond tomorrow. And given his resourcefulness, that surprised her. She finished off the joint, went to the shower, knew he'd join her when he heard the water.

After they'd showered and were drying off Trixie said to Duffy, "Don't you ever get tired of hustling, Duff? I sure as hell do. I'd like to start living like regular people for a change."

"Brady Bunch," he sputtered to Trixie. "You watch too much television, girl. That shit's only real for white folks and niggas that think they white—no offense, baby, but that's reality in America. Don't need no college degree to see that."

Trixie finished toweling off, slipped on panties, tried on a bra. She said to Duffy, "Maybe so. But folks like us ought to have a chance to live like that, don't you think? Get us a house with neighbors we got something in common with." Duffy thought that was funny and said so.

"What Brady Bunch people you know got anything in common with us, Trixie?" Duffy asked, laying out clothes on the bed.

Trixie said, "We could have us a kid maybe. That would be something in common?"

Duffy shook his head violently, dreads sending out pinwheel remnants of water in a circle that caught the mirror and Trixie's cheek.

"Look," he said pulling on shoes, edge in his voice rising. "I ain't down with no marriage and kids and shit, alright? You wanna play house like the Huxstables, go play it with someone else— not with me!"

'*Go play it with someone else?*' Trixie couldn't believe he'd said that. But he had. And although the words stung, she heard them loud and clear, like the tolling of a bell, warning citizens to flee approaching disaster. Trixie looked at Duffy as if seeing him for the first time. Had she been this blind, or was it the drugs? She couldn't be sure which. But she could see him now for what he was more clearly than at any time in the past— cold, uncaring and selfish. She realized now more than ever that a change was in the wind and it was blowing with gale force intensity. Once again her mind turned to Crane. Perhaps she was giving up too easily and that wasn't like her.

She discarded yet another bra, slipped on a one-piece body dress so short and tight it left nothing to the imagination. She pulled her hair into a ponytail, swiped on a smattering of lipstick, rouge, sprayed on cheap perfume. She looked at Duffy, incredulous eyes stabbing his with the hurt of disbelief, her voice latent with the bitterness of resignation. She said sourly, "I guess it can't really change for people like us after all." She stepped to the door, opened it, walked into the corridor and throwing words over her shoulder weighted in sarcasm said, "Crane is waiting for us at the club. Let's go make us some motherfucking money."

Crane's table at the Baby Doll was front row dead center of a three-sided stage that extended out from a wall of red satin and velvet decor.

Erotic oversized cutout caricatures of thumb-sucking, diaper-wearing, large-breasted females striking provocative poses around a playpen hung on the walls. Loud recorded music filled the club over the din of conversation from a patronage of mostly Asian men, some whites, few blacks, scattering of women. Banks of colored lights bathed the girls on stage, intermittent flashing strobes turning their routines into slow motion pantomimes.

Crane had been waiting more than an hour. But he didn't mind. It had been an experience. He'd seen a dancer by the name of Holley Woods, a tall, round-faced black girl of about twenty whose oversized implants, large pink wig, skinny legs and uncoordinated movements gave her the appearance of a flamingo wandering loose in the Everglades. Dressed in a retro outfit meant to resemble Diana Ross' days with the Supremes, her routine was cumbersome and boring and was lost on the customers who, almost to a man, ignored her. They talked in low muted drunken chatter during her routine. Catcalls. Whistles. Shouts to get off the stage and vulgar comments of derision didn't help her confidence. Crane slipped a C-note in her G-string out of pity, watched her leave the stage in tears.

Duffy and Trixie arrived just as the next dancer was introduced, a thick, big-boned Dutch girl who danced as Sunsett Stripp to Gene Autry's *Don't Fence Me In*. She was dressed somewhat more imaginatively as a cowboy including a pair of holstered cap pistols she discarded as the last item of clothing. The Asians loved her, whooping and hollering and slapping their butts, trying to slap hers, as if riding horses in a western.

Duffy apologized for being late, put it on Trixie. Trixie's apology was a simple kiss on Crane's cheek, the one facing Duffy. But she stuck her finger in the ear Duffy couldn't see, felt Crane's slight jerk, sensed all was not lost. She sat down in a chair facing Crane and Duffy, her back to the stage. They ordered drinks—Duffy red wine, Crane a beer—complimentary since Trixie worked there, and launched into the details of Crane's plan while Sunsett Stripp fired her cap pistols.

"You bring the notes from this morning?" Crane asked Trixie.

Trixie produced folded sheets of yellow from her purse and laid them on the table.

"You took real notes?" Duffy asked, surprised.

"Of course I took real notes, Duff. Why wouldn't I?"

Duffy said, "Figured you just frontin' like the rest of us. And anyway, what good they gonna do us? Can't nobody get in that mutha-fucha unless they stayin' there, and they sure as hell ain't gonna let no whole bunch of black folks just walk in and walk out through the lobby with all their shit! Know what I'm sayin'?" Duffy was looking at Trixie, but his words were meant for Crane. "How you figure it, bro?" he said to Crane directly. "You told us that first night we picked you up we was gonna hit the top floor of the Duchess. Get us some seven figure money. Right? Ain't that what you said?" Yes, that's what he'd said that first night. But he hadn't told them how. Not until he'd scouted the Duchess, knew what obstacles he faced, what risks were involved, reliability of the team he'd have to put together and if he could trust them.

Crane said to Duffy, "That's still the plan. Every room, lock, stock and barrel—cash, jewelry, clothes … everything."

Duffy looked at Crane as if he was crazy. He said incredulously, "That's still the plan? You must be insane. How you gonna do that? I mean, even if we could get in … even if we could get niggas up to the muthafuckin' fifteenth floor, which with all that high tech security they got I don't see how, but if we *could* get up there, what about all the people? They ain't just gonna open their doors and stand around while we rip off their shit. We need them rooms completely empty—the whole floor has to be empty to do what you talkin' about," Duffy sputtered, sipping his wine, eyes occasionally drifting to Sunsett Stripp's routine.

Crane sipped on his beer. "That's right," he said casually.

"That's right, *WHAT?*" Duffy retorted, knowing he should be able to see it, frustrated at not being able to.

"We need the entire fifteenth floor empty. Deserted," Crane said.

"How you gonna do that?" Duffy said. "What you got in mind gonna make a bunch of rich white folks just open their doors and walk away without sayin' shit? Tell me!"

"A diversion," said Crane. "Fire."

"FIRE?" Duffy cried out louder than he wanted to. He jerked up in his chair, his hand accidentally knocking over his glass of wine and sending a slow moving malignant red stain across the white tablecloth. Pulling lazy eyes away from the big sexy legs of Sunsett Stripp now inviting his attention just above the table, he put them on Crane and said, "Fire? You gonna set the muthafuckin' Duchess on fire? You must be out yo' muthafuckin' mind, Crane, you know that? Fire. Jesus! Let me get the fuck up off a' you!" Duffy pushed himself away from the table and stood up. Trixie started to laugh as she came part way out of her chair. Her breasts accidentally smashing into Crane's face, she reached up and pulled Duffy back down in his seat, righting his empty glass and placing a napkin over the stain all in one motion.

"Just chill, Duff," she said, cutting eyes at Crane to see if he enjoyed the peep show, satisfied he had. "Nobody's gonna set the Duchess on fire."

"I'm not deaf. I heard what this nigga said," Duffy said, flicking tiny droplets of wine off his shirt with his finger. "Fire gonna kill up a whole lotta muthafuckas, an' I ain't down for that. And there might be kids too? Aw hell no. Not me!"

Crane saw what he knew Trixie had to see, that Duffy wasn't a man who could think in abstract terms. They'd both seen it this afternoon at the Duchess when it was obvious Duffy was out of his league. He could see now that he'd have to spell things out for him. He said to Duffy, "Ever see a movie called *The Towering Inferno?*"

Duffy thought for a moment, trying to remember. "Yeah," he said, tentative. "When I was a kid. High-rise caught on fire ... something like that."

"Something like that is right," Crane said leaning back in his chair, eyes drifting past Trixie to Sunsett Stripp's inviting legs, back to Duffy. He said, "But did the high-rise really catch on fire or do you just think it did?"

"That was a movie."

"My point exactly."

"What point?"

Crane drew in a deep breath of exasperation, tried not to let his irritation show.

"He's telling you not to worry about the fire," Trixie said coming to the rescue. "Cause it's gonna be faked like in the movies," she added, having caught on long before.

"For real?" Duffy exclaimed, the light finally coming on. Crane nodded, caught Trixie's telling glance, her raised eyebrows, ever so clever smile, so subtle, so dangerous now. "Alright," Duffy went on looking at Trixie, amazed not only by the concept, but that she could see it and he couldn't. He began to sense Crane and Trixie had something in common. Wondering now if he could trust them. He said, "Let's assume you can do that ... clear out the whole floor with some kind of fake fire. Where you gonna put the people? They be screamin' and hollerin' and shit ... Five-O be on our ass quicker than shit go down a toilet."

Trixie's face answered for Crane. Suddenly the whole plan came to her. Flashed before her eyes like a photographer's camera ... clear, in the way a complex math problem is suddenly made simple. She saw it all now without his having to tell it. Understood how he would use the elevator, garage, the roof.

"He's gonna put 'em on the roof, Duff," Trixie blurted out. "Simple as that."

Duffy looked at Crane, raised his eyebrows. He said, "That right ...?"

Trixie's quickness surprised Crane. Cocaine, he guessed. He nodded. Duffy looked at Trixie, curious.

"How you know that? Crane tell you the plan?" Duffy asked, suspicious now about them, feeling left out. "What else he tell you?" His suspicious eyes darted back and forth from Trixie to Crane to Trixie again, searching their faces for signs of betrayal.

Awe and jealousy ... powerful enemies, powerful allies. Trixie read both in Duffy. So did Crane, drained his face of any emotion, brought his eyes back to Sunsett Stripp. Trixie started damage control. She reached over, started rubbing Duffy's neck, blew him a kiss with puckered lips and said, "Where else would you put them, Duff? Said yourself they'd be all over the place. Don't need to talk to Crane to figure that out." Her voice was soft and reassuring.

Duffy's face softened, the suspicion on his forehead and in his eyes gone. He nodded, not fully convinced but wanting to be. He said to Crane, "How much you think we gonna get?"

Crane said, "You were there. You saw the suites. Nothin' but seven figure people. Sixty rooms with sixty safes. They could be full. They could be empty. But don't forget we're also looking at jewelry, luggage ..." Crane had to include luggage to cover Moffett's trunk. "Laptops, anything we can carry. Best case scenario: We walk out of there with ten, maybe fifteen million. Worst case: Half that or less."

Trixie said, "And after the fence?"

Crane said, "After the fence, half."

"So tops could be anywhere from five to seven million ... bottom, two and a half on up," Trixie said, doing the math despite loud music and cap pistols. "Divided by how many?"

Crane counted on his fingers. He said, "Seven so far. Gonna need at least two more for some specialty work. That's nine."

Trixie's computer didn't miss a beat. She said, "That's nine-hundred-thirty-seven-thousand five-hundred on the top end ... hundred and twenty-five grand on the bottom."

"That's a lotta work for just a hundred grand," Duffy said, disappointment edged in his voice.

"How much you got now," Crane asked.

Duffy held out his fist in concession. Crane touched it with his. "Word," Duffy said.

Momentarily a loud round of applause filled the club, the Gene Autry music gone. Sunsett Stripp stood and took her bows, fired off the last of her caps, sauntered off stage with a G-string full of money. Trixie gathered her purse, garment bag of costumes and stood to leave. "I gotta go get ready, guys. I'm on in thirty minutes." She moved behind Duffy, let her arms fall around his neck, bent down to kiss him on the ear and neck for reassurance. But all the while she was looking at Crane, winking.

In the thirty minutes before Trixie's show, Crane gave Duffy more details of the plan, using Trixie's absence to bolster Duffy's role, make him feel more important than he really was. "We'll rent a truck and pose as vendors," he began, spelling it out slowly for Duffy. "We enter through the garage. Accessing the penthouse suites through the service elevator we'll cut all power to the fifteenth floor, drill into the air conditioning ducts that run through the elevator shafts and drop in smoke bombs. That'll set off the sprinklers and send the hotel guests into the corridor in a mass of confusion. We lead them to the roof. After that its all we can carry, load it on the service elevator, unload it on the waiting truck and we're home free."

Duffy liked the idea now and wanted to hear more. Crane said they'd need a locksmith to key the service elevator, the rooms and the sixty digital safes. Duffy said he knew someone he could get—Smith, a man he'd met in Lompoc doing time for stealing government checks. He'd sold him *chronic* since they'd been out. He'd talk to him first chance.

Crane also needed someone who knew electricity and could cut off the power to the penthouse. Duffy said he knew someone who could do that too. C.J. Jones. An older man, a crack addict who'd been high up with the City and got fired because of his habit. He owed Duffy a lot of money, was sure he'd jump at the chance to clear his bill.

He didn't tell Duffy, but Crane didn't like the idea of using an addict, then remembered he hadn't liked Trixie at first. This afternoon had changed that, but it didn't mean he trusted her.

Backstage Trixie was dressing for her show. She put finishing touches on her makeup, arranged her hair and when satisfied with her look, poured out a small packet of cocaine on a small vanity mirror and drew four lines into her nose through a straw. She felt the high rushing to her brain. She knew she looked good. And she knew Crane liked her. She was convinced of that now. All he really needed was just a little push. And what she was planning tonight, had been planning since his arrival would be more than just a little push. She was going to give him a shove. The buzzer in her dressing room sounded three times. It was show time and she was on.

Suddenly the lights dimmed and the announcer's voice came on loud.

> *"... Ladies and gentlemen, the Baby Doll*
> *is pleased to present our featured attrac-*
> *tion for this evening ... all the way from*
> *Boise, Idaho ... will you please put your*
> *hands together and welcome middle*
> *America's one and only Trixie Treat ...!"*

Crane said, "Trixie Treat?"

Duffy said, "Stage name. That was my suggestion."

It was the music that showcased Trixie's genius. The haunting repetitive melody of Ravel's *Bolero* brought the audience to silence, their eyes to the curtain beyond that marked her entrance, ushering the start of Trixie's routine. And Trixie did not begin her routine by prancing and bounding on stage with the typical leaping, fast-paced gallop of a gazelle in heat. Rather she slithered on stage like a snake, undulating in perfect synchronized movements that brought her forward to the center of the stage in slow mesmerizing steps.

She was beautifully dressed in sheer layers of flowing silken gowns, sleeves embroidered with cuffs of red and gold satin, her headpiece glittering with costume jewelry that anchored a veil hiding all but the powder-blue eyes ... the harlot in a sheik's harem, a role she was born to play.

And play it she did. Trixie understood choreography if none of the other girls did. She moved from one side of the stage to the other, each time discarding another gown, playing to the audience until she was topless in spiked heels, G-string and veil, remnants of Scheherrazade strewn about the floor. She embraced first one pole then another, fondling it, straddling it, sliding up and down masturbating it, simulating orgasm, and not one time in all her movements did the snake-like undulations stop or fall out of sync with the music. She would be down on all fours crawling to the edge of the stage, reaching out fondling one man's cheek, patting another's forehead, wrapping her legs around the head of a third, simulating sex on the table of a fourth, simulating masturbation in the face of a fifth, burying the face of a sixth between the enormity of her breasts. Back to the pole, embracing it with her breasts, climbing it, spinning around it as she lowered herself to the floor, jacking it off and all the while still keeping up the rhythmic motions in sync with the music.

Trixie had saved Crane's table for last and by the time she reached it her G-string had become a money belt of folded cash. She undulated to the edge of the stage. Ignoring Duffy, she stood directly in front of Crane so he would have to look up, framing him with long willowy legs. Swaying from side to side Trixie suddenly dropped down on her heels, swaying sensuous thighs opened wide, hands gently caressing her breasts, playing with nipple rings, moving down to caress toned and muscled thighs with soft delicate fingers ringed in gold, long painted nails.

The beginning had been interesting as far as Duffy was concerned. He'd seen her routines before, always different, always unique and creative. But the Arabian Nights was the most elaborate costume she'd ever worn and he wondered when she'd had any time to fashion it in such detail. He was impressed as he watched her G-string fill with big faces of

Grants and Benjamins, tried to count them as she worked her way to his table. And when she got there he'd expected she would acknowledge him as her man. She always did, picking him out of how ever many men were seated and performing her routine for him. And as she approached he smiled and started to stand and wave at her with a C-note, but stopped when he realized she had chosen Crane for the routine. Duffy sat back down embarrassed, crushed the bill into an angry ball in the palm of his hand and took a long sip from his glass. What the fuck was this girl doing, he wondered to himself, giving Crane a private show in front of others, disrespecting him like that? And earlier, when she and Crane seemed in league about Crane's plan, leaving him out as if they had worked it all out ahead of time. What the hell was going on here? He wondered if they'd been together when he wasn't around, but couldn't believe Crane would disrespect him like that. He couldn't really believe that Trixie would betray him like this, not with Crane, not with the man he idolized. But there it was right in front of him as plain as the nose on his black face.

But wait a minute. He was drunk, imagining things, twisting what he saw to mean something it didn't. That was it, wasn't it? He was just drunk, that was all. She didn't mean anything to him. Trixie was just a common ordinary street whore. Why should he care who she danced for? He never did before. It was just business … cash money for a little play fantasy. That's all it was. After all, she'd brought home money from tricks she'd turned … in the beginning. Then after she started dancing he didn't want her to turn streetcorner tricks anymore. Said she could do just as well or better on stage. And she did, coming to him with offers of sex from millionaires she turned on with her dance routines. He went for it at first, five grand a night. Not just a quick plunge and come job, but a full night. Then he saw the movie *Indecent Proposal* with Demi Moore and

Robert Redford and put a stop to it, rationalized to himself she might be tempted to leave him for greener pastures and Trixie was a cash cow he didn't want to lose. At least that's what he told himself. But inside he knew different. Knew he'd begun to care for Trixie in a way he wasn't supposed to care for a whore and he hated himself for it. How could he have let this happen ... getting his nose opened behind one of his whores. He couldn't believe it. It had to be the alcohol. That was all. People said booze made you feel crazy. He didn't give a shit about Trixie, who she fucked or who she danced for. Still, for her to give Crane a show like that right in front of him ...

If Trixie was aware of Duffy's growing paranoia about she and Crane it didn't show. She reached out, took Crane's hand and placed it on the inside of her right thigh just over the tattoo, guided its direction in slow, circular, ever closer movements toward her crotch until his fingers could feel the softness of her cushion and the building moistness beneath the cloth that hid it. She suddenly leaned forward, grabbed his ears, pulled his head to her chest, guided it around the surface of first one breast and then the other. She then rotated on her back, simulating oral sex holding his head tightly between her legs, moving her crotch up and down a breath away from his mouth. From the scissors of her crotch Crane looked between the mountains of her breasts into the invitation and willingness of powder-blue eyes wise beyond their twenty-one years. He could feel his desire for her grow bolder, his erection stiffen, could feel the building of his passion and desire for her overriding his basic distrust, overriding better judgement. He could not stand, could not turn, could not withdraw. He wanted to reach out, feel the roundness of her breasts, grab the cheeks of her butt, kiss the mouth so skillfully hidden behind the veil, slip his fingers through the tangle of blonde hair framing her face. There was no one but the two of them. Duffy no longer counted. He did not feel he could help himself. Control seemed to be slipping from his grasp. He felt weak, drained of all will to resist.

"Oh hell no," Duffy shouted, one screaming voice in the midst of hundreds, trying to stand and pull Crane away from the stage and the lock of Trixie's thighs, but falling to the floor in a drunken stupor. What did she think she was doing? Crane couldn't be doing Trixie behind his back. Not the Godfather? He wouldn't do that. They were friends. He was Crane's dog since Marion. Crane wouldn't do that, no matter how much she put on him. He wouldn't do that to his dog. Not to Duffy. "Muthafucka," Duffy shouted again, tried to stand but couldn't.

The powder-blue eyes continued to speak to Crane, calling to him, fleshy white thighs offering false sanctuary. He could hear Duffy calling him. And if Trixie did, she didn't care. Neither could hear envious voices cheering them on, the pad of folded cash stuffing her G-string. Even Crane was only distantly aware of putting cash in her G-string. He didn't know how much. The screaming crowd seemed muted, like the over-modulated volume of a transister radio. His head just below her crotch. Unseen smile behind the veil. Ravel's Bolero. Paradise.

Suddenly Trixie released him, rolled flat across the stage to the pole, stood embracing it, then collapsed on the floor at its base in the final crashing spasm of the Bolero's end ... the harlot returning to the harem.

Thunderous applause. Even Crane stood, tried to at least, blushing, embarrassed, clapping his appreciation, fending off back slaps of envy. Trixie stood, bowed. It wasn't Sadie Thompson this time. It was Trixie. And if Crane didn't get the message now, he never would. She sent a telling smile in his direction, gathered up her costume and quickly scampered off the stage.

When Crane's euphoria had subsided he dropped back in his seat and turned to Duffy, but Duffy was gone.

Chapter 10

IN THE DAYS THAT FOLLOWED TRIXIE'S SCHEHERRAZADE performance at the Baby Doll, Duffy went about his daily routines with an uncharacteristically leaden effort, divided between his own hustle of weed, rocks and hookers, and the ever increasing demands on his time from Crane in preparation for the assault on the Duchess. And while he never slacked up from doing either one, his mind had become obsessively preoccupied with Trixie and what he perceived to be her waning allegiance to him in favor of Crane. Yet there was no real evidence to support his feelings.

Or was there? In hindsight he remembered the Rendezvous Lounge at the New Otani Hotel. They were all drunk. At least *he* was. But he wasn't so drunk he didn't notice Trixie and Crane dancing next to the piano. His vision was blurred true enough, but he hadn't missed Trixie's bare feet playing footsy with Crane's leg. And when she'd wanted to dance she didn't ask him, she'd asked Crane, and he'd seemed a little too willing. There was something in the way they'd moved together, in the way Crane had held her, in the way Trixie's head rested snug on his shoulders, her eyes closed while thirty fingers stroked his neck and ears, and their occasional echo of laughter. He hadn't thought much about it at the time, put it down to Trixie's nature.

And then there was the Duchess. How well she and Crane had got on together, working the white boy together like they'd rehearsed it. It was as if he wasn't there, that they didn't really need him. He wasn't drunk *that* time, had put it down as an act, Trixie's showbiz talent. But at the Baby Doll, when Crane asked if she'd brought her notes, he was surprised. How'd she know to take real notes unless Crane had spent time teaching her? How'd she know the details of the robbery unless Crane told her? Put 'em on the roof—she couldn't have known that unless he'd told her. Why'd they leave him out the loop like that unless …?

And the dance for Crane? True, he may have been a little drunk … well more than a little, but he wasn't blind, her choosing Crane for a lap dance instead of him, knowing that would upset him, causing him to fall out on the floor in a drunken stupor like that, embarrassing himself. He knew then … knew they'd been together ever since they'd met that day at Union Station, Crane's thing about not trusting white girls nothing but bullshit. He could see that now. The dance proved that.

Or did it? Trixie had scarcely been out of his sight since Crane's arrival, so if they'd gotten together he'd of certainly known. Wouldn't he?

Maybe not.

And Crane? Why would Godfather do that to him ... go behind his back like that? Why? He trusted Crane. He'd always trusted Crane, ever since that day at Marion when that big ugly-ass nigga Mack and his punk posse cornered him in the fourth tier shower and tried to turn him out. They would have too if Crane hadn't interceded, knew Crane was Bear's dog and took his threat seriously. He respected Crane. He learned so much from him in those three and a half years. Crane was the only man he could ever really call a father. There was a lot of love there. And respect. He just couldn't believe Crane would betray him like that, go behind his back and player-hate with Trixie.

Then again why not? And why should he care if he did? So what if they were fucking? She was just a whore, one of several he pimped and not the only white girl. She was just a bitch he found in a Payless Shoe Store, felt sorry for and pimped. Wasn't anything special about Trixie. She was just a thick white girl with big titties. And he had lots of whores like Trixie, thick girls with big legs, firm tight asses and big titties. They didn't mean anything to him but money. And neither did Trixie. How could she.

But she did and he hated himself for it ... hated not been able to handle this weakness for her that haunted him, this control she had over him. But the one thing he hated even more was being played for a fool. And if that was what they were doing, gaming him, playing him from one end to the other like an accordion, his two closest friends betraying him behind his back, then he would have to kill them both. He wouldn't want to of course. It would be a hard thing to do, but if his suspicions were true, he'd have no choice, really.

But he couldn't do it on suspicion alone. He'd need proof first,

watch them like a circling hawk watches rodents, give them enough rope
to hang themselves. And to do that he'd need another pair of eyes. A
woman's eyes.

Romero finally delivered the C-4 near the end of Crane's second
week of freedom. So far things were going smoothly, all things considered. There had been progress but it was troubling. His former partners
were hostile and sullen, their movements slow and unmotivated in their
resentment. He'd expected that, of course, knowing none of them felt any
obligation for the ten years and anonymity he'd given them. It still bothered him, their feeling this way, but they were doing their part and he was
on schedule, just barely, so there was nothing he could say.

More disturbing however was Duffy. He'd come through on every
task assigned but he'd suddenly become moody and distant, brooding as
if preoccupied with something. He carried out instructions but it was not
with the kind of zeal and energy Crane was used to seeing. He'd asked if
something was wrong but Duffy said no. He was just feeling the stress
and pressure. Trixie said Duffy was always moody. She didn't think it
meant anything. But Crane wasn't convinced. Something was wrong.
There was something Duffy wasn't telling him, and not knowing settled
hard in Crane's gut.

The locksmith was Nate Smith, a heavy-set Jamaican with long
dreads he wore under a cap, a full bushy beard and greedy marijuana
eyes. Using his own truck to pass for a vendor, he keyed the service
elevator one day, returned the next day with a young girl he sent up to the
penthouse dressed as a maid and a key blank she used to get computer

coded for a master key to all the suites. He assured Crane when the time came he could open the safes in the suites with the power off. All he'd have to do was build a battery operated circuit board to activate the micro-computers in each one.

C.J. Jones on the other hand was a problem from the get go. A Creole in his early sixties with straight hair and fading good looks from weight loss due to his cocaine addiction, he was a stone basehead who was suspicious and paranoid from the moment they'd been introduced. Two coke addicts were more than Crane had bargained for and started to pass, but Duffy reminded him he had the skills. He was familiar with the Duchess because he'd inspected it numerous times when he worked for the City, said cutting off the power and the telephones to the fifteenth floor was a piece of cake if you weren't afraid of heights. However, by-passing the water flow from the sprinklers to avoid alerting the fire department was another matter, but he could solve it if he had enough time. Crane said he had ten days, wondered if C.J. could hold up the forty or so minutes of the heist without the glass dick, told Duffy it was on him if he didn't.

Trixie found just about everything on Crane's list at various motion picture supply houses. Tables, portable laundry hampers and luggage racks from a studio prop house, smoke bombs from a special effects company, and from a costume supply outfit the firefighter uniforms complete with helmets, gas masks and red hatchets. If Marcus' van had been a taxi he'd of made a fortune running Trixie here and there to pick up supplies, making daily runs to the LAX storage hangar.

Near the end of the week Henry T delivered a five-ton diesel semi-trailer that had seen better days. He'd stolen it from a repair yard in El Monte along with plates from another truck he figured had been sitting for months. When he disconnected the cab from the box it fit snugly in the hangar but didn't leave much room for anything else. It needed a lot of work … radiator, muffler, brakes, cracked rear wheel rim … and a paint job. Henry T said he'd need at least two weeks to get it in shape. Crane said ten days was all he had. Henry T said he couldn't promise anything but he'd try. Trixie said she knew someone who could paint a logo, found a graffiti artist up in Hollywood who asked no questions and drove out to the LAX storage hangar every day for fifty bucks and a Blunt.

By week's end Crane had finished his balsa wood model, held the first of several meetings at the storage hangar where he began to outline details of the robbery. The model was a beautiful replica of the Duchess that impressed Trixie even more once she saw its finished form. It was complete with doors, windows, elevator shafts, stairwells and toy cars for the garage. It was especially helpful to C.J. Jones who used it to explain the complex layout of the electrical, water, telephone and air conditioning systems they'd have to neutralize before gaining entrance to the penthouse suites.

By the start of the third week only two major details remained outstanding before Crane felt he could begin rehearsals, both of which he would have to handle alone. The first was the cemetery.

The mausoleum at Compton's Washington Memorial Cemetery was a large, free-standing stone edifice with a pair of rusted steel doors, one of which was off its hinges and propped against the side. Crane parked, entered wearing coveralls, hard-hat and carrying a large shopping bag. Floor to ceiling burial crypts lined the walls on three sides and in the center, three double-sided coffin-filled marble walls stretched the entire length of the mausoleum. Vented stones supporting the roof offered the only natural light. The light switch next to the door was frozen. From his bag Crane withdrew a flashlight and swept the gloomy interior, trying to match MMWC-2 written on the paper with those on the crypt. He found it on the second level of the first center wall at the rear of the mausoleum. The numbers matched and below them, the inscription *CRANE*. He wondered if he had located his future.

He found the ladder, positioned it to the side and pulled hard on the handle above his name. Lighter than he'd expected, the plain metal casket slid out with little effort. He pulled it out as far as it would slide and still be self-supporting, got off the ladder and bracing it with his weight, brought the casket its full length, lowering it to the stone floor. He removed the top, inspected the austere interior. From his bag he removed several items including a saw, drill, hammer, nails and a small combination CD player-cassette-clock radio boombox. He turned the radio to KKJZ-FM, listened to a few riffs of Miles Davis' *Sketches of Spain* and set to work.

'WILLIE NANCE'S PAWNSHOP' was deep in South Central on Wilmington Avenue. A post-Rodney King heavy duty steel security door, burglar bars on the windows and a shuttered steel screen that rolled down the entire width of his premises said it all.

Willie Nance looked like a fence. Crane could read ex-con in the frown lines around his mouth, on the old scars on his jaw and cheek. Puffy age sacs hung below tired greedy eyes magnified twice their size by thick bi-focals that seemed to rest on the wide flat bridge of his nose. There was no hair on his head except for a rim of gray that circled from ear to ear. Short and stocky, he walked in slow discomfort with a cane that favored his right leg in the manner of a football player way past his prime who'd taken one too many hits.

Crane waited to one side while Nance finished with his last customer, ushered her to the door and locked up. He led Crane into a back room that served as both office and storeroom, taking a seat behind a cluttered desk, offering Crane a battered couch. Crane dropped down on the only cushion that didn't have springs showing.

"You say Bo Bo sent you?" Willie began, lighting a cigarette, offering one to Crane, Crane declining.

Crane said, "That's right."

Willie said, "How's old Bo Bo doin' these days? Get use to walkin' on a nub where they took the nigga's leg off?"

Crane smiled. Willie was testing him. He said to Willie, "Bo Bo never lost his leg. May have lost his nerve one or two times ... never lost a leg."

The old man half-grunted, half-laughed, half-coughed through a curtain of smoke. He went on, conceding the first round to Crane and said, "Missed his birthday party. Wife sent a nice invitation. What's he now ... near sixty?   I forgot, been so many years."

"Bo Bo never had a wife," Crane said, "and I make him forty if he's a day. How long we gonna play this game?"

"Till I'm satisfied you the nigga you say you is. Till I know fo' sure it was really Bo Bo sent yo' black ass here."

"Fire away."

And Willie did. He was finally satisfied midway through his third cigarette.

"So what you want?" he asked Crane.

"I need to fence some property."

"What kind of property?"

"You name it."

"No," Willie said. "You name it. You the nigga needs a fence."

"Jewelry. Lots of jewelry. Top of the line. Cartier stuff. Tiffany. Laptops. Furs. Luggage. Suits. Cell phones. Big screen TVs—eighty inch types ..."

Willie fished around on his desk for something to write with, found a white pad under a pile of magazines, pen in the desk drawer.

"Can't do shit with furs," he said to Crane writing on the pad. "Animal rights white folks see baby seals clubbed on TV, go crazy."

Crane laughed and said, "What's on their feet—leather!"

"They don't see cows. They see baby seals clubbed on TV. No more than ten, maybe fifteen cents on the dollar, tops. What about the jewelry ... any loose stones?"

"Can't say just yet. More than likely not."

"If it's high quality shit ... give you ... maybe sixty, sixty-five cents. Seventy on the laptops. I can move those real quick."

The crackle of gunfire suddenly erupted in the distance, screeching of tires, blare of fast approaching sirens, helicopter. Crane ducked by instinct. Willie never moved, kept writing, blowing smoke.

"Traveler's checks, gold cards," Crane added when he'd regained his composure, sat back up. Willie was still writing.

Willie said, "People cancel gold cards. Platinum cards too. Traveler's checks be worth something though ... maybe fifty, fifty-five on the dollar. Give you forty on the luggage if it's Louis Vuitton. Same on the cell phones. What about VCRs, camcorders?"

"Camcorders, yeah. Don't know about VCRs."

"Camcorders get fifty, fifty-five. Any weapons?"

Crane thought for a moment, remembered five soldiers in suite fifteen seventeen and said, "Few. Don't know what kind."

"Any kinda weapon move fast," Willie said. "Give you least seventy, seventy-five cents on the dollar. What about collections?"

"What?"

"Collections—you know, baseball cards. Stamps. Coins. Records."

"Oh," said Crane stupidly. "Don't know about records. CDs probably. Can't say about stamps and shit. Probably not."

Willie looked up for an instant, pen still moving on the pad and said, "So what you tellin' me, is you don't have none of this shit yet?"

"I will in about two weeks," Crane said proudly.

Willie pulled a small calendar close to the bi-focals, flipped through the pages with his pen. He said to Crane, "Halloween."

Crane hadn't realized Halloween was two weeks away.

He suddenly laughed and said to Willie, "Trick or treat time." Willie didn't see the humor, returned to his pad.

"What are we lookin' at?" Willie asked.

Crane remembered Trixie's figures and said, "Anywhere from fifteen to twenty million. I figure on fencing half that, say … seven mil, maybe more."

Willie nearly choked on his spit. He stopped writing, removed his bi-focals and leaned back in his chair, laughing. He said to Crane, "Seven million in cash. You must be insane. You want me to get you seven million cash money on shit you don't even have? Nigga, please!"

Crane stayed cool. He said to Willie, "Of course if you can't handle it—?"

Willie stopped laughing, put on his bi-focals and leaned the scarred face forward on the desk. He lit another cigarette, blew smoke in Crane's face and said, "Where's a con like you cop this kind of merchandise?" And before Crane could answer he added, "Oh, yeah. You a con, alright. Spotted you for one right off. Con can't never hide that. Know what I mean?"

Poker playing time. Crane kept his cool. He crossed tired legs, cushioned his head with clasped hands and said to Willie Nance, "I got my sources, you got yours. I know what I'll have in two weeks … figure you can do the same—*IF* you the man Bo Bo said you were. You know us cons gotta stick together, right, Nance?"

Crane called, made Willie pay to see his cards.

Enormous lids blinked several times behind the bi-focals. Willie folded. He sat back in the chair, blew smoke to the ceiling, studying Crane.

"Two weeks, you say?" Willie said, thinking. "I'll have to make some calls. Put a group together. Seven million lotta cash …"

Crane said, "But you *CAN* get it?"

Willie said, "Need trucks, warehouse space …"

"Not really," said Crane. "Just take over my place when the time comes."

Willie said that was good thinking and picked up the pen. He said to Crane, "Where you located?"

"I'll let you know in two weeks," Crane said. "You in, Nance, or we jackin' each other off?"

Willie said through a laugh, "You ain't pretty enough for me to jack you off, Crane." He stood and offered Crane his hand. "Of course I'm in, you stupid ass muthafucka. What the fuck you think?"

Crane unwound from the couch like a snake, shook Willie Nance's callused hand, wondering if he'd just shaken hands with the Devil.

He said to Willie, "I only think for myself," and left the office for the store, Willie following. "Halloween, Nance. I'll have my shit together—just make sure you got yours?"

Willie slid back several large steel deadbolts, opening the door for Crane to pass. "Yeah," Willie said. "Halloween. I go out on a limb … get your seven figures and you don't have my inventory, I'm gonna ride in there on a muthafuckin' broomstick and cap yo' black ass. Know what I'm sayin'? Trick or treat, muthafucka!" and he closed the door hard behind Crane, steel deadbolts sliding into place one after another.

Chapter 11

L ISTEN UP, PEOPLE—BE BACK HERE AT MIDNIGHT," Crane said on the eve of Halloween, the posse breaking up at twilight, drifting out of the storage hangar and into the deafening crescendo of a 747 stealing down the glidescope. All were exhausted from nearly two weeks of twelve to fifteen hour a day rehearsals, Crane's unexplained ranting and raving and name calling when they made mistakes, Duffy's constant threats when they got out of line. "I want us into disguise and at the Duchess no later than three. Twelve hours from now you'll be richer 'n Bill Gates."

"Say, homie, you run Trixie home for me?" Duffy asked Crane as they straightened up. "Got some runs to make before tonight," he lied, setting up the trap. "Left my Rolex at your place day before yesterday. You pick it up on the way, give it to Trixie?" Crane remembered Duffy asking about the watch earlier, said he would, not thinking it might have been left on purpose. Nothing in Duffy's voice or smile betrayed his true intentions. For a change he seemed like his old self and Crane, consumed with events of the next twelve hours, failed to sense Duffy's sudden agreeable nature for the con it was.

Duffy was the last to leave. He dropped into the soft comfort of the Regal's expensive leather seats, pulled out Zig-Zags and rolled a joint, the buzz creeping into his brain as the taillights of Crane's Lexus disappeared in the night. He put OUTKAST on the CD player and from the glove compartment withdrew a fifth of Boone's Farm wine, popped the top and took it to the dome. He was in no rush now. Everything was in order. The trap was sprung. He took another swig from the bottle, turned on his cell phone and waited for the call.

Trixie didn't question her unexpected good fortune. By the time Crane brought the Lexus through the gate and onto the street she was halfway through a Blunt. Crane asked if she wanted dinner. The freckle face smile and powder-blue eyes found yes easy to say, suggested Denny's in nearby Culver City.

It was after seven when they arrived at the *Hardcore,* climbed stairs to the second floor balcony reeking of marijuana. Princess and a white trick were just leaving a room as Crane and Trixie approached.

"Hey, penthouse man," Princess said swiping on cheap lipstick, stiff blonde wig slightly off center, gold incisor gleaming in the dull glow of her trick's cigarette lighter. "Ain't seen you 'round lately. Where you been keepin' yo' self?"

Slowing but not stopping Crane said, "Busy, Princess. Just handling my business, that's all."

As they passed on the balcony Princess gave Trixie that knowing look from one whore to another and said to Crane, "I see you into pink pussy, huh? Me and blondie there could put on a real show for you?"

Crane said, "Ain't that kind of party, Princess."

"Well *EX-CUSE* me if it ain't!" said Princess, feigning insult. "Enjoy yo' self anyway."

Once in the room Trixie threw herself across the bed and said, "Place sure stinks like hell, but at least the bed is comfortable. You bring what's-her-name, Princess, up here?" she asked, twinge of jealousy creeping in her voice.

"Oh, please," Crane said sarcastically.

Trixie laughed and said, "Got anything to drink?"

Knowing he should've said no, Crane said, "Sure," and began searching in his closet for the shoes where he'd hidden the Rolex. "Bottle of wine in the frig," he said. By the time he found it and turned around to go, Trixie was back on the bed, her shoes off, bottle of Night Train in one hand, two empty glasses in the other.

Trixie said, "Since we gonna be rich after tonight, may as well toast. Put on some music, why don't you?"

And again, knowing he should have refused, knowing he should have pulled her off the bed and out of the room but couldn't because she was so beautiful and because he desired her so, he nodded, put on a CD by Toni Braxton and plopped down beside her.

Trixie handed him a glass. When she'd filled it and they'd toasted to success she pulled out a joint and lit it, passed it to Crane, waited for him to pass it back. By habit she began to undress. She started to pull off her tube top, suddenly stopped with a hint of forgotten embarrassment, then pulled it up over her head and off, freeing her breasts and said, "You've seen them before." She crossed her legs and looked at Crane as if seeing him for the first time, knowing she'd been waiting for him all her life, knowing too they were about to make love and that when they did, her break from Duffy would be complete. Now in the harsh glow of the room's only light his face was softer, the hardness of prison life drained away in his four weeks of freedom. They'd worked well together since that day at the Duchess and she had come to understand why Duffy had said he was smart. The boldness of his plan and its complexity was not only smart, but seasoned and mature. And for a man who'd been locked up for ten years to still be capable of this kind of thinking said everything.

While Crane and Trixie were getting high, Princess was sitting in the lobby of the *Hardcore* next to a window that had an unobstructed view of the penthouse. Doing as she'd been instructed, she checked the clock on the wall above Antonio's makeshift registration desk every fifteen minutes from the time Crane and Trixie had entered the room. After an hour of boredom and four primos she pulled out her cell phone, punched in Duffy's number and waited for him to answer.

Back in the penthouse Trixie and Crane were talking all around what they both knew was inevitable.

"What are your plans when this is over, Crane?" Trixie asked him, the Night Train and weed easing the awkwardness between them. Crane let the smoke settle around him. He looked at Trixie through half-closed eyes, turned away thinking.

"Move away from here. That's first on the list. Desert maybe. Get me a ranch, place where I can walk around and be free." He closed his eyes, tried to imagine Toni Braxton singing only to him but kept seeing Marjorie's face interchange with Trixie's face, their sultry lips mouthing lyrics only he could hear.

Trixie removed the elastic from her ponytail, blonde hair springing back to life, framing her web of freckles. She uncrossed long shapely legs and stretched them out in front of her, falling back on a brace of elbows, draining her glass.

"Alone?"

"Alone," said Crane repeating her question, understanding its meaning. "Man been alone long as I have can't figure on much company. Know what I mean?" Crane drained his glass, took a drag on the joint and said, "Maybe I'll go back to school, be an architect or engineer like Uncle Joe said."

A builder. So that was the source of his vision. Trixie sat up, pulled the blonde mop out of her face.

"That what you wanted to be—an architect?" she said, genuinely impressed.

"Yeah," he said. "Could've been if it hadn't been for the streets."

"That explains the model you built."

"Use to build a lotta things like that as a kid. Prison too. Built a replica of Marion out of matches and tissue paper. Took me four years. It's still on display in Moffett's office," he said proudly. "Moffett's the warden."

"Then go back to school, Crane," Trixie said thickly, words beginning to slur. "Be an architect or whatever, but not alone. You get someone understands you—"

Crane looked at Trixie in the haze of Night Train and weed, the spell of Toni Braxton's lyrics. Not sure he was seeing Marjorie or Trixie, nor which one he wanted more and not really caring, he could no longer control himself. Slipping from his grasp, unchecked emotions spilled from his gut like water from a broken glass. "Oh, Trixie—" he said, his lips suddenly drawn to hers, hands filled with the soft mass of her breasts, feeling his erection rise out of control, grasping her like a magnet drawn to its opposite.

Matching Crane's uncontrollable desire with her own, drenching his face and neck with kisses, fingers caressing his ears, studded tongue driving deep in his throat, hands freeing his sex from the prison of his pants and taking him inside her with all the passion and wanton desire she'd waited a lifetime for, whispering softly in his ear when his moment had finally exploded and he lay on top of her soaking in the rapture of exhaustion.

"It's okay, baby," she said, bathed in the warmth of her own orgasm, holding Crane tightly in the midst of his fading spasms. "We're gonna be together a lifetime. We have plenty of time."

But they didn't. An hour later a heavy-booted foot splintered the door at the lock, ripping the safety chain from the molding and sent the door slamming loudly back against the wall on its hinges. Crane and

Trixie bolted upright and into the barrel of the executioner's wavering, unsteady 9mm. It moved between them.

BLAM! BLAM! Two rounds intentionally missed, whizzed between their heads, splintered the headboard, wall behind.

"You chickenshit muthafuckas, both of you!" Duffy shouted over Trixie's scream, his words thick and slurred, glassy eyes attached to a head that was weaving unsteadily back and forth. "I trusted you!" he cried, words meant for Crane but eyes holding on Trixie, holding back tears that wanted to come. "I trusted you. You been talking 'bout me all this time, haven't you? Why? I trusted you. Why you player-hate behind my back like this, muthafucka? WHY?"

Crane's worst nightmare come true.

"Wasn't like that, Duffy," Crane said feebly, trying to gather his senses up out of the muck. He cursed his own weakness, couldn't believe he hadn't seen it coming—Duffy's sudden pleasantness, suggestion he take Trixie home, the watch. Had she blinded him that much? He just couldn't leave her alone, could he? He'd known this could happen. Had in fact warned himself on several occasions when she was so inviting and he thought he might weaken. If he'd only waited. Now it had all blown up in his face. Duffy was hurt, angry and drunk. That made him dangerous. He felt betrayed by both of them, and that made him twice as dangerous. It made him homicidal. Crane had seen it all before. In Marion ... recognized that look, that stare of a man on the edge reeking of revenge. He learned early on the most dangerous man on the yard was a man betrayed by a homie.

"Behind my back, Godfather!" Duffy was saying drunkenly, respect for Crane still present despite the hurt, "You player-hatin' behind my back! I'd of taken a round for you, Crane. I was your dog," he said, struggling to hold back tears of disbelief and disappointment. "Why you do this to your dog?"

"Still my dog, Duffy," Crane said desperately, not knowing what else to say and too scared to move from the bed, eyes glued to the 9mm, feeling Trixie's frightened nails bite into the flesh of his leg under the sheet. "Wasn't intentional, dog," Crane lied. "Just happened."

Duffy laughed out loud. "Yeah, right," he said facetiously, "I'm so dumb I'm not suppose to believe my eyes. I'm suppose to believe this ain't really happenin', that all this shit I'm lookin' at ain't intentional? Nigga, give me a muthafuckin' break!"

"Maybe it was, and maybe it wasn't," Trixie said honestly, thinking truth might help.

Duffy said, "What you mean '*maybe it was*'?"

Trixie said, "What you and I had was over, Duffy. You've known that for a long time. It was just a matter of time. If it hadn't been Crane … someone else."

Crane couldn't believe his ears. Was she insane? The man was seconds away from killing them and she's playing Truth or Consequences. Didn't she realize the spot they were in?

"Maybe so," Duffy conceded. "But it was my call, not yours. I say when we through. Not you, you white bitch!"

"*WHAT?*" shouted Trixie, her anger suddenly overriding fear, coming naked from under the sheet standing to face him next to the bed, making Duffy back away slightly. "What did you just call me?"

Duffy said, "I called you what you are, a scandalous white bitch," and as she reached out to hit him Duffy brought the back of his gun hand hard across her cheek in a pimp slap, knocking Trixie to the floor, her mouth drawing a trickle of blood at its corner. At this distraction Crane lunged forward and tried to grab Duffy's gun hand, but his legs were entwined in the sheets and his forward movement, though sufficient to knock Duffy to the floor, did not allow him enough leverage to turn the gun away. Duffy and Crane rolled over and under one another, the 9mm still pointed at Crane's head.

BLAM! As they rolled across the floor Duffy fired again, sending a round past Crane's ear and into the refrigerator, its deafening noise and Trixie's scream filling the room.

"DON'T BE A FOOL, DUFFY!" Trixie screamed from the corner, her face numb and bleeding. *"WE'RE ABOUT TO GET PAID! MORE CASH MONEY THAN YOU'VE EVER SEEN. MILLIONS, DUFFY. CASH MONEY!"*

Duffy's face was contorted in a drunken rage, struggling with Crane on the floor, trying to get a bead on Crane's head with the 9mm, Crane's hand on Duffy's gun arm, his other pressing violently up on Duffy's neck, his legs kicking air behind him. Crane twisted violently on the floor, managed to throw Duffy to the side, got a slight advantage with his legs against the wall and powered himself up still keeping Duffy's 9mm out of his face. Duffy turned, and bringing his weight to bear, slammed Crane so hard against the adjacent wall Crane saw stars, thought he'd pass out. But he held on, muscled Duffy against the table, both of them crashing down on top, rolling off and crashing heavily to the floor, Duffy on top, Crane on bottom, his legs kicking air again.

Through it all Crane somehow found his tongue and sputtered desperately through clenched teeth, "She's right, Duffy. Kill us behind bullshit, it all goes down the toilet!"

"Tired old men," hissed Duffy through Crane's choke on his windpipe, arm struggling against Crane's for position. "Get me some niggas

off the street know how to take orders, do the job myself, muthafucka!"
Frothy saliva from Duffy's mouth sprayed itself across Crane's face.

"You can't," said Crane trying to bargain for a few more seconds of
life, arm beginning to tire in the struggle with Duffy's. "Ain't time, dog.
Gotta be tonight. The money. Seven to fifteen million in cash. Fence
won't deal with no one but me," Crane lied, knowing Willie Nance would
deal with anyone after he'd checked them out. "And if something goes
down, something goes wrong I'm the only one knows the way out. Kill
me, dog, you kill the deal and your seven figure future—"

Dazed, all modesty gone, Trixie crawled painfully over from the
corner, put her hand on Duffy's shoulder and pleaded, "Don't kill him,
Duff. Think about the money. We get paid in a few hours," she said
desperately, holding her jaw, words tumbling out awkwardly through the
pain of a cut lip. "Millions. Remember, the Pharaoh of Crenshaw ... ?"
she said to Duffy's profile, appealing to his twisted ego. "Think about
how much dope you could sell if you had that much extra large cash
behind you? The money." Desperate to penetrate the fog of his rage, she
screamed in his ear, *"FOR GOD'S SAKE, DUFF, THINK-ABOUT-THE-
MONEY. PLEASE!"*

He must have, for Duffy's arm suddenly went limp and he jumped
up, still weaving over Crane in the stupor of alcohol but still very
dangerous and hungry for revenge. He lowered the 9mm, reached down
and roughly jerked Crane's naked frame to his feet, Trixie coming up
beside him.

"Alright," Duffy said, bitterness filling his voice, looking at both of
them with the disappointment of betrayal burned deep in his eyes. He was
looking at Trixie for a moment, her nakedness once lovely now lost on
him in the cruelty of her deceit. But his words were venomous and cold

and harsh and meant for Crane. "I should bust a cap in both yo asses right now," Duffy said cruelly. "But we gonna do this just like you planned," he said. "Every step of the way you laid it out, alright? You still in charge ... for now. But after tonight, after we get paid—?" and he waved the 9mm in Crane's face, "—better watch yo' back, you player-hatin' trick-ass nigga. Gonna be you and me." He looked over at Trixie again, almost fondly but said viciously, "You want this trashy white bitch, you can have her—" and he turned once again facing Crane and added prophetically, "—for as long as you stay alive. Know what I'm sayin', muthafucka? Get dressed, both of you. I'll wait for you down in the car." Duffy turned and walked through the half-open door without closing it, the residue of his threat still heavy in the room.

Chapter 12

REESE BROUGHT THE DIESEL OFF THE NORTHBOUND 405 onto Sunset Boulevard heading east five minutes ahead of Henry T's stretched Mercedes limousine. The caravan wound slowly through the hills of Bel Air, past estates bordering UCLA's campus, caught the light at the Beverly Hills Hotel. The truck looked like new money with its side now broadly covered by a tapestry of color and graphic design depicting a large mattress and the words: <u>HOTEL MATTRESS CORPORATION</u> arching above it from end to end like a McDonald's sign. Inside the box Crane and six others, suffering the oppressive discomfort of weighty firemen's uniforms, huddled together in the dark on makeshift seats, struggling to maintain balance against the constant swerving and swaying of traffic maneuvers. Only Trixie dressed otherwise in a caramel-colored maid's outfit. No one spoke. Breathing was shallow and fast, heartbeats keeping time with destiny.

The diesel began to slow. Reese tapped the horn three times in quick succession. They were approaching the Duchess. Everyone stiffened. A beam of light from Crane's helmet splashed onto his watch for no more than a second, washing away darkness. 3:07 am. Right on time. Crane punched a number on his cell phone and spoke softly.

"We're at the Duchess, Henry T," Crane said. "Close up fast. I need that garage blocked for two hours." He clicked off, said to vague restless shadows, "Listen up, people—from now on it's a race against the clock. Trixie, C.J.—you're up first. It's show time!"

Reese downshifted roughly, separated passengers from seats as he made a hard left into the driveway and headed for the garage. There was no one to stop him but a single parking attendant walking back from the garage who waved him through with hardly a glance in the truck's direction. Air brakes whistled as the truck floated down the incline, slowed, shifted hard again to the right as he made a wide arc past the elevator, maneuvering several times until the box faced its doors less than six feet away.

Reese shut off the engine, stepped down from the cab, walked to the rear of the truck. He was dressed in white coveralls, blue long-sleeved shirt with embroidered emblem that matched the logo and lettering on the truck. He looked around. The parking structure was empty of attendants. He knocked three times on the door of the box, waited thirty seconds and knocked another three times, drew back the locking bolt and swung open one door. It was time to get paid.

Trixie jumped out first. C.J. Jones followed, helped lower the housekeeping cart and followed her into the service elevator. He was dressed in a navy blue fire Captain's uniform with gold badge, shiny stiff-brimmed cap, clipboard and a sidearm of tools. The elevator rose to the fifteenth floor without interruption. The doors opened to an empty corridor. Trixie pushed off her cart, C.J. followed, passing her. Neither spoke. They were strangers.

A door opened suddenly. Its owner, dressed in a silk robe, asked for a shower cap. Another door wanted more towels. A third wanted condoms. If you didn't know Trixie, you would think she'd worked at this job her entire life, she was so smooth.

C.J. went straight to the passenger elevator console, pulled open the familiar panel door, began de-activating the fire alarm and water flow systems so they'd by-pass the front desk computers as well as the fire department. The elevator bell rang, floorlight blinked on. Several drunk couples stumbled off, staggered down the corridor to their suites. If they saw C.J. it didn't register. The elevator returned four more times with hotel guests, some drunk, some sober. No one paid any attention to the fire Captain working officiously on the panel.

While Trixie was handing out towels, shower caps and condoms, Henry T brought the stretch limo to a stop in front of the Duchess, got out, chatted briefly with familiar bellboys, bored parking attendants. He said he wanted to turn around, got back in the limo and headed for the parking structure. Once beyond their view he maneuvered the limo across the entrance just above the incline to completely block all passage in either direction. He shut off the electric fuel pump by a switch hidden under the dash, let the engine die of starvation. As instructed he tapped the horn a quick three times and walked back to the hotel entrance cursing.

When Reese heard the limo's horn he drew back the locking bolt a second time, helped Marcus, Bo Bo and Smith manhandle the massive canvas tent and piles of blankets into the service elevator, sent them skyward, beeping Trixie on her walkie-talkie to alert her. Their luck held. No one on any floor interrupted their ascent. When they reached the penthouse level Smith used his key to override the door control, keeping them closed, the elevator frozen.

The wait inside seemed like an eternity, though it was only a minute or so. Trixie stopped her cart at the console, signaled C.J. silently the tent had arrived. C.J. held up one nervous finger, made a last adjustment on the panel and closed it. He walked back to the service elevator and knocked on the door three times. Inside, Smith released the doors to open. C.J. pressed the same nervous finger to his lips for silence, keyed off the alarm on the fire door exit, motioned for them to move quickly into the stairwell.

Twenty minutes on the roof and the tent was up, blankets in place. Another seven in the stairwell waiting for C.J.'s signal to re-enter the elevator, join them in the drop down to safety, climb back in the truck.

It was 3:45 am and by Crane's calculation he was already fifteen minutes behind schedule. He helped C.J. back into his fireman's uniform, grabbed toolbox, bag of supplies, joined him in the elevator and watched the floor numbers fly by. They suddenly stopped on the eighth floor. A janitor got on, asked if there was a fire. Crane said no—Fire department checking out a defective sprinkler that malfunctioned during a routine test. The janitor seemed satisfied, asked if the department was hiring. Crane said they were, gave him a fake name, phone number, told him to call in the morning after ten, let him off on the twelfth floor with a smile.

Two floors later Crane froze the elevator, steadied C.J. as he pushed light panels aside, swung open the access door, maneuvered his thin body up and through the tight space onto the beveled roof, pulling Crane up behind. C.J. cautioned Crane which cables to hold, which ones had power. They replaced the light panels and closed the access door, sealing them in a closet of darkness whose bobbing motion was like a boat floating on water.

Helmet lights defined the space above them as an elongated capsule held together at both ends by a forest of cables. At the top was the massive ventilation duct that curved out of the darkness of the elevator shaft and into the wall, the high-pitched whine of its fan like the purring of a cat. In another corner a massive tangle of cables snaked up from the darkness, coursed underneath the ventilation duct and buried itself in the wall. It was as C.J. had described, but the platform was smaller than Crane had imagined and certainly couldn't seat two men side by side in bulky firemen's uniforms.

Suddenly the elevator buzzed. C.J. pointed to the ladder on the wall, stepped off the bobbing roof after Crane, began their climb to the platform. Crane beeped Trixie, told her to release the elevator for use. They'd be a while. He didn't know how long. A few seconds later the floor of the capsule dropped out from under them, disappeared down a well of blackness. Crane made the mistake of looking down, became dizzy, lightheaded, told C.J. he thought he'd faint. C.J. grabbed his arm, held him steady until his head cleared, continued their slow labored ascent to the platform.

Crane reached it exhausted, manhandling the heavy toolbox ahead of him, hanging the sack on a protruding pole. He threw off his heavy fireman's coat, slung it over the shallow rail, pulled himself up until seated just below the ventilation duct's entrance into the wall. C.J. followed the same routine, found himself in cramped quarters on the platform with little room for movement.

Facing the actual ventilation duct instead of a model presented a major problem that hadn't been anticipated—the duct fit inside a thick steel sleeve anchored to the wall and would take much more time to cut through than Crane had allotted. He looked at his watch. 3:55 am. Time was evaporating like ether. He opened the toolbox, took out drill, saw, can of oil and set to work. He wrapped a large towel around the body of the drill, pulled the trigger switch and satisfied it was muffled, bore into the steel sleeve.

Outside the Duchess, Henry T and several parking attendants were gathered under the hood of the limo, each passing thoughts as to why it wouldn't start, but all saying it would have to be moved once the driveway filled up with cars, and especially by five when the vendors would begin arriving. Henry T agreed, played off ignorance, continued checking his watch. Crane had said he needed two hours. One had already passed. He wondered if he could stall for a second.

Inside the diesel's box four restless shadows shifted about in darkness with ever increasing tension. The heavy firemen's suits were claustrophobic. Duffy needed a primo. Smith wanted a blunt. Every time a helmet light fell on a watch the tension escalated. 4:15 … 4:20 … 4:25 … 4:30 … 4:35—Crane had said they'd be gone by five. Maybe something had happened. He'd been caught. Or fell down the elevator shaft. Whatever it was, none of them planned to stay in place after five. No word from Crane by then—he and his plan were history.

At 4:41 Crane's voice crackled through the walkie-talkie as if he'd read their thoughts of mutiny.

"Everyone—into the elevator. *NOW!*"

Only moments before the call he and C.J. had finished what they hoped would be a successful diversion. C.J. had severed all power and phone systems to the fifteenth floor when he cut through the bundle of 'hot' cables that fed power to the penthouse suites. Crane had managed to cut a hole in the ventilation duct large enough to slip in five smoke grenades, sent Trixie down with the elevator to change uniforms and collect the others. He knew he'd lost his battle with time, but there was no turning back. Not now. He didn't know if it would work, remembered Schwarzenegger in *Raw Deal,* figured it was as good an idea as any he could think of. If it worked, he'd get the trunk and let the others fight over the cash. If it didn't, well—he still had Duffy to deal with either way he cut it. He called Henry T, asked if he could stall another fifteen minutes. Henry T said the front of the Duchess was a parking lot. They were pressing him to send for a tow truck, didn't know how much longer he could stall, but he'd try. Bo Bo beeped him on the walkie-talkie to say he was staying behind to help Reese unload merchandise but the others were on their way up.

It reached the fifteenth floor at 4:45 am. As he'd been instructed, Smith kept the doors closed, the elevator frozen. Almost as soon as they arrived, Crane and C.J. stepped from the ladder onto the roof, dropped awkwardly through the access door to rejoin the team in a tight closet of darkness. Crane fastened his gas mask, switched on his helmet light. Five others did the same. Axes in hand, they stood motionless in complete silence like garish figures on display in a wax museum.

"Okay, Smith," Crane said, his voice muffled by helmet and mask. "Open the doors."

No one, not even Crane, was prepared for the sight that greeted them. The doors slowly opened to a ferocious wall of freezing water hidden in darkness and wrapped in a swirling cloud of thick black smoke visible only in the short narrow beams of helmet lights. In the faint distance, over the hiss of sprinklers, high-pitched blares of battery operated smoke detectors, they could hear the feeble shouts and screams of fear and panic.

It was beyond anything Crane had ever imagined. So startling was the effect, so eerie and shocking its impact, the group stood mesmerized at the elevator door, paralyzed by the surreal landscape that faced them.

But only for a moment. Suddenly out of the veil of darkness a half-dressed woman in her fifties stumbled blindly, desperately into the six beams of light. Coughing, sputtering in the cold drenching shower that matted long strands of graying hair to her face and back, she threw herself into the elevator crying out desperately, "Help me. Please! Dear God, help me!" Her pleas brought them out of their collective trance, sent them exploding out of the elevator and into the lightless corridor, fanning out along the length of its arc and the chaos that waited.

Trixie brought the hapless women to her feet, pulled her to the fire exit and directed her up to the roof, her light now serving as a beacon to others filling the corridor, groping blindly along its walls, crawling feebly over and under one another like animals stranded in a flood.

They did not have to use axes or card keys so convincing was the ruse, so realistic its effect—the sudden blaring of smoke detectors, immediate cascade of water, loss of power, absence of any light—that guests spilled out into the blackened, smoke-filled, water drenched corridor without prompting. Few if any were clothed beyond underwear or nightgowns. Many were nude, dragging water-soaked blankets or sheets behind them in an effort at modesty in the midst of sheer terror, bumping shamelessly into one another, confused and frightened.

Because the combination of smoke and water was so obscuring, the penetration of helmet lights so limited, the team on many occasions stumbled or tripped over guests crawling aimlessly about in the corridor. Some guests, so panic stricken and terrified at events they were immobilized, had to be forcefully pulled along the corridor to the fire exit. Crane had underestimated the number of children staying in the penthouse. Smaller children were terrified and hysterical with fear—older children so frightened they couldn't move. But his generalship had prepared team members, as best he could, to be particularly alert and attentive to their safety, personally escorting them to the fire exits.

It was this fear that eroded his time, slowing movements along a waterlogged carpet, some guests hesitant to move along the wall until the sporadic splash of a helmet light glimmered through sheets of chilling water, choking smoke.

Laughing stupidly, five drunk guests staggered out of the elevator into the downpour. Three men, two hookers. Halloween masks, little bags of candy. Mistook Duffy's uniform for a costume, asked where the party was. Duffy said the roof, frisked them for cell phones, led them through drenching blackness to the refugee column.

From the very beginning of the evacuation Crane had positioned himself between suites 1512 and 1517, needing to see what if any surprise was achieved with the Feds, degree of cooperation and danger posed by the Mexicans.

The Feds blinked first, five men in boxer shorts stumbling blindly through the door of 1514, seven more from 1512. No shoulder holsters. Totally convinced of fire, they fled panic stricken and shivering through the unseen matrix of artificial rain and choking smoke, groping their way blindly along the wall, grateful for an occasional flicker of light from a helmet leading the way. One of them had managed to grab a cell phone, dropped it into the dark abyss of water and smoke when Crane slammed him against the wall in the pretext of shouting instructions for safety.

Six Mexicans emerged from 1517. Fully dressed and soaking wet, they were not frightened or disoriented. They didn't stagger or stumble out clumsily as so many others—they walked out calm and deliberate one after another, stood together in a tight defensive knot just outside their door under an invisible deluge of water, waiting. The light beam from Crane's helmet found them before the others, cut a path across hardened brown faces blinking away the wet sting of never-ending spray, corrosive smoke that burned their lungs.

Crane approached them cautiously, touched the arm of one in a show of recognition and motioned for them to follow. They were hesitant at first, reluctant to leave the room unsecured, not completely sure how much was planned, how much was real. He led them past a caravan of slower moving guests, heavy-booted feet sloshing through deep saturated carpet to the fire exit, motioned for them to follow others to the roof. Once in the stairwell they stopped as a unit, spoke among themselves, looked suspiciously at the figure hidden in the disguise, shook their heads in disgust. One of the Mexicans, Crane figured the leader, cocked his finger at Crane in the manner of a gun as a silent warning and turned away motioning the others to follow him up the stairs. He couldn't tell if they were armed, but smart money said they were.

At 5:02 am the fifteenth floor of the Duchess Hotel was totally evacuated of all guests. Crane secured the door to the roof, sent the service elevator down to the garage for laundry hampers and luggage carts, called Henry T to check his time. Henry T said several tow trucks had arrived and drivers were arguing among themselves as to who would get the job. He'd parked at such an angle that who ever prevailed wouldn't have an easy time of it. Fifteen minutes—twenty at the most. Thirty if he started a fight, got the police involved. Crane wanted no part of 5-O and said so.

Bo Bo rode up with the first three laundry hampers out of curiosity. On his way down the elevator stopped at twelve. The same janitor Crane had seen earlier got on, pointed to water dripping down the elevator shaft in ever increasing amounts, asked if they'd have the sprinkler fixed any time soon. Thinking on his feet, Bo Bo said they would, called Crane on the walkie-talkie when the janitor got off, told him about the problem. If the janitor had noticed, it was just a matter of time before someone else would. Crane agreed, pulled C.J. aside, repeated Bo Bo's warning, asked if there was some way to shut off the water.

"There's a valve in each stairwell!" C.J. shouted to Crane over the din of blaring smoke detectors, hissing of water. "I'll do one—you do the other. Look for a red handle, turn it till it stops."

Crane said, "Alright," and throwing an armful of laptops into a nearby hamper he disappeared into the soupy quagmire of the corridor.

In the stairwell his helmet light slashed walls till it fell on a series of pipes coursing up from the floor below, disappearing into the ceiling above. He saw dials, the red handle, turned it hard to the right at least four times, heard the hiss of sprinklers soften, waited for the deluge of water to finally stop.

Marcus and Duffy were manhandling the first overloaded hamper onto the service elevator as Crane stepped back into the corridor, almost unfamiliar in the absence of drenching downpour. But the pall of thick black smoke trapped in its long curving arch still limited his field of vision to the helmet light and its maximum penetration of little more than a yard, if that. His watch read: 5:16 am.

Nate Smith performed spectacularly. To keep his circuit boards from shorting, the safes dry, he had fashioned himself a hood similar to the kind turn-of-the-century photographers used. He'd already done three suites by the time Crane returned. And with the water off he was even faster, outpacing Trixie who followed him with a plastic bag collecting cash and jewelry, the men behind her loading luggage and electronics into hampers and carts.

And that's the way Crane's team looted the penthouse—one suite after another. One bedroom after another … the team didn't miss a beat. If there was anything to slow the operation down it was heavy overloaded laundry hampers and luggage carts whose narrow wheels bogged down in the entrapment of thick water-saturated carpet. It would take at least two men, sometimes three to get hampers to the elevators. But it didn't discourage them, and after a while they fell into a rhythm with one another that enabled them to clean out a suite with ever increasing speed.

Down in the parking structure Reese and Bo Bo worked at fever pitch to unload the steady stream of loot into the truck. They took turns accompanying empty hampers and carts back to the penthouse, riding shotgun against possibility of discovery and hijacking by curious hotel maintenance crews, room service personnel or housekeeping maids. The last time Bo Bo looked at his watch it read: 5:25 am.

In front of the Duchess the driveway was so filled with cars, attendants were now parking on Sunset Boulevard in spots usually reserved for taxis. Vendors were beginning to arrive: grocers, liquor distributors, linen suppliers, meat and poultry trucks, refrigerated produce trucks— lined up one behind the other, horns blowing their irritation. At the entrance to the parking structure Henry T and a tow truck driver were arguing over where to attach chains and tow bar on the limo. His watch read 5:40 am and daybreak was just minutes beyond the horizon.

Up in the penthouse they were down to 1506. Crane's team had moved this fast despite smoke, water and darkness because some of the suites were empty, or the guests lightly packed with only one or two pieces of luggage, empty safes, no electronics. 1517 had been like that ... only three small pieces of cheap luggage and the steamer trunk. They had told him correctly—it did look like the kind of trunk one expected to see on the Titanic. It was a tall, weathered two-tone brown and beige turn-of-the-century wardrobe trunk usually seen in antique shops or the movies. It was tied together from top to bottom with frayed cords of thick rope and was standing in a foot of water in the middle of the sunken living room. So this was it, thought Crane when he first saw the trunk, trying not to appear overly interested. So caught up in the mechanics of his plan, he'd almost forgotten why he was here. But his continued freedom lay in its safety and for an instant he wondered about its contents.

Not so Marcus. Because of its size, weight, trouble it would take to transport it to the elevator, he suggested they leave it, move on to another suite in the interest of time. Still being casual Crane insisted, helped Marcus load it onto a luggage cart and manhandle it down the darkened corridor. More importantly Crane had noticed the absence of any weapons in the suite, knew instantly the Mexicans on the roof were armed.

1514 and 1512 on the other hand, yielded a cache of arms, ammunition and body armor that absolutely delighted Marcus and Duffy. There were AK-47s; TEC-9s; MAC-10s with laser sights, infra-red night vision scopes; 9mm GLOCKS; twelve gage shotguns; 357 MAGNUMs; SWAT body armor, untold rounds of ammunition and a box of flash grenades. Marcus felt they had stumbled across an illegal arms deal. Duffy, putting his hostility aside for a moment, agreed with Crane's deception, said they may have interrupted another North Hollywood-type bank robbery in the planning.

They entered 1505, started their practiced routine behind Smith. No one noticed the faint rays of dawn stealing out from behind edges of thick drapes. It was 5:55 am.

"Crane? Henry T." Henry T's nervous voice crackled through the walkie-talkie.

"Yeah, Henry T?"

"They movin' the limo, bro. Niggas better get the fuck outta Dodge, know what I'm sayin'? Pick me up at the curb."

Crane clicked off, looked at his watch, cursed at his carelessness, clicked back on and said, "Reese? Crane."

"I heard," Reese said. "Motor's running. Come on with it, my brother!"

Crane pulled off his helmet, coughed violently at the irritation of lingering smoke, shouted over the dying blare of smoke detectors.

"THAT'S IT, PEOPLE! PARTY'S OVER! LET'S MOVE OUT—NOW!!!" and he rushed around the suite rounding up team members, pushing them toward the corridor, dropping laptops, cameras, cell phones in the watery abyss on their way out.

No one saw the Mexican until he was right up on them, Trixie knocking into him, nearly losing her balance as she ran through the door and into the corridor. Beams of light rolled over a dense brown face, caught fragments of long black hair tied in a ponytail, teardrop tattoo below his left eye. Except for his shoes and pantscuffs he was completely dry, stood just outside the door holding a handkerchief to his face.

Everyone figured he must have wandered in from the passenger elevator. Crane knew different, knew he was one of Romero's soldiers left behind as insurance, probably hidden in the shower stall judging by his dry clothes. Crane also knew from years in the joint, teardrop tattoos on young Mexicans were notches on a gun.

So did Duffy. He instinctively sensed something was wrong, hung back, working the heavy zipper down the front of his uniform.

"Where's the trunk?" The lilting accent was pure East L.A. The caravan of curious lights that circled about him began trotting away in smoky darkness.

Crane continued the ruse, put his helmet back on, took the Mexican's arm, urged him into the rapid cadence of fleeing thieves and said, "Sir, you'll be quite safe on the roof with the others."

The soldier wasn't buying it for a second. He jerked his arm away and still trotting alongside Crane, repeated his question.

Crane repeated his answer and added, "Fire's not down yet, sir. It's not safe for you down here. But on the roof—"

"Ain't no fire, homes," the Mexican said irritably. "I know what this is about. *WHERE'S THE MUTHAFUCKIN' TRUNK?*" he suddenly shouted, coughing as he spoke but still trotting at speed in midst of the group.

"Just relax, sir," Trixie shouted at his elbow, trying to calm him down, thinking he was worried about his luggage. "We've made every effort to protect your belongings. Now if you'll just follow me to the roof—?" and she took his arm in a gesture of guiding him but the Mexican became incensed.

"Fuck the roof, puta!" the Mexican cried out angrily, still coughing. He jerked his arm from her grasp and said to Trixie, "I'm tired of these games. My orders are to go with the trunk—that's where I'll follow you!" And before Trixie could answer his insult, or Crane bring his authority to bear the Mexican suddenly produced a 9mm pistol from the darkness, kept it at arm's length by his side out of Crane's view and without breaking his stride, grabbed Trixie's arm and pushed her forcibly in front of him. But Trixie lost her balance in the unexpected movement, stumbled and fell to her knees. As the Mexican tripped over her, losing his own balance, spinning around in an effort to stay on his feet, Duffy caught the glint of the 9mm in his beam of light.

The coat of his uniform now open, Duffy withdrew his own 9mm, fired five rounds at the Mexican point blank. *BLAM! BLAM! BLAM! BLAM! BLAM!* Four hits in the chest, one in the neck that severed his spinal cord.

"Ughhh!" The Mexican staggered back in wide-eyed surprise into the vacuum of darkness, fell out of Duffy's field of vision, splashed down on a hard cushion of water, his finger jerking the trigger in uncontrolled spasms, firing wildly until the clip was empty of all sixteen rounds, the firing mechanism clicking like a solenoid on a dead starter.

The sudden shock of gunfire sent Crane's hands fumbling in his uniform for his .357, dropping to the ground defensively until he put together what had happened, then stood up again cautiously.

The retreating column ahead had not heard the exchange between the Mexican and the others. But when they heard the shots behind them, they too instinctively dropped to the ground in panic, Marcus struggling clumsily to get at his .45 COLT under the heavy uniform.

Duffy and Crane helped a shaken Trixie to her feet, asked if she was okay, saw her nod inside the mask. Duffy pulled off his helmet and coughing, said to Trixie, "Don't think I did this for you, bitch! But I ain't gonna let no muthafucka rip me off, not after I come this far." He said to Crane, "Now you see why I told you ain't no nigga dumb 'enuf to go into something like this without being strapped, know what I'm sayin'?" Crane nodded gratefully, thought it best to say nothing. His helmet light found the Mexican's corpse a few yards away. Duffy kicked him to make sure he was dead. He was spread-eagled on his back, eyes and mouth still open in shock. All he needed was a cross.

Fearing the Mexicans on the roof heard gunfire, that they'd break down the door, shoot out the locks if necessary and come streaming down the stairwell after them, Crane grabbed Trixie's arm, pulled her along behind and said to Duffy, "We gotta get the fuck outta here!"

Duffy said, "Word," and jammed a full clip in his 9mm, sliding the action.

They rushed up on an array of scattered forms still on the ground, beams from their helmets rising up like stage lights. As they approached, Marcus was the first to stand, waving his .45 like a flag in the wind.

Marcus said, "What the fuck was that all about?"

Duffy said, "Guess someone didn't want his shit stole," and he looked at Crane, the anger and hostility in his voice more intense, knowing now Crane hadn't told them everything.

"Who cares," Crane lied, playing it off. "But if he has friends, we don't wanna be here when they show up. Let's go, everybody. Into the elevator!"

But as Marcus turned to follow he noticed the two remaining lights on the ground didn't move. He said, "Hey, come on, people. C.J.? Smith—?" He bent down to help Smith up, realized his form was limp, that he was dead. He reached over and shook C.J.'s shoulder, felt no movement in the uniform and knew he too was dead.

"CRANE! HEY, CRANE," he shouted over his shoulder and realizing Crane hadn't heard him in the tight confines of his helmet, removed

it, coughed in the smoke.

"CRANE!" he shouted again. *"THEY BEEN SHOT, MAN! C.J. AND SMITH ARE DEAD!"*

Crane and the others rushed back, stood beside Marcus, peering down.

"Muthafucka." Crane removed his helmet and kneeled beside C.J., rolled him over on his back, saw three bullet holes in the front of his coat. Smith had been shot two times in the head, his visor so covered in blood they couldn't see his face.

"Oh, God!" cried Trixie, a storm of nausea washing over her. She ripped off her helmet, turned away and vomited.

Sorry it wasn't Crane lying dead on the ground, Duffy said reluctantly, "We gotta go, Crane," and tugged at his coat sleeve.

"DAMN!" mumbled Crane, feeling remorse, the tic returning, punishing his face. It wasn't supposed to be this way. Crane had told Moffett and Romero he could do the job, just leave him alone to do it his way. Why didn't they trust him?

Suddenly everyone heard the commotion at the top of the stairwell. Muted shouts, heavy pounding on the door. Then a fusillade of shots poured into the door, echoed down the stairwell, filtered into the corridor.

"That be their friends, probably," said Marcus readying his .45, Duffy his 9mm, moving back to the elevator, pulling Trixie with them.

"Crane?" Reese's anxious voice crackled again through the walkietalkie. "You'd better come on, my brother. They beginnin' to park cars … ask questions."

Marcus clicked on and said, "We on our way," his eyes riveted on the fire door. Then to Crane he shouted, "We gotta go, Crane! You and Reese can pray over them niggas later if you want, but we gotta go—

NOW!!!"

They heard the door on the roof give way, a rush of heavy boots into the stairwell, flowing down stairs like water from a ruptured dam. The Mexicans reached the fire door, began firing point blank, showering the corridor with steel splinters, shards of broken glass.

That the Mexican Mafia would be so bold in the midst of the heist confused Crane. Why would the M & M's be firing away like that ... taking a chance on fucking things up? It didn't make any sense, Crane thought—unless they'd planned it all along and needed someone to take the fall? And who better than a con whose presence couldn't be explained—again, unless he's listed as an escaped con by Moffett? Unless he'd been set up ...?

"CRANE!!!" shouted Duffy as the fire door broke open, soldiers of the Mexican Mafia threatening to storm through. *"C'MON, YOU STUPID ASS MUTHAFUCKA!"*

Like marines in a John Wayne movie Duffy and Marcus rose to the occasion, lay down a blanket of covering fire that peppered the fire exit, keeping the M & M's at bay as Crane dove into the elevator, firing even as the door closed.

As they began their slow descent they heard the assault on the elevator door above and once forced open, braced for a blistering barrage of fire roaring down the elevator shaft, rounds ricocheting off the beveled roof, splintering cables, chipping concrete walls. But the floor lights still winked and the elevator continued its unmolested fall.

When the shower of rounds tapered they knew their pursuers would join others already in the stairwell bounding down after them, hoping the elevator would stop at one floor or another and not really caring who might see them or the consequences. Soldiers of the Mexican Mafia were prepared to die. Always prepared to die.

Eleven. Ten. Nine—

Floorlights passed unbroken as if divined. Marcus, Crane and Duffy reloaded and ready, guns trained on the door, eyes watching floor numbers like lights on a keno board. Trixie—her mouth dry, throat raw from smoke—swallowed hard, eyes blinking in terror.

Eight. Seven. Six. Five—

Crane's face jumping like a stick puppet on a tethered string, his breathing rapid and shallow, .357 at the ready. No one spoke. Hearts racing together, pounding in chests about to explode. Beads of salty sweat bathed foreheads, played at the edges of dry lips.

Four. Three. Two. Lobby. Parking—

They stepped out of the elevator into an orchestra of blaring horns, squealing tires, profanities of parking attendants. Vendor trucks beginning to arrive, jockey for position, unloading. Reese and Bo Bo pacing frantically by the rig, engine starting to belch a sliver of smoke.

Reese swung open the heavy door, space to sit at a premium in a box more than three quarters full. Bo Bo jumped in, helped pull in the others.

"Where's C.J. and Smith?" Bo Bo asked.

Duffy said, "They got shot."

Bo Bo said, *"SHOT?"*

"GO!" Crane shouted.

Reese closed the door, secured the locking bolt, climbed in the cab. He pushed in the clutch. First gear … jerking the aging diesel out of its spot, snorting up the incline and into the dull gray mist of early morning. He maneuvered carefully but quickly along a driveway narrowed by double and triple parked eighty thousand dollar imports, vendor trucks and waiting taxis, saw Henry T standing at the curb. Without downshifting he braked only slightly when he reached the street, swung a hard right west onto Sunset, opened the passenger door for Henry T all in one motion. Henry T hit the runningboard like Superman, slipped in beside Reese, cursing.

Henry T said, "What took you niggas so long?"

Reese said, "Left two behind dead—Smith and C.J."

"Five-O?"

"I didn't get that impression."

"Guess that means we rich," Henry T said. "And two less to split with means we not only rich, we *real* rich," and he began laughing irreverently.

Reese said to Henry T, "You should have more respect for the dead."

"That's your department. You the preacher. I just wanna be rich."

Reese said, "But I am poor and needy. Make haste unto me, O God. Thou art my help and my deliverer. Oh Lord make no tarrying—Psalms seventy, verse five."

Chapter 13

WHEN REESE PULLED THE RIG INTO THE STORAGE HANGAR it was just after seven. The first thing the group did, even before unloading the box, was trade firemens' uniforms for FuBu, Phat Farm and Tommy Hilfiger. It was party time. The pungent aroma of Blunts soon filled the hangar along with CDs of NAS and DMX competing with LAX's glidescope every five minutes. Nobody seemed to miss C.J. or Smith. The men were playing gangster with the weapons Crane knew belonged to the Feds, trying to get a rep, pumping it up on shit that never went down.

Wearing jean cutoffs that showed too much butt, a DKNY tank top a size too small and a nose layered with cocaine residue, Trixie wasn't worrying about Duffy's threat that still hung over her and Crane. She danced, spun and gyrated to the beats, her arms dripping with gold, silver and diamond bracelets retrieved from a nearby plastic bag.

It had taken them an hour and a half to loot fifteen suites and load the truck. Crane reasoned they could do the reverse in half that time, sort through, inventory. But in fact it went much slower than anticipated. Without the pressure of time, worry about discovery and mounting fatigue, their pace was almost leisurely. Frequent breaks for food that one or another would take turns going out for, even more for Blunts, rolling Zig-Zags with *stress* or *chronic* ... Trixie's cocaine fix—slowed the pace even more.

Still Crane was able to bring a semblance of organization to the process. He put Trixie in charge of the small stuff: plastic bags filled with jewelry, credit cards, cash-fat wallets, purses, Traveler's checks. She was assigned two tables and instructed to separate the stash into piles of like items. Henry T, Bo Bo and Reese had the task of unloading attaché cases, laptops and electronics. They had four tables. Crane, Duffy and Marcus handled the luggage, placing it in rows along the rear wall of the hangar. Crane kept his eyes on the steamer trunk as they worked their way to it, thinking what he would say to keep them away from it, what he would have to do if he couldn't. And all the while sensing Duffy knew he hadn't been straight with them from the get go. Knowing too he'd have to watch Duffy's every move after Nance's payoff, unless Duffy had a change of heart and Crane didn't think that was likely to happen. Since the trunk was one of the first to be loaded, they reached it last, decided as a group to let it stay in the box for the time being because of its size, their growing fatigue ... getting back to it when they'd opened the rest.

And opening the rest took some doing. The rich travel with the best: Louis Vuitton, PRADA, Samsonite, Coach. Three quarters of the luggage was locked. They had to use crowbars … shoot off the locks on some, cut through thick leather on others, the results disappointing: lots of socks and underwear, a few silk ties, custom made shirts from Hong Kong, silk handkerchiefs, alligator shoes, a few crocodile belts, more than enough cosmetics in the smaller pieces. Plane and cruise ship tickets in every suitcase along with portable clocks, electric razors and stashes of weed. Every other suitcase had condoms and a deck of cards. Five had freebase pipes. They needed a separate box to hold all the rolls of film.

The attaché cases were filled with legal and financial documents nobody understood. But five of them yielded an unexpected surprise: displays of unmounted jewels. Crane guessed they'd stumbled across the stocks of diamond importers … maybe in L.A. for a convention at the downtown jewelry mart. The unloading stopped. Everyone gathered to look, noticed the handcuffs attached to the handles.

"How much you figure they worth?" Duffy wanted to know.

Turning stones over in his hand, rolling them between fingers, Crane was guessing. "I dunno," he said honestly. "Million each case, maybe more. Fence'll tell us."

Trixie said, "Definitely more. Saw a documentary on TV once. Said diamond couriers have to be bonded at least five million dollars."

Bo Bo said, "Bonded?"

"Insured," Trixie said. "That means these are worth at least three, four million each."

While Crane was more surprised than anyone, he felt it prudent to keep quiet. But Duffy did the math … five cases at four million each was twenty million.

"Damn," he said to no one in particular but looking at Trixie with dollar sign eyes, the hardness displayed toward her softening. "We sure 'nuf gonna be seven figure niggas, huh?" But the softness was only temporary, hurt and anger returning to a face that sneered at her and Crane as they resumed work.

They were halfway through by noon, moving at a snail's pace, exhausted. No one was in the mood to go back in the box for the steamer trunk. Marcus and Duffy took a break during Method Man's *Judgement Day*, smoked a Blunt and fell asleep on top of unused tables. Henry T and Bo Bo didn't need any dope to sleep, the floor of the hangar a hard mattress they wouldn't notice. Reese fell asleep in a chair reading his Bible, Trixie still bouncing to the beats, in Cartier and cocaine heaven.

Crane went outside, surprised by the brightness of the sun. He climbed into the Lexus, called Willie Nance on one of the stolen cell phones and when he answered, told him where to come. He asked about jewelry. Crane said there was a lot. Nance said he'd have to call his jeweler and the money man. He'd be there when he got there.

Crane's next call was to Romero. It rang seven times.

"Romero."

"This is Crane. I've got your trunk."

Romero said, "Is it damaged?"

Crane said, "No. Little wet at one end is all."

"Has it been opened?" Crane could hear the unspoken threat in the question.

"No," Crane said. "It's not my property. Why would I open it?"

He could hear Romero interpreting to others in the background.

"Be glad you don't have to answer that question, homes," Romero said. "Where do we pick it up?"

Trunk more important than the three lives it cost. Crane couldn't believe it and said, "Your man killed two of my people, esé."

There was a long period of translation before Romero answered.

"So what?" Romero's voice, devoid of any compassion, sounded almost cavalier.

"It wasn't necessary."

Romero said, "You're right, homes. It wasn't necessary. If you'd let Luis go with you I wouldn't be sending money to Mexico for his funeral." Crane was surprised he knew the soldier's name.

Crane said, "Who pays for my two?"

Romero said, "That's your problem, homes."

"We had a deal," Crane said, pressing the Mexican. "Your people were suppose to cooperate—?"

The Mexican's voice exploded over the cell phone. "Listen, miyaté!" Romero shouted. "The only deal was you get our trunk. Don't come to me with some punk-ass shit like that! You understand? You be glad you had any deal at all. Know what I'm sayin', homes? 'Cause if you'd of fucked up, lost all our shit to the Feds—?" Romero half-grunted, half-laughed facetiously. He said, "Shiiit, homes ... your life expectancy wouldn't be worth talkin' about. Now, like I said before ... where do we pick it up?"

Crane gave him directions and said, "How'll I know it's you?"

Romero said, "Damn, homes ... you got a short memory. I said I'd be with someone you know, remember?" Crane thought back, recalled the conversation with Romero that first night at the *Hardcore*. "Once we have the trunk," Romero was saying, "our business is finished. You get a new lease on life. Simple as that, homes."

But Crane knew that a new lease on life was never very simple. He clicked off, rubbed fatigue out of sleepless, bloodshot eyes, caught the glitter of diamonds walking toward him. Trixie dropped into the passenger seat wearing Rayban wraparound sunglasses and weighted down by untold strands of diamond necklaces, her tanktop covered with diamond brooches, ears dotted with earrings rimmed with sapphires.

Queen for a day.

Trixie removed the sunglasses, and before he could protest pulled herself over and on top of Crane all in one motion, sending her probing tongue deep in his mouth. Powder-blue eyes and freckles sparkled with a smile. Trapped in the facets of a blanket of diamonds, the sun exploded across her face in a brilliant rainbow of color.

"Everyone's asleep," Trixie said, fingering a brooch that caught the sun, splashing its rays over Crane's face and eyes, playing with him. "They won't wake up for hours." Crane looked at her, raised his eyebrows, smiled slightly. "You've got three hundred and seventy thousand in Traveler's checks, two hundred and fifty seven thousand in cash. I counted both twice, tucked the cash away. Don't figure your fence has any right to that."

Crane kissed her and said, "You figured right."

Trixie sat up, crossed bare legs and leaned into Crane, shoulders just barely touching. She leaned forward and cocked her head in an attitude, chin jutting out in profile and said, "How do I look in all these jewels, Crane?"

Crane said, "Like a million dollar lady."

Trixie giggled like a schoolgirl, leaned over and kissed Crane on the cheek, let her fingers linger around his face where the tic usually appeared when it did. She pulled away for a moment, looked through the windshield past the storage hangar to the distant strobe lights, descending jets on the glidescope. She said, "Lady," thinking about being one and how to go about it. "Tired of being a whore, Crane," she went on, fingers frozen around a ruby necklace, eyes moving to Crane's. "Tired of fucking strange men ... tired of going on stage shaking my titties, wiggling my ass ... rubbing my pussy, strangers feeling all over me—" Trixie sent her eyes back to the glidescope and the tail of a 757. She said, "I'd like to get on one of those jets, fly outta here and never look back. Don't care where ... long as it's with you."

Crane laughed softly. "We're a team now," he said shaking his head in agreement, blush of guilt about Marjorie stabbing him. "Find us someplace we can start over together, where nobody knows us." And with bitter memories of Marion—the 'Hole,' the 'Committee,' beatings, rapes, torture—all flooding back for an instant, he added, "Cause I'm never going back to prison. Not in this lifetime. They'll have to kill me first ... if Duffy doesn't."

"Duffy doesn't scare me," Trixie said boldly. "I know him. Once he gets his hands on some big money he'll forget all about us."

Crane said, "I wouldn't count on that. We hurt his pride. With him it's like living in the days of King Arthur ... you wound a man's pride, he demands satisfaction."

"You mean like a duel?"

"Something like that."

"So what do we do?"

Crane said, "Get as far away from him as we can."

Trixie glowed at being included. She hugged him and said, "And we're gonna do just that ... together. Go somewhere on that big jet ... buy us some land you can build a house on ..."

"Ranch," Crane said interrupting, caught up in the fantasy of the moment.

"I wanna design a big ranch house with a stream running through it like Frank Lloyd Wright's *Falling Water*."

"I like Taliesin better," Trixie said.

Crane turned and looked at her, eyes open in never ending amazement.

He said, "In Wisconsin. You know about that?"

Powder-blue eyes blinked in modesty. Trixie went on, "We'll live like normal people do in the movies ... have lots and lots of kids ... invite our friends over for dinner."

In the face of so much danger it was fun, this fantasy—planning a better life the way it was on TV and in the movies. But movies are make-believe. And Crane knew from personal experience, if Trixie did not, that life imitating art didn't always have a happy ending.

Chapter 14

"KING SOLOMON'S MINES," Willie Nance had exclaimed when he first saw the piles of glittering jewels in the dull glare of overhead flourescent lights. His arrival at ten in a battered 1986 Cadillac Sedan DeVille missing it's front bumper and left headlight, was announced by squeaking brakes and a cloud of choking smoke that lingered after the engine was shut off.

His jeweler was Mickey, a thin, baldheaded white man in his late fifties with a sunken face he tried to hide in the thickness of a graying mustache. His teeth were stained by years of Cuban cigars, the unlit *Cohiba* filling a mouth that moved mechanically from side to side. He wore a pair of rimless bi-focals with a loupe attached and who, next to Willie Nance's faded jeans and sweatshirt, looked almost respectable in his cheap Strafford suit.

Crane asked what took them so long. Willie Nance said he was busy, leave them alone so they could work. Crane and the others did—for two hours.

No one spoke. Marcus and Duffy played cards. Reese read his Bible, Bo Bo and Henry T smoked *stress*, grooved to Ginuwine. Trixie paced nervously the entire time, made occasional trips to the head for a snort, pouted when Mickey demanded the jewelry. Crane watched everyone watching Mickey and Nance, but especially Duffy.

The white boy was nothing if he wasn't methodical. He set about the task of appraising each pile in order—necklaces first, then bracelets, brooches and pins third, earrings fourth, rings and gold chains fifth, watches last. Meticulously fingering each item one piece at a time, searching it with the loupe for flaws and discarding costume jewelry in its own pile on the floor. And all the while making notations on a small pad … description, estimated value …

And while Mickey was doing that Willie Nance went about the process of assessing the worth of what was left—electronics, cell phones and miscellaneous items like golf clubs, tennis rackets, cameras and weapons. The weapons, more than anything, impressed him. But he didn't see them all. Marcus and Duffy had taken some—the TEC 9s, GLOCKS and MAC 10s. Of the weapons that were left Willie told Crane he'd get top dollar like he'd promised.

He wanted to know how much there was in Traveler's checks and cash. Crane fed him Trixie's numbers on the Traveler's checks, said the cash was none of his business, told Willie to deal only with what he saw.

Willie Nance saw a lot: thirty-three top-of-the-line laptops, thirty-two digital cell phones, fourteen CD players, seven pocket TVs, twenty-three Mastercard Gold cards, forty VISA Platinum cards, twenty-one American Express Gold cards, thirty Discover Gold cards. There were forty-five sets of travel documents for destinations outside the U.S. including one round-the-world cruise. The fence said he could move those as fast as Traveler's checks, weapons and the thirty-four German and Japanese cameras he counted.

Most of the luggage was now junk, trashed in the process of opening, a few with water damage.

"What's that?" Willie Nance was standing at the door of the box, looking at the steamer trunk.

Crane said, "Someone's trunk. Just ain't got to it yet. Figure it belongs to one of those cruise tickets probably."

Willie said, "Probably." He returned to the tables, poked around with his cane, looked at some things more closely through bi-focals thick as Mickey's, said he couldn't take a chance on Gold or Platinum cards.

Mickey finally got to the five display cases, spent another thirty minutes appraising unmounted stones. When he finished he stood up, handed the pad to Willie. Willie adjusted bi-focals across the flat bridge of his nose, scanned the list.

"You got eight million in jewelry," Willie said. "Another six in unmounted stones ... electronics, about a hundred grand ... guns, fifty ... Traveler's checks, three hundred seventy thousand ... airline tickets, ten grand. That's fourteen million five hundred thirty thousand all total. I'll give you half on the jewelry and stones, half on the electronics, Traveler's checks and airline tickets, seventy-five on the weapons ... can't do shit with the rest," and he waved his hand back toward the wall to include the luggage, sports equipment and furs. "So that's seven million two hundred seventy two thousand five hundred ... I keep the hangar. We got a deal?"

Trixie did the math. She said, "Only six million dollars for the cases? That's little more than a million apiece. Ought to be worth more than that...?"

Willie looked at Trixie over the rim of his bi-focals. He said, "You got a degree in appraising, white girl?"

Trixie let the words pass. She said to Willie, "I saw this thing on TV ... about diamond couriers, you know—said they always carry at least five million?"

Willie said, "They lied, white girl." He turned to Crane and said, "TV. That's the trouble now days, bro," and he handed Crane the pad. "People watch too much TV ... think it's the Bible."

Reese said, "There's only one Bible," and he held up his Bible for Willie to see, saying, "But my God shall supply all your needs according to his riches in glory by Jesus Christ—Philippians, chapter four, verse nineteen."

Willie said to Crane, "Where you find these people ... a Jesus freak, coke-sniffin' TV expert? We got a deal or not ...?"

Crane handed the pad back to Willie and said, "Show me the money."

Willie Nance pulled out a cell phone. "At the other end of a phone call." He punched in a number, waited for a voice. He said, "This is Willie Nance. Looks like everything's in order. Come on with it."

Sighs of relief filled the hangar. Muted laughter, slapping of hi-fives, relaxed congratulations mixed with Brandy and Monica's 'The Boy Is Mine,' a late arriving 747 on the glidescope.

"Seven million Benjamins makes each one of us seven figure

niggas," Henry T said, separating out seeds from the *chronic* with a stolen VISA Platinum card.

"I'm not a nigger," Trixie said, lighting a Primo, drawing it in deep, holding it for the buzz.

"Ain't you?" asked Reese howling with laughter, others joining in. "You may be white, snowflake, with your blonde hair and blue eyes. But in America, if you ain't rich, educated or powerful, you considered poor white trash, which is just another term for nigga. And on top of that you a ho, but there's still time for you to repent," and Reese picked up his Bible and began waving it in the air saying, "Therefore I tell you, her sins, many as they are, are forgiven her, because she has loved much. But he who is forgiven little, loves little—Luke seven, verse forty seven."

Willie Nance said to Crane, "Philosophizing Jesus freak … I'll be outside."

Crane followed Willie and Mickey into the chilly night air, walked alongside Willie's slow crippled pace to the Cadillac, opened the door for him. Mickey opened his own door, dropped into the worn leather seat. He pulled out a dime bag of *stress*, Zig-Zags, rolled a joint, fired it up, settled in for the buzz.

Crane stood by Willie's door, waited for the window to lower and when it did he said, "You didn't tell your money man how much to bring?"

Willie said, "Didn't need to. You told me that first day we met … remember?" He took a drag from Mickey's joint, passed it back.

Crane asked, "How long we gotta wait?"

Willie turned on the overhead light, looked at his watch.

"He's 'bout half-hour away, maybe sooner."

Suddenly the hangar exploded with shouts of laughter and excitement, the way it sounds at a Las Vegas crap table when the shooter makes his point. Crane grunted and said to Willie, "Celebrating."

Willie said, "I always say you shouldn't celebrate 'till money's in your hand."

"Word," said Crane. "They young ... getting paid for the first time ..."

Willie laughed. Crane laughed. Mickey too.

Momentarily Marcus appeared in the hangar door, his massive frame silhouetted by dim light. He was waving his arms wildly, suddenly bounding towards them like the fullback he could've been, shouting, *"CRANE! CRANE! COME HERE, HOMIE! YOU GOTTA SEE THIS!"*

"Later, dog," Crane said when Marcus reached the car. "After everyone's—"

But Marcus cut him off, grabbing his arm and jerking him away from the Cadillac back toward the hangar.

Marcus said excitedly, "Can't wait, homie. You gotta see **THIS** with your own eyes! You ain't gonna believe it. You just ain't gonna believe what you see!"

What Crane saw when he stepped in the hangar was a death sentence that made Duffy's threat seem childish. The steamer trunk had been pulled from the box, its ropes cut, locks broken and was sitting in the middle of the floor wide open. It was a bank. Literally.

The two sides had been gutted of shelves, the spaces now packed tightly with stacks of money wrapped in plastic. Hundreds of stacks, thousands. Trixie, Bo Bo, Duffy and Reese were pulling out stacks of money as fast as they could. Crane picked one up, saw the figure $10,000 scribbled across the top and below that a name, Robert Lake ... and a city—Angola, Louisiana. He picked up another stack, $15,000 ... David Lewis ... Attica, New York. A third, $8,000 ... Richard Lang ... Leavenworth, Kansas.

Didn't take a genius to figure it out. Angola. Attica. Leavenworth—prison towns. Prison gangs paying off debts: Judges, prosecutors, wardens, guards ...

Henry T rushed over to Crane, embracing him. He said, "You a beautiful nigga, Crane. Beautiful. Knew what you was doing from the get go. Sorry I gave you such a hard time. But this shit is off the hook—!"

Crane came to himself, found his tongue. He said, "Put it back," pushed Henry T aside then shouted, *"PUT IT BACK!"* and waded into the knot raiding the trunk, pulling Trixie violently away ... jerking Bo Bo by the arm and pulling him to the side, pushing Reese on top of him ... and without thinking, manhandling Duffy away from the trunk then trying feebly to replace the stacks before Marcus reached down, grabbed him under the arms and flung him halfway across the room.

"What the fuck is wrong with you, Crane?" Marcus said. They were all looking at him now, like he was something strange that had stepped into their midst. Crane picked himself up off the floor, wiped his pants clean.

"We can't keep it," he said to the group.

Convinced now more than ever that Crane was holding back, that he'd been holding back from the very beginning, perhaps in league with Trixie, Duffy said, "Who says?"

Crane said, "It don't belong to us, Duffy. Trust me."

Duffy walked over and stood directly in Crane's face and said, "Trust you? You must be crazy. Trust you ...? After what you did— nigga, please! Trust you ...?" Duffy sneered turning away, wishing he could spit in Crane's face but knowing now was not the time, hating the fact he couldn't, that Crane was still in control.

"Who then, if not us?" said Henry T. "We found it."

"You mean we stole it," said Bo Bo, correcting Henry T.

"Not this," said Crane pointing to the trunk. "We didn't steal *this*. We just moved it for safekeeping. That's all."

Marcus said, "You know who it belongs to?"

Crane nodded. "The ones that sent me here to get it. They own it."

Henry T said, "You ain't makin' any sense, Crane. What do you mean '*sent you here to get it*'?"

Trixie saw the whole picture before the others. She knew what Crane was trying to say, said it for him. "That's how he got out of prison ... isn't that right, Crane? Agreed to get this trunk in exchange for your freedom," she said, not liking the revelation, offended he didn't trust her and wondering now if she'd made a mistake with him. "This whole thing was just a cover for the trunk. Just lucked up on the jewels—right?"

"You crazy, Trixie," Duffy said, forgetting her betrayal for the moment, admiring her reasoning now more than ever, peeping Crane's hold card the way she did. "What they let a nigga out the joint for just to get a trunk? They get it themselves. What they need him for?"

"Maybe they can't get it themselves," Trixie said, her mind putting everything together now. "Look at it—" and she waved her hands at the trunk, stacks of money on the floor. "Got to be dope money, payoff money probably ... going by the labels. Why should they take the risk when they can get someone's got nothing to lose? Spring Crane, let him take the heat. He succeeds, better for them. He doesn't—oh well!"

Trixie's explanation made sense. Crane didn't refute it. He just stood there with nothing to say.

Bo Bo said, "I wondered how you got out the joint doing just a dime of a twenty-five to life ...?"

Reese said, "That true, Crane ... what she said—you used us from the beginning just to get this trunk? You weren't gonna tell us what was in it … just split it with who you working for, keep your share to yourself? That's wack, my brother, going behind our backs like that." In a rare display of emotion Reese sounded hurt and betrayed, the silence of others signaling agreement.

"Yeah," said Duffy sourly, "Crane been doin' a lot of that lately."

Crane said, "I'm not working for nobody but myself and my freedom. I had a chance to get out the joint and I took it. I ain't apologizing to none of you niggas for that! I didn't wanna do another ten years of **YOUR** time, straight up!" Crane was looking at Reese, but his words, calculated and unapologetic, were meant for the group. He said, "And no, I wasn't gonna tell you, none of you … 'cause it wasn't important. I got nothing to do with this trunk 'cept to get it here. I never knew what was in it. Not 'till now. Besides," Crane went on, hands in his pockets, pacing slowly in front of them as he spoke, "it doesn't make any difference—we got seven million Benjamins all our own comin' with no drama attached."

"Fuck the drama," said Marcus. "Now we got even more."

"I'm telling you," Crane said, "We can't keep it. These people are not the kind you steal from."

Marcus said, "You said '**THESE PEOPLE!**' Who are **THESE PEOPLE?**"

Crane said, "The M & M's."

"Mexican Mafia," Reese whistled, alarmed, swallowing hard. "You telling us this is mob money, Crane?"

Crane nodded. He said, "Now let's just put it all back, okay?"

"Not okay," said Duffy speaking for everyone except maybe Reese, pulling out his GLOCK, waving it back and forth. "Ain't gonna put shit back! I don't give a fuck who it belongs to, M & M's or no M & M's! Let them Mexicans try and take it," he said boldly. "I know how to protect *my* shit." He walked over to the box, lay the gun down just inside the door and returned to pulling out stacks from the trunk.

"Word," said Marcus, slapping hi-fives, beginning to count stacks.

"We can't keep this money," Crane repeated desperately. "I had a deal—"

Bo Bo said, "You right, Crane. *YOU* the nigga had a deal. Not us. We ain't got a deal with anybody. And seeing as how you held out on us, you ain't got shit to say about it. We stole it ... we gonna keep it."

Marcus said, "Word," and continued counting. He stood up and said to no one in particular, "How much you think is here?"

"*SEVENTY-FIVE MILLION DOLLARS, MIYATÉ*!"

The group turned around as a unit. The voice belonged to one of three Mexicans who'd stolen in silently behind them. They were young, early twenties. Baggy clothes, tattoos, jet black hair faded at the temples.

"Who's Crane?" the taller one with a ponytail said.

Crane stepped forward. He said, "Who wants to know?"

"I'm Romero."

"I don't know any Romero," Crane lied, recognizing the voice now.

"We've talked. I'm here for the trunk."

"I still don't know you. Suppose to be with someone I know?"

The Mexican smiled. But only for an instant. He said, "I am. He's outside."

"Then bring him in," Crane demanded.

Romero said, "No reason to. You know him. Willie Nance."

"Willie—?" Crane stammered in shock. "Willie Nance is your man

…?" Crane felt the tic crawl onto his face, turn it into mush. Willie Nance. He couldn't believe it, couldn't figure the connection …? Bo Bo perhaps? But then Bo Bo knew nothing about Romero. It didn't add up. Or did it?

Romero didn't give Crane much time to work on it. He said, "Why is it open?" and stepped to the side for a better view of the trunk.

Crane said, "Accident. I was outside talking to Willie—"

"Wasn't no muthafuckin' accident, esé," Bo Bo said, talking boldly in the marijuana haze, walking over to the trunk, picking up several stacks of cash, waving them in the Mexican's face. "We opened it 'cause we wanted to," he continued on foolishly, "Like we did the rest. And look what we found—?"

Romero said to Bo Bo, "What you found doesn't belong to you, miyaté."

"Bullshit it don't," said Bo Bo. "Ain't possession nine tenths of the law?"

Romero said, "Whose law?" and moved back to his position beside his two lieutenants, reaching under his shirt as he turned.

From the moment they'd announced themselves—other than Crane and despite his ongoing virulent hostility lifted on Blunts—only Duffy's razor sharp street smarts had sensed the danger. During Crane's brief exchange with Romero he'd slowly backed himself up to the box, slipped his hand inside, let it rest on the 9mm.

And perhaps it was the years in prison that allowed Crane to appreciate danger, knew the direction it would come and how. From the beginning Crane had noticed Romero's two lieutenants appraising Marcus, never taking their eyes off the massive black frame that intimidated them, knew he'd be their first target. And caught up in the specter of money, so much money ... perhaps lulled by the easy exchange between Crane and Romero—Crane didn't know which—Marcus had lost his edge. By the time he'd gotten it back, realized what was about to go down and went for his .45 it was too late.

It lasted seven seconds.

Three TEC-9s roared simultaneously. Two of the Mexicans poured fire into Marcus. Crane pulled out his .357 and dove headlong over Trixie, knocking her to the ground and behind the protective cover of Marcus' huge body crashing down on a table of laptops. Firing over Marcus's lifeless form Crane put three rounds into the face of the nearest Mexican, watched his head explode in a shower of bone and blood and without stopping, sent six rounds into the chest of the second Mexican. Grunting, the gunman spun around, fell backward and folded over on himself like an accordion given out of air as he hit the wall and toppled over onto the floor with a heavy thud.

At the same time, Romero's TEC-9 had cut a deadly path across the chests of Bo Bo, Henry T and Reese—the three of them collapsing together in a bloody pile on a carpet of payoff money. Duffy swung his GLOCK out of the box and in a single motion lunged forward into and behind a mountain of luggage, firing a trail of rounds into Romero's belly, up his chest wall and into his neck. Romero staggered back on reflex until he hit the wall. His gun hand fell limp to his side. Leaving a narrow path of blood in his wake, he half-walked, half-rolled along the wall to the door where he stumbled through, took three awkward steps into the night then collapsed on the ground like a pretzel.

The sudden quiet in the hangar seemed unnatural. There was no music. The boombox was shattered by bullets. No planes were landing.

Crane stood up and said, "Yo, Duffy ...? You alright?"

Duffy stood up cautiously, reloading.

"Yeah, muthafucka," Duffy said derisively, reluctant anger toward Crane still burning, but knowing in the midst of battle they operated well as a team and hating it. "I'm alright. But all yo' dogs is dead. Too bad. Should've been you. Yo, Trixie …?" he shouted. "You still with us, you scandalous white bitch, you?"

Trixie was still on the ground. Curled into a tight knot, hands covering her ears she was speechless, shaking in fear. The smell of vomit was on her chin. Crane reached down and pulled her to her feet. He said to Duffy, "She's okay," and reloaded his .357.

Trixie regained her composure and said to Duffy, "My name is still Trixie, motherfucker!"

"Whatever." Duffy walked over to the killing field, peered down at former partners, turning them over with his boot—Henry T's eyes still open; Reese clutching his Bible; Bo Bo's mouth wide open as if he was about to shout. "Esé's play rough," he said moving to Marcus stretched across the table, long black arms dangling inches above the ground, blood dripping down his fingers like water from a leaky faucet. "Just didn't know who they was fuckin' with. Same as you two," and he looked at Crane and Trixie with cold impassive eyes.

Crane said to Duffy, "You need to check all this hostility till we get the fuck away from here and—"

Suddenly they heard the screeching of tires.

Crane looked at Duffy for an instant. He said, "Willie Nance. That double crossin' muthafucka—!"

They bolted for the door still a smoothly operating team, rushed through it, saw the single headlight of the Cadillac backing rapidly away in a swirl of smoke. Crane began running after it, Duffy a step behind.

Both men firing at the light as they ran, saw a muzzle flash from the driver's side, heard the light popping of a .38, felt the hot air of rounds whiz past.

No evasive action. They continued running straight ahead still firing, saw sparks fly off the radiator, the windshield shatter, the headlight explode in a brief shower of burnt orange fireworks, coughing sound of a damaged engine. Suddenly the driver lost control, the Cadillac swerving in a slow wide arc that sent its rear end crashing hard into the corner of another storage hangar, its radiator belching steam, dying engine sputtering into silence and orange flames under the hood beginning to feed a shroud of thick black smoke.

They rushed up on the Cadillac still firing, reloading.

Mickey was dead. Slumped forward on the dashboard amid his shattered bi-focals, a .357 round had gone through his right eye, took off a third of his skull when it exited.

Willie Nance was dying from a chest full of 9mm rounds that exploded his lungs. His gun arm hung limp down the side of the door, the .38 dead on the ground. His head was propped back on the headrest, bi-focals still intact across his nose. It was amazing he could still talk, let alone breathe. But he could … in short spurts between even shorter, more labored breaths.

"You chickenshit double crossin' black ass muthafucka," Crane was saying, his .357 cocked at Willie's ear. "Why you set me up like that, nigga? How you come by workin' for my people?"

Willie coughed, or grunted—Crane wasn't sure which. Willie said, "Accident. Went lookin' for yo' money—" He coughed again and continued, saying, "They one of my sources—"

Willie coughed again, harder, bringing up a mouthful of blood. He said weakly, "Said you didn't need no fence 'cause you'd be dead—"

Coughing again. More blood. "Didn't care 'bout no jewels—stupid Mexicans ... said I could have 'em and anything else if their trunk was there ... that's all they wanted ... that trunk. Just cut myself in on the jewels—"

Willie still coughing. More frequently now. Voice dropping to a whisper, Crane having to lean closer to hear him. Willie said, "You dead when you took the job, Crane. Shoulda known that—"

Another cough. More blood. Desperate breathing, gurgling like he was trying to talk under water. Eyes opening and closing in slow motion. He said with difficulty, "May as well keep the trunk. They gonna kill you anyway and—" Willie began to laugh, rising up in the seat and looking at Crane in one final act of arrogance. The laugh turned into a violent spasmodic cough that took his last breath of life. You could say Willie Nance died laughing.

They stepped back, watched the Cadillac become a crematorium. They stepped back even further waiting for the gas tank to explode, knew when it did police and helicopters would be on their way.

They returned to the hangar. Trixie was in the bathroom. Lighting a primo, she said she couldn't look at the dead faces of people she'd once known. So they rounded up blankets, covered the heads of dead comrades. Even the Mexicans.

A pager went off. Another one. Then a third. All belonged to the Mexicans. If no one answered they'd know something was wrong, send a team to investigate. Then they'd send an army.

Willie Nance had sold him out for jewels. And Moffett—Moffett was pure double cross from the beginning. What was it Willie had said, " ... you dead when you took the job ...?" He was right—Crane should've known that. He couldn't believe how stupid he was not to have seen the reality when it was staring him dead in the face. Something for nothing. Freedom for—what? A trunk. He was so desperate to get out he'd of believed anything Moffett said. What a fool. They never intended for him to live, the few weeks of freedom all he was due.

Well then. The fence was right a third time, his words ringing in Crane's ears as if just spoken from the ashes of the crematorium, " ... *May as well keep it—they gonna kill you anyway ... "*

Duffy seemed to read Crane's mind. He said, "Alright, muthafucka ... we got seventy-five million dollars we ain't suppose to have, and I ain't givin' shit back to the Mexicans, know what I'm sayin'? Now you said if shit went down dirty, you had a way out. Well it's dirty as a muthafucka, so let's hear it." Duffy always reduced things to their lowest level. Clean and simple, but never well thought out. He was that way in the joint ... that way now. For him the only issue was keeping the money.

Well, yes. Only how do you keep seventy-five million dollars of the mob's money and live? The answer of course, is that you don't. But he couldn't tell Duffy that.

The pagers went off again. One. Two. Three ... Crane looked at his watch, said they had fifteen minutes, twenty at the most, suggested they start repacking the trunk, said he'd explain things on the road, stalling Duffy for time, trying to figure a way out of a bottomless pit.

Trixie came out of the bathroom, color back in her cheeks, the primo half-gone. She said, "Shouldn't we count it?"

Crane laughed. He said, "May not be able to speak English—but they can count. If he said seventy-five million I'll take his word on it." He bent down to grab a stack of bills, suddenly felt lightheaded and sat back up.

Duffy saw the blood before Crane, the left sleeve of his sweatshirt blotched red above the elbow. A thin river of blood trailed down his arm, collecting in slow measured goblets at his fingertips that splashed in tiny sunflower bursts on the floor.

"You been shot, Crane," Duffy said without emotion or concern, hating the fact they were tied together, that he still needed Crane to get away safely.

Crane looked at his arm, felt the pain for the first time, the tic return.

"OH SHIT!" Trixie walked over, helped Crane out of his sweatshirt, saw the dark ugly hole in the thick muscle of his shoulder. "You need a doctor," she said.

"We take him to a hospital, they start askin' questions," said Duffy.

Trixie said, "Where then?"

"I know a vet?"

"Dog doctor," said Trixie in disgust. Pulling a handkerchief from her pocket and rolling it tight, she looped it under Crane's arm and tied it as best she could over the wound to stem the bleeding. "It's the best I can do," she said apologizing, winking at Crane, wetting her lips.

Duffy said to Crane, "Think you can drive?" Crane tried moving his arm, winced in pain.

Crane said, "I'm right handed. Be okay long as I don't pass out."

Duffy said, "Maybe your *new* girlfriend can suck your dick while you drivin'. That oughta keep your black ass awake." He spit out the words like a mouth full of rancid milk, continued repacking the trunk.

Crane ignored Duffy's hostility, joined him on the floor where they finished repacking the trunk, securing it with ropes and dragging it across the floor to the door and outside. Trixie wanted to take the jewels. Crane said they'd be too easy to spot when she tried to pawn them. Trixie said she didn't want to pawn them ... she wanted to wear them, threw a dozen strands of diamond necklaces around her neck, emerald-crested bracelets on her wrists over protests.

Romero and his men had come in a Dodge Ram van. Crane said they'd be looking for it, so they put the trunk in Marcus' battered Ford Econoline van. Duffy said he'd drive the van, Crane and Trixie to follow in the Regal. Crane said the Lexus belonged to the M & M's too. He removed his wallet from the glove compartment, clothes from the trunk and locked the doors. But he kept the keys.

Duffy put all the weapons and a few cell phones in the trunk of his Regal, a GLOCK and TEC-9 on the passenger seat of the van. Crane paid a last quick visit to the hangar, made sure nothing was left that could identify them. He had always liked Marcus, apologized silently to his spirit for the outcome, vowed to get some money to his widow and kid. He turned off the lights, locked the door and joined Trixie in the Regal. They stole single file past Willie Nance's smoldering tomb, turned onto 104th Street and sped rapidly away.

Chapter 15

KRUGER'S ANIMAL HOSPITAL was in the shadow of Sony Studios on a Culver City street heavily lined with an umbrella of shedding maple trees. The vet, Wilbert Kruger, D.V.M. was a white man in his late fifties with long blond hair whom Duffy had said stayed wired on primos twenty-four-seven. He did not appreciate being awakened at 2:00 am. But when he saw it was Duffy, understood the situation and the chance to bargain his services for more dope, he relented, ushered them into the examining room, called for his nurse.

It took Melissa all of two minutes to get from the upstairs bedroom of the attached apartment down to the examining room. Wearing a

Victoria's Secret teddy she was trying unsuccessfully to cover with a nurse's smock, the busty adolescent brunette—not a day over nineteen—stumbled sleepily into the examining room behind a yawn, breath reeking of weed. She cast shameless glances at Crane on the table, Duffy on a chair ... a cautious one at Trixie pacing in the corner. If Melissa was a nurse, Trixie was a heart surgeon.

The doctor inspected the bullet wound at both ends, moved Crane's shoulder and arm in all directions, made clucking noises with his tongue that said he didn't like what he saw. The pain brought tears to Crane's eyes before he passed out. The vet said he wasn't equipped for this kind of emergency, that Crane needed to be in a regular hospital with better facilities. He insisted Crane couldn't stay with him, picked up the phone to call an ambulance.

Hating himself for being tied to Crane, but knowing there was no place else to go, that Crane had to stay there and recover, plan their escape like he'd promised, Duffy reached in his pocket and counted out three thousand dollars, slapped them in Dr. Kruger's hand saying, "Can't go to no regular hospital, doc. He's gotta stay here."

The vet didn't say anything right off, but at sight of the money slowly lowered the phone to its cradle. Melissa's doe-eyes came to life translating cash into Nordstroms and Macy's, her sugar-daddy translating it into rocks, primos and sex.

Dr. Kruger drew in a deep breath of reluctance through the space in his front teeth, bit his bottom lip. He said absently, "Question is, where could I put him?"

Melissa said, "There's a den downstairs with a sofa-bed, daddy ...?"

Daddy. That said it all.

"No more than four days," the vet said reluctantly, reading Melissa's eyes, bulging chest beneath the smock.

"Four days?" Duffy said, surprised.

"He's sick," the vet said, hanging a bottle of IV fluids on the stand, slipping a needle in Crane's arm. "Needs to be transfused, shoulder has to be X-ray'd ... see if any bone was hit, the wound cleaned, watched for infection. He allergic to anything?"

Duffy didn't know and said so. Neither did Trixie.

"I'll need a blood sample from everyone," Dr. Kruger said. "You too, Melissa. Me included."

"What for?" asked Duffy.

Dr. Kruger said, "Can't give him animal blood. I need to see who matches his blood type."

"And if don't none of us match up?" asked Duffy.

"I'm a vet, not a mortician."

Duffy said, "Like to park the van in your garage if it's not a problem?" and he counted out another three thousand dollars, waiting.

This time Melissa saw Liz Claiborne, DKNY and BeBe. She said, "Put the van next to the Benz. I'll move the Blazer," and immediately left the examining room. Duffy smiled for the first time that evening, shoved the cash into Dr. Kruger's hand. High maintenance young girl, pussy-whipped old man—Duffy knew, if no one else did, that cash was always the key to that combination.

When Melissa returned from moving the Blazer the vet had already drawn blood from Duffy, Trixie and Crane. He drew it from Melissa then handed her the cash, told her to secure it and set up the tray. Melissa took the money with a smile and easy familiarity. She folded the wad, started to put it in her bra, smiled sheepishly at remembering she wasn't wearing one, put it in the pocket of her smock and went about the business of preparing the tray for surgery.

When Crane regained consciousness it was to daylight seeping in behind curtains in a darkened room. He was disoriented and slightly nauseous. There was a distant throbbing pain in his left shoulder that seemed to worsen as his head cleared. He came to appreciate the comfort of the sofa-bed, tried to move his right arm but found it trapped by Trixie's soft fleshy form lying next to him, arm across his chest, lips buried in the crux of his neck and her breathing synchronous with his own. He tried moving his arm again, woke Trixie. She asked how he felt, said she'd given him a pint of her blood so they were tied together for life. Remembering Marjorie, Crane said he didn't think that would be so bad, wanted to know what time it was. Trixie told him he'd been asleep close to twelve hours, it was nearly two in the afternoon. Crane said his shoulder hurt, asked if the doctor had left anything for pain. Trixie pointed to a vial of codeines on the table, but said she had something better. Crane asked what she meant, so she showed him. When she climbed off him five minutes later he agreed and said the pain was gone. It wasn't of course, but he loved the treatments.

From the time he'd gotten out of Lompoc Duffy, a wannabe big time gangster with small time means, had floated through the underbelly of L.A.'s black criminal life with the singed reputation of a perpetrator. But now, with seventy-five million dollars behind him and an even bigger ego lacking in judgement, he was bound and determined all that would change. But four days was too long. He couldn't wait that long for Crane to heal up. They could all be dead by then. He'd get out on his own, the hell with Crane and Trixie. He'd deal with them later if they were still alive. And if they weren't—oh, well. Less work for him.

And so, when he awoke Thursday at noon, he was already seeing himself in grossly inflated terms that had yet to be thought out. An hour later he brought the Regal south on Crenshaw to the CD of *'Lil Kim,'* crossed over the Santa Monica Freeway to Adams, headed east to Montclair Street.

Blood country.

He parked on a side street, put on his alarm, checked the clip in his 9mm and rang the buzzer of a familiar security gate at a graffiti-marked two-story apartment building. A distorted voice he didn't recognize on the intercom wanted his four-one-one. When he said Pharaoh the gate swung open.

He knocked on the door of an upstairs apartment that yielded a dimly lit room with the shades drawn despite a day of bright sunlight. The room reeked with the odor of *stress*, deafening rap of a *'Missy Elliott'* CD. Several infants in diapers and sucking on bottles they dragged with them, scampered across the floor chased by half-dressed teenaged mothers ... most black, one or two Mexican, token white girl. Somewhere there was a kitchen and the odor of frying fish.

Seated around the only table on dilapidated chairs and worn couches were half-dozen or so black gangbangers wearing red bandannas or some other article of red clothing. They were all young. Most around twenty, twenty-two. But they were hard-core killers.

All were smoking—some *chronic* ... most *stress*. A few smoked primos. The one Duffy knew best ... the leader whose street name was 'Street Killer' stood up. Hi-five's. Shoulder hug. Chest bump. He said to Duffy as they sat down, "Ain't seen the Pharaoh around lately. What's up with that?" He offered Duffy a primo.

"I been around. Just takin' care of biz-nez." Duffy lit the primo, waited for the buzz.

"Word," said Street Killer. "Still slinging?"

Duffy laughed hard, proudly. "Still slinging," he said. "Off the hook."

"Word," said Street Killer. "Thought you might be in jail."

Duffy said, "Naw. Just doin' what I gotta do. Makin' plenty cheeze. That's why I'm here—" Duffy reached inside his jacket, pulled out a stack of cash meant for a prison guard at Pelican Bay and slammed it down hard on the table as if it were a game of dominoes.

The stack impressed everyone. One reached over and counted Benjamins. He said to Street Killer, "Twenty-five thousand—"

"And more where that came from," said Duffy unwisely, flossing big time. "If you come in with me, we can take over all of L.A."

Everyone in the room laughed.

Street Killer said, "You come in here flossin' with twenty-five G's and want me to help you take over L.A.? You been smokin' too many Blunts, Pharaoh. Need a whole lot more than twenty-five G's." Street Killer was laughing so hard he dropped his primo on the floor, touched fists with the others.

Duffy said, "I know that, muthafucka." He waved his hand across the stack of money as if dismissing its importance. "This ain't shit compared to what I come across, nigga. I come across more money n' you'll ever see."

"Yeah, right," said Street Killer, still laughing. "What you do, homie, rob a bank?" The group exploded in more laughter.

"You could say that," Duffy said when the laughter had waned. "Got a hundred times this little chump change ... a thousand times more than what's on the table," Duffy said, jamming his index finger on top of the stack.

One of the gangbangers did the math. He said, "That's twenty-five million dollars … ?" and looked at Duffy curiously.

"Three times that," Duffy said insistently, his ego out of control now, wanting them to take him seriously for once. But he hadn't meant to reveal that.

Suddenly the room grew quiet. Street Killer looked at his posse, then looked at Duffy. He said, "So what you tellin' us is you got seventy-five million dollars from a bank?"

Something in the way Street Killer had asked the question didn't feel right. Duffy backtracked. He said to Street Killer, "Not me, necessarily. But maybe I know someone who does."

"Who?" Street Killer wanted to know.

"Friend of a friend of a friend," said Duffy, more cautious now.

"He the one rob a bank?" Street Killer asked.

"Ain't really my biz-nez how a nigga come by his money, know what I'm saying?"

Street Killer said, "You the one said he robbed a bank?"

Duffy said even more cautiously, "Figure of speech. All I know he lookin' for muscle to watch his back."

"That's what this twenty-five G's for—muscle?" Street Killer asked. "'Cause if it's what I think it is, you can't buy shit!"

Suddenly Street Killer sat up straight, called toward the bedroom. "Yo, Lo-retha …?" A big-legged black girl all of sixteen appeared at the door holding a partially hidden newborn nursing at her breast.

"What?"

"Bring me that piece of paper I got this morning."

Loretha disappeared, returned with a piece of paper she handed to Street Killer. Street Killer gave it to Duffy and said, "That your friend who robbed a bank?"

Duffy choked on his shock, tried hard not to let it show. The paper was a crude 'Wanted' flyer with a picture of Crane—his driver's license photo, Duffy guessed. Above Crane's photo was an inscription that read: $5,000,000 REWARD FOR INFORMATION ABOUT THIS MAN, ALONZO CRANE. Below the picture was a pager number. The reverse side of the flyer was identical, only printed in Spanish.

Five million dollars. Duffy had to work at not saying it out loud. The robbery was only forty-eight hours old and already a contract on Crane's life was public knowledge. If they knew who Crane was, how long before his own picture would be on a flyer.

"That the nigga you dealin' with?" Street Killer was saying. "'Cause if it is, give up the four-one-one and make you a quick five mil."

Duffy played it off. He shook his head. Still holding the flyer he said, "Naw. Ain't never seen this nigga before. Who's lookin' for him and what he do worth five million dollars?"

Street Killer lit another primo and without taking his eyes off Duffy said, "Ripped off the M & M's and BGF—"

"Dope?" Duffy asked, playing dumb.

Street Killer shook his head and said, "Benjamins."

"How much?" Duffy asked.

Again not taking his eyes off Duffy, Street Killer said, "It don't say. Must be a lot they gonna pay five mil, though."

"Word," said Duffy, laying the flyer down. He shook his head and said, "Don't know anything about this. My shit's straight up. Just lookin' to buy some muscle, that's all."

Street Killer said, "Ain't a nigga in this town dumb enough to go up against the mob … if that's what this about. Bin Laden ain't got nothin' on this muthafucka. Them esé's lookin' for this nigga all over the world!"

"I wouldn't either," said Duffy playing it out to the end. "But my shit somthin' different … ain't got nothin' to do with no mob."

"But if it is, Pharaoh, and you know this muthafucka—?"

"I told you this here nigga ain't no part of what I got going," Duffy repeated, playing poker with a hand weaker than when he first walked in. He picked up the cash, put it back inside his jacket and said, "But if you niggas ain't interested—"

Street Killer said, "Not goin' against them esé's and the BGF, we ain't—"

"Like I said, don't know nothin' 'bout no esé's or BGF," Duffy repeated too insistently, cutting Street Killer off.

Street Killer said, "Now if you want us to help you flip them twenty-five G's …?" He escorted Duffy to the door, flyer in hand.

"'S all right," Duffy said. "I can handle my own shit."

Street Killer handed Duffy the flyer as he walked out and said, "Here, bro—you keep this. They ain't gonna stop lookin' for this nigga 'till he dead. You run across him—drop a dime and make yourself a quick five mil tax free."

"Word," said Duffy. "I see him, I'll be sure to do that. Peace, out."

Duffy hadn't realized how much he was sweating until he reached the car. He hated dealing with gangbangers. You just couldn't reason with kids. What he needed were professionals, now that he knew what he was really up against. Older men, experienced, ex-felons mostly, men he knew he could rely on. Only this time he'd be careful how much he'd tell them, wouldn't mention the money, only that he was building an organization and needed muscle. He started up the Regal, put on a CD by *Da Brat* and headed for the mean streets of Compton.

Five million dollar bounty. And they were looking for Crane—not him! He thought about dropping a dime on Crane, letting the M & M's take him out. But he decided against it, realizing Crane might roll over on him to save his own skin. Then too he'd have to move the van first. And for the moment at least he could think of no safer place to hide it. Besides, he wanted that pleasure for himself—and that was a pleasure whose anticipation he savored. And doing Trixie. He'd been thinking about her replacement from the moment he learned of her betrayal.

Lola. Tall, coal-black honey with a chest he could live with and kinky hair she kept in a fingerwave perm with a tight curl looping over her forehead. Party girl who loved cocaine and swung both ways. She modeled for 'girlie' magazines and did movie extra work to pay the bills. Duffy called her answering machine on a stolen cell phone, made a date for later that night—dinner, dancing, some coke and a fuck afterwards.

Ten hours later they stepped off the elevator and into the typically darkened fourth floor corridor of the Whitley Street apartment building. Lola was lit up on Hennesy and *chronic*, turning in Duffy's arms to fondle and embrace him, kissing him about the face and neck, legs giving out and having to be propped up at the door as he fumbled blindly with his key, missing the lock in the effort to keep her upright … trying again, her tongue licking his face and neck, probing his ears.

Finally the door opened and he half-walked, half-carried the stoned hundred and fifteen pound beauty into the darkened apartment, kicking the door closed but not turning on the lights. Laughing with her in anticipation, his erection already building he found the bed, the two of them falling together onto the soft mattress, Duffy removing her jacket, raising her tanktop above full supple breasts.

Lola grunted deep in her throat and said thickly, "Fuck me, Pharaoh. Just fuck me, baby. Fuck me. Fuck me ..."

Duffy threw off his coat, ripped buttons from his shirt, slipped unzippered pants down to his ankles, returned hands and mouth to waiting breasts, hardened nipples.

Suddenly the room filled with light. Duffy bolted upright on his knees like a startled cobra, head weaving in confusion, mouth agape, speechless. Dilated pupils in bloodshot eyes constricted at the shock of light, brought five strange men into focus—three Mexicans, two blacks—standing at various points around the room.

Duffy said, "What the ...?"

"Yo, miyaté," one of the Mexicans said, spinning a .45 on his finger like Roy Rogers. "You wanna tell us where our money is?"

Instinct for survival is the most powerful emotion there is. Having appraised his only chance for escape during the few seconds of his initial shock, realizing he would have to sacrifice Lola, knowing the two of them were dead no matter what he told them, Duffy suddenly sprang off the bed and hurled the full weight of his body into the chest of the man standing directly in front of the window. The two of them crashed violently through the window as a unit, the black gangster first—screaming in panic and terror, Duffy on top, falling together in darkness amid splinters of wood and shards of glass. Two floors down Duffy braced for the blow he knew was coming, as his assailant's back hit the concrete wall of a balcony with a thud, the snap of his spine ringing out like a broken twig folded over on itself. The gangster's limp form, arms and legs dangling spread-eagled across the corner of the balcony, served as a cushion for Duffy, but not completely. He felt the pain of a row of cracked ribs as they hit, the force of the blow stunning him for an instant of stars and pinwheels as he bounced off the human cushion, realized he was still falling when he regained his senses, heard shouts, the vague popping of smallarms fire, felt the heat of their rounds whiz past. He felt a sharp pain in his left arm, knew it was broken just as he crashed down hard on the tops of slanted garbage bins and fell painfully to the ground in a dazed heap of the building's shadow.

Somehow Duffy's mind continued to function. The gunfire had stopped, but there were screams and commotion all around the building. Duffy knew someone had called Five-O, that the gangsters were coming down the stairwell after him. Only four floors. He didn't have much time. Dazed and bleeding, his head spinning, his vision blurred, left arm an orchestra of pain and useless, he somehow managed to pull his pants up, struggled to his feet and hobbled close along the side of the apartment building until he reached the street.

Cursing himself for having parked so far away, he half-ran, half-staggered across the street and down the block, limping between cars and sometimes falling, getting up again and going until he reached the Regal. He reached for his keys by habit, realized both pager and cell phone were smashed, keys still in the apartment. He reached under the right front fender and felt desperately for the magnetic box that held the spare key. He heard loud hostile voices burst through the front door of the apartment building, screams and angry shouts of tenants knocked to the side in their wake. He opened the Regal's door, was hit by the loudness of the alarm's voice he knew would give him away, fumbled desperately with the only hand left to him and managed to start the engine, peel away into the protection of Hollywood's back streets accompanied by the dull thud of rounds striking the Regal's trunk. With his knee holding the steering wheel, Duffy reached inside the glove compartment and hit the emergency switch that shut off the alarm. He turned a corner, realized no one was following him. So far luck was on his side.

He reached Wilcox, crossed Sunset down to Melrose, breathed a little easier as he drove west along the deserted trendy street to LaBrea. But just as he turned onto LaBrea for his run south, Duffy's luck ran out. He heard the familiar loud burst of a siren playing with octaves, saw the flashing red and blue lights that turned the inside of his car into a disco, the blinding halogen lights that put him center stage, the ever so familiar voice of unwanted attention. Duffy knew the routine, pulled the Regal to the curb and stopped.

"DRIVER, PUT BOTH HANDS OUT OF THE WINDOW!"

Chapter **16**

CRANE SPENT A RESTLESS CONVALESCENCE in the shuttered seclusion of Dr. Kruger's downstairs den waiting for his strength to return. That it did was a testament to Trixie's surprising ability as a cook, the vet's professionalism … checking on Crane in the early morning just before office hours, and again in the afternoon inspecting the wound, changing the bandages—though this was left to Melissa who, when she wasn't in 'training' with the vet caring for sick animals, proved surprisingly adept as a nurse. She and Trixie hit it off right from the get go, discovered many things in common—sex, MTV, involvement with older men, drugs. Youth, Crane thought. Melissa even lent Trixie some clothes to wear until Duffy brought hers from the apartment.

But Duffy never returned and he hadn't called. He hadn't answered his page, the phone at the apartment was out of order and there was no answer on his cell phone. Twenty-four hours later and still no word from Duffy. Crane wondered if Duffy had sold them out to the Mexicans, realized they'd already be dead if he had. Crane knew something was wrong. He didn't know what but they couldn't afford to stick around and find out. He said they'd already stayed at the vet's too long, that it wasn't fair to put him and Melissa in anymore danger than they already were.

Crane's idea was to move to Uncle Joe's, plan their escape from there. Hoping to catch Uncle Joe sober so he wouldn't have to repeat himself, he called to make arrangements. Uncle Joe wasn't drunk. But the slurring of his words said he was on his way. Crane told him he was thinking of getting married, wanted him to meet his *fiancée*. Could they come by and chill a couple of days before the wedding? Uncle Joe, delighted at hearing from his only living relative, agreed. Said he looked forward to the company, wanted to know if Crane could pick up a fifth of Chevas Regal on the way. Crane didn't tell him Trixie was white, but figured it wouldn't really make any difference. With a fifth of Chevas Regal on the table Uncle Joe would like anyone Crane brought over.

Trixie said she needed her clothes from the apartment before they went anywhere. Crane said if that was the case and since they were so close to Santa Monica, he may as well drop some money off at Marcus' widow on the way. But he didn't like the idea of driving all over the city in the van. So Friday evening he asked the vet if he could borrow the Blazer to make a run, said the van needed a part. Dr. Kruger said it was too soon after surgery for Crane to drive, worried about his strength, the risk of bleeding and infection. Crane lied and said he was feeling much better, that his strength was beginning to return, his appetite improving.

Thirty minutes later he pulled the Blazer into the Santa Monica trailer park where Marcus' widow lived.

She was an eighteen year old Chicana named Carmen. With her newborn in her arms, she cried. Trixie cried too, arms around her shoulders for support. But the crying suddenly stopped when Crane put a hundred thousand dollars on the table—ten stacks of ten grand each. Crane lied and said he didn't know what happened to Marcus' van, guessed the police would eventually find it and contact her, waved good-bye as they drove off.

When the Blazer had cleared the trailer park Carmen went inside and fished around a pile of junk mail collecting on the sink until she found Crane's 'Wanted' flyer. She called the number listed and said the man they were looking for had just left her trailer in the company of an 'anglo' girl with blonde hair and very large *chi chi's*. She described the Blazer, remembered all but the last number of the license. She said they probably had her dead husband's van and described it in detail. But she didn't mention the hundred thousand dollars sitting on her table.

♦♦♦♦

They arrived at Trixie's former residence on Whitley Avenue just after eight. Loud blaring reggae music from a Ziggy Marley CD and the odor of *stress* filled the fourth floor corridor. Crane wondered why the corridor was so dark. Trixie said drug dealers usually stole the light bulbs, dug around in her purse for her key.

Even before she turned on the light the smell of death filled their lungs. Crane's hand found his .357 as the door to the tomb swung open, the light flickering on.

What they saw resembled a series of black and white photographs taken at a crime scene. The window was completely broken out of its frame, the chest of drawers turned on its side amid scattered contents, and a semi-nude black woman of about twenty-three was stretched on her back across the end of a blood-soaked bed, head and arms draped over the side barely touching the floor as if she were doing a Yoga exercise. She was looking at them upside down with lifeless eyes wide open. A single gunshot wound was in the center of a large curl on her forehead. Two rivers of blood coursed over her ears and matted her fingercurl perm from a massive knife slash across her throat.

Trixie vomited, felt faint. "Oh, God," she said weakly.

Crane caught her before she hit the floor, took her out into the corridor and sat her down against the wall. His .357 in hand he returned to the tomb and searched it cautiously. No Duffy. Clothes from the closet were strewn about the floor, the apartment ransacked. Crane walked over to the missing window and looked down. If there had been anything on the balcony below, glass, wood, or a body—it was gone now. He wondered if there had been a struggle, who or what went through the window. He started to return to the corridor when his eye caught a blood-stained crumpled piece of paper on the floor at the dead woman's fingertips. He teased it apart from its knot of dried blood, felt the vicious bite of the tic return to a face in complete shock when he read it. He returned to the corridor in disbelief and kneeled next to Trixie.

"No Duffy," Crane said. "But I found this—?" and he handed Trixie the 'wanted' flyer.

"Jesus," said Trixie, still ashen and shaking. "What'll we do now?"

Crane said, "Disappear. Vanish like we never existed, only with this," and he pointed to the flyer, "it'll be much harder."

Trixie said, "What about Duffy?"

Crane said, "If he isn't already dead they must have him somewhere trying to sweat him. Either way we gotta get the fuck up outta here." Snatching Trixie to her feet Crane turned off the light in the apartment, closed the door and rushed to the elevator still holding the 'wanted' flyer.

"You think he told on us?" Trixie asked, shaking fingers pulling out a joint from her purse and lighting it, calming her fear, passing it to Crane to calm his.

Crane pounded on the elevator button and said, "If he did they'll be waiting for us at the doc's. Of course with this," and he crumpled up the flyer in disgust, stuffing it in his pocket. "They don't really need him. Esé's send this all over the world ... someone spot my shadow—I'm dead!"

It was nearly ten when Crane brought the Blazer down the hospital driveway, parked in front of the apartment. He'd driven by the hospital three times to make sure it was safe, no suspicious cars or vans on the street, strangers loitering nearby. The hospital and adjacent apartment were dark, but on the second floor they could see the flickering light of a TV creeping around edges of shuttered blinds. Once inside and with Trixie in tow they bounded upstairs and burst into the vet's master bedroom without knocking.

The flickering light belonged to a porno film, *Debbie Does Dallas* ... the odor belonged to *stress*. Both were butt naked on the bed. Dr. Kruger, his back up against the headboard, legs spread out in front of him was smoking a joint while Melissa was giving him a head job better than Debbie ever dreamed of.

"Say, look—?" Dr. Kruger said at the interruption, holding the joint with a roach clip, reaching for the sheet.

Melissa sat up unembarrassed and smiling. She said, "Hi. You wanna party?"

Crane said, "Sorry to interrupt, doc, but you gotta get a move on and get the fuck up outta here. *NOW!"*

Dr. Kruger said, "What?" He was trying to adjust his vision to see Crane against the dim light of the TV. He found the sheet, pulled it across his middle and stood facing them. He said, "I don't understand. What's happened?"

"Someone's looking for us, me and Trixie … Duffy too, if he's still alive," Crane said. "You too, if they find us."

Melissa, shameless in the beauty of her nudity, suddenly lost her smile and penchant for fun and games. She jumped off the bed and said, "Can't we just call the police?"

The distant squeaking of car brakes alerted them to someone in the driveway.

"Shhhh!" Crane said whispering, bringing a finger to his lips, walking to the window. "Cut the TV off!" he hissed over Debbie's groans, arm waving for Melissa to plunge the room into darkness.

Crane moved the mini-blinds a finger's width to the side, saw a Ford Bronco with its lights off roll to a stop next to the Blazer. Two Mexicans got out. One older, one in his twenties. The older one wore a long trench coat that was open and a Dodgers baseball cap. The younger one was dressed in a thuggish-ruggish way with Nike tennis shoes, baggy pants and a white T-shirt. His hair was longer than the older man's but wasn't in a ponytail.

They walked over to the garage, tried to see through narrow frosted windows with a flashlight, made a half-hearted attempt to open it before returning to the Bronco. One of the Mexicans, the younger one, opened the Bronco's door and handed something to the older one who promptly concealed it under his trenchcoat—a shotgun, Crane guessed. The younger Mexican took something else from the Bronco, then closed the door softly. For a moment Crane couldn't make out what he was holding, then realized it was a cat. Crane knew their plan instantly.

"FUCK!" Crane said to the apprehensive shadows behind him. He said, "Doc, you and your honey get dressed. Quick!" and he heard the sudden hurried rustle of clothes, the sliding of dresser drawers.

Down in the driveway the two Mexicans were conferring with one another by the Bronco. Momentarily they walked over to the door together and the younger one began ringing the doorbell.

Crane left the window. Eyes adjusted to darkness he grabbed the vet by the shoulders and pulled him into the bathroom. When the door was closed he turned on the light. The vet's face looked craggy and drawn, his cheeks sunken and shadowed with lines of fear. Crane sat him down on the commode. They could still hear the muted ringing of the doorbell through the door.

"What you do from now on determines whether we live or die," he said firmly to the vet. "You understand me?" If Dr. Kruger did, he wasn't saying. In shock, he just stared at Crane in the dull glow of vanity lights that formed a collar around the mirror. He started to speak but Crane cut him off saying, "You do like I tell you, *EXACTLY* like I tell you—we got a chance to get outta here alive. Understand?"

Dr. Kruger shook his head and said weakly, "Yes."

The doorbell continued to ring as Crane laid out the plan for the vet. But when he'd finished and before Crane could ask if he understood, the terrified vet jumped up in a panic and said, "I don't know if I can do this!"

Crane brought the back of his hand against the vet's face in a pimp slap that knocked Dr. Kruger to the floor. Crane reached down, grabbed his coat collar, snatched him to his feet and slammed him hard against the door.

"Listen to me, muthafucka," Crane spit out harshly. "Listen. *You listening to me?"* and before the vet could respond Crane pimp slapped him again only holding him up against the door so he wouldn't fall. "I'm sorry Duffy put you in this shit, but you're in it. We all are. And you're the only chance we got to get out alive! You understand me? You're the only chance we got! So don't punk out on me. You pull yourself together, go down there and do exactly what I told you. You hear me?"

Dr. Kruger shook his head violently in agreement.

"Good," said Crane. He turned off the light, opened the door, followed the ashen-faced vet into the bedroom.

As he crossed Melissa's shadow she said fearfully, "Daddy ...?"

The vet started to turn around but Crane pushed him forward and said, "Daddy's gonna be fine. But start packin' for a long trip. You too, Trixie."

Trixie said, "Crane ...?"

"Stay up here. Both of you," Crane said, voice disappearing down the stairs behind the vet. "No matter what happens, don't leave this room!"

Dr. Kruger opened the office door nervously, saw two angry Mexicans on the other side of the security gate, one holding a cat.

"What took you so long? The cat is sick!" the younger one in the thuggish-ruggish outfit said, hand trying the door handle, waiting for it to be released.

Dr. Kruger faked a yawn as he'd been instructed and looked at his watch. The older Mexican tried the door and demanded harshly, "Open it."

Dr. Kruger said, "What's wrong with the cat?"

"Just sick," the younger one said. "Won't eat—?"

"Shits all the time," said the older Mexican, still trying the door handle.

Dr. Kruger pointed to another door and said, "Meet me over there." He closed the office door, headed out through the examination room and, on his way, unscrewed three lights as he'd been instructed. His heart was pounding, his breath short, his mouth so dry he wondered if he could talk.

He opened the thick padded soundproof door to the hospital and walked into a small zoo. Filled with wire cages of every size, the room was lit softly from above by low hanging fluorescent bulbs and the animals, now disturbed from sleep, began an orchestra of deafening howls, barks, hisses, chirps and meows.

He walked over to a padded side door, drew back a heavy locking bolt and swung the door open. His impatient angry cat owners were waiting at the security gate. With apprehension he was sure covered his face, he unlocked the deadbolt and swung the security gate open so they could enter.

The older one came in first, his right arm hanging down as if limp. The thuggish-ruggish one followed, thrust the cat into the vet's hands and waited until he'd closed the door. It was clear they weren't prepared for the noise. Dr. Kruger put the cat on a nearby table and began to examine it. It was an alley cat. A plain, healthy alley cat. Just as Crane had predicted.

"How long has it been sick?" Dr. Kruger asked, not looking at them.

"A week," the thuggish-ruggish one lied. He noticed the door to the examining room, motioned to his older partner with a silent nod. "Where's that lead to?" he asked.

Dr. Kruger turned to look at them for the first time, saw the younger one pointing to the door. "Another examining room," he said, returning attention to the cat.

"Nice place you got here," said the older man. "Mind if we look around?"

"No," said the vet apprehensively, "I don't mind. Cat had its shots?"

They chatted in Spanish. "No," said the younger one, hand on the doorknob, turning it cautiously. "No shots I know of."

Inside the examining room Crane watched the door swing open, saw two silhouettes fill the space, a hand trying the light switch, the other holding a pistol. He saw the silhouette of a shotgun come out from under the trenchcoat.

"HEY, ESÉ!" Crane shouted from hidden shadows, saw the pistol rise up, the shotgun swing out.

Crane's heavy .357 roared out of the darkness, put five rounds into the door space, saw both stagger back under the force of impact, crash together into a wall of cages and drop to the floor in a bloody heap. The sound of the .357 was nothing compared to the panic cries of terrified animals pacing, fluttering and jumping around their cages.

Crane rushed in to fire more rounds, saw it wasn't necessary. The thuggish-ruggish Mexican had taken three rounds in the chest, was in his last stages of sucking breath. The older man caught a round in his neck that turned his carotid artery into a loose cannon, and one through his left eye that took off the back of his skull.

Having dropped to the floor at the sound of gunfire as instructed, Crane found Dr. Kruger in a tight ball under the table, hands covering his head, shaking violently in fear, his pants wet.

"You alright, doc?" Crane asked, pulling the shaken vet to his feet.

Dr. Kruger stared blankly at the two corpses, fought the urge to vomit.

"Sobering, isn't it?" said Crane. "Ain't nothin' like in the movies. You played it off great, doc. Saved our lives. But we ain't got much time to celebrate. They got friends know they're here. Gotta make it appear you weren't home … away on vacation when they came by. Get me a mop and bucket of soapy water … clean up all the blood, put the place back in order. We'll dump these guys in the Bronco, take 'em out to LAX and leave 'em in some long term parking lot—Won't be safe for you to come back for a long time though," Crane added.

"What's a long time?" Dr. Kruger wanted to know.

Crane said about six months. The vet thought Crane was kidding, said he was crazy when he realized he wasn't. He had professional responsibilities. He couldn't leave the animals unattended. Crane suggested he call the Humane Society. Dr. Kruger said if he decided to go along with the six months he'd have no other choice. But said he'd have to think about it.

The pagers going off on the two corpses helped make up his mind. And Melissa. She said she wasn't going to wait around for him to get killed. If he stayed, he'd stay by himself. The vet remembered *Debbie Does Dallas* and decided the real thing was infinitely better. He told Crane he'd need time to pull together some cash for them to live on. Crane said there was no time, got cash from the van and gave the vet two hundred and fifty grand. Dr. Kruger called the Crown Plaza Hotel at LAX and reserved a room, told Melissa they'd make flight reservations for Rio in the morning. Melissa called him 'daddy' and said six months in Rio would be a good vacation.

Ten minutes later the four of them were southbound on the 405 in three vehicles headed for LAX. Crane was leading in the Bronco, the dead Mexicans covered by a blanket in the back. Melissa, with Trixie as passenger, followed in Dr. Kruger's cream colored Benz 500 S, Dr. Kruger bringing up the rear in the van. Dr. Kruger wasn't happy about leaving his toy in a parking lot for six months. He was even more disconcerted at having to abandon his sick animals, although he guessed the Humane Society would see to their welfare under the circumstances. Crane said the only thing that would happen to the Benz 500 S would be a layer dirt and a dead battery.

It was nearly midnight when the caravan pulled into LOT C on 98th Street behind the Crown Plaza Hotel. Crane parked the Bronco in a far corner of the lot crowded with cars, suggested Melissa and the vet park the Benz and van closer to the shuttle terminal if they could find a spot. After they'd parked and unloaded hastily packed bags, Crane and Trixie accompanied them on the long walk through November's cool night air to the Crown Plaza's entrance.

Trixie suddenly remembered her purse she left in the Benz, asked

Crane to get it as she'd been instructed. When he got to the Benz and retrieved the purse he'd told her to leave, Crane switched the keys and alarm remote with those of the Lexus. Dr. Kruger wouldn't need the Benz for six months. But Crane would. If the thin, pitiful plan he was formulating worked—and he had to admit his chances of surviving this were remote at best—he'd return to the lot and retrieve the Benz, make it a part of his new identity for six months, have it back at the lot just before Dr. Kruger's return. *If* he survived.

If he didn't, Dr. Kruger would need the Auto Club and a car wash when he returned.

Melissa cried. Trixie cried. They hugged. Dr. Kruger said he still didn't like the idea of being away for six months. Crane said it was necessary, but Carnival and Melissa's never ending presence would help make it bearable. Dr. Kruger smiled at the thought of Melissa doing her rendition of Debbie on Ipanema beach, implored Crane and Trixie to join them, badgered Crane for a reason why they couldn't. Crane knew the vet still hadn't seen the flyer, knew they'd be relatively safe as long as he didn't. He knew too he'd freak out if he did, become panicky and unstable and blow it for everyone. Maybe even rat them out for the five million, buy Melissa her own shopping mall. Crane explained he and Trixie were wanted by some very dangerous people. He couldn't give them any details because the less they knew the safer he and Melissa would be. Melissa said she was a firm believer in her personal safety, was sorry they couldn't have met under different circumstances.

They said their final goodbyes under the screaming belly of a 757 passing overhead. More tears. Hugs. A handshake. And then they were gone.

"It's just you and me, Trixie," Crane said as his one arm manhandled the van east on Century Boulevard just beyond the 405 underpass headed for Uncle Joe's, hoping no one would spot the van, recognize him from the flyer. He turned on the radio, the silky smooth voice of Luther Vandross crooning '*Superstar.*' "Still time to get out," he said after several blocks of fast moving traffic. "They're looking for *me*, not you. You want, I'll give you as much money as you can carry, take you back ...?"

Trixie laughed, shook her head. She said to Crane, "Can't get rid of me that easy. Gotta protect my investment."

"Investment?"

"You got a pint of my blood in your veins, remember?"

Familiar images of Marjorie flashed before him, dissolved more quickly than before. His sense of guilt beginning to fade, Crane grunted appreciatively and said, "Can't promise you a long future."

"How much time you figure we've got?" Trixie asked.

Crane thought about it over Luther's falsetto whisper voice, realized his plan would have to be modified for two and wasn't sure it could.

"Few days. Week maybe," he said to Trixie after a moment, not telling her the flyer meant it could be even less, that he was being hunted down like an escaped animal from a zoo.

Trixie didn't answer for a long time. She hummed along softly with Luther and stared out of the window at passing cars, thinking about the future. Luther segued into the melodic, lilting rhythm of Bob Marley taking them to Jamaica with '*No Woman No Cry.*' When Trixie finally spoke it was in the manner of a last request from a death row inmate.

"Get me pregnant, Crane—please?" she suddenly blurted out as they passed Hollywood Park. "I'm not using anything now and if I'm gonna die in a week I wanna be pregnant. Try. Please?"

Crane hadn't realized Trixie was so fatalistic, but figured she had a right to be.

"Now what man in his right mind would refuse a request like that?" Crane said, imagining himself with long flowing dreadlocks, walking the beaches of Jamaica with Trixie, waves licking at their feet, ocean spray in their faces.

In the passing shadows of amber street lights, river of red flashing turn signals and pulsating rhythms of Bob Marley, Trixie's powder-blue eyes still sparkled even when brimming with tears. She took Crane's hand in hers and smiled.

"Yes. What man—?"

Chapter 17

THE IDEA CAME TO HIM IN THE WAKE of his fourth orgasm as Trixie, careful to avoid touching his shoulder, rolled off Crane, exhausted and spent. Fractured rays of early morning sunlight broke through unpatched tears in Uncle Joe's age-old window shades filling the tiny bedroom with bursts of lasers. And as always when Crane was under pressure, the solutions to problems had somehow seeded from movie images that flashed constantly across the screen of his mind. It was not a complete solution as yet. But as the passion of their moment receded, Trixie's arms and legs stretching out alongside his own, Crane could see the plan's potential in greater depth. It was risky, of course. But with so little time left to them he saw it as the only real chance for escape they might have. And so, dozing on and off for the rest of the morning in the languid embrace of blonde hair, freckles and a stream of seemingly endless orgasms, he turned the plan over and over in his mind developing, refining, changing, discarding, and polishing it until he felt it was workable. Only then, in the final minutes of the morning, did he present it to Trixie.

"So," he said when finished. "What do you think?"

She didn't answer right away. She was lying on her back, head resting on a carpet of blonde hair that covered the pillow, powder-blue eyes transfixed on a chipped and faded ceiling. Momentarily she sat up, back against the headboard, rays of light slashing across pale freckles in three places, their shafts filled with billowing clouds of dust from movement of the bedspread. She reached over Crane to the only nightstand, grabbed a joint from her purse and lit it, filling the air with *stress*. She passed it to Crane, pulled her legs up to her chest and wrapped arms around her knees.

"Long as you drive that van, you'll be a target?" Trixie said after a while.

Crane said, "I'll dump it on the streets after dark, take Uncle Joe's truck."

Trixie nodded, seemed to look through and past Crane, thinking, trying to organize her thoughts in the haze of desperation building around them.

"Whatever you may think of me, Crane—" she began, taking a drag on the joint, passing it back, "—trailer park trash, whore, hooker, addict … whatever," she went on openly, for she had no illusions about herself or how people saw her. "I'm here with you 'cause I want to be," she said honestly. "And if we die tonight, or tomorrow, or the day after … I want you to know that last night with you—" she stopped a moment and looked away, recalling her meeting Uncle Joe for the first time and the instant acceptance she felt from him. Envying the warmth and unconditional love he had for Crane, the sense of family that bonded them together in the way it had never happened to her back in the trailer park, she wondered for an instant what her life would have been like if it had. But only for an instant. "—If we only have one day or three days left together," she went on fatalistically, "then it's my destiny and my choice and I'm down for whatever happens. I want you to know that."

Crane didn't answer. As a sign of his appreciation and growing affection he raised his hand, let the back of his fingers gently grace her thigh for an instant then fall back to the sheet.

◆◆◆◆

It was noon when Princess brought Duffy's Regal to the curb in front of the Twin Towers, waited for him to show. When she finally saw him limping toward the car she hardly recognized him … his lips swollen, face bruised and cut, eyes blackened and his left arm locked in a massive L-shaped upper body cast made firm by a metal bar running from his wrist to the center of his chest. She let the weight of the passenger door swing open as he maneuvered the heavy cast through the door and closed it.

"FUCK!" Princess said pulling the Regal away from the curb and into traffic, frowning under a row of blonde bangs, flashing gold incisor. "Five-O do that?"

Duffy lied and said they did.

"Ought to get you Johnnie Cochran and sue they muthafuckin'

asses!" Princess said. "What kinda case you catch … impound your car and shit? Cost me twelve hunnert dollars for yo bail and three to get yo car out? And them bullet holes in the trunk? What you get yo'self into?"

Duffy lied again, made up another story. In truth, when the cops had stopped him that night it was on a hummer. He was driving without taillights, knocked out apparently by some of the rounds fired by the Mexicans. They didn't believe his story about being assaulted by robbers. So they ran a make on the car, found twelve hundred dollars' worth of tickets that had gone to warrants and arrested him. They took him to the jail ward of County U.S.C. Hospital first to get his arm set. A day later, after he'd recovered from the anesthetic, he'd tried calling Dr. Kruger but got nothing but an answering machine. So he'd called Princess, told her to bring him money for bail and his car.

"You check out the vet like I told you?" Duffy asked.

Princess said, "Yeah. But ain't nobody home. Bunch of white people from the animal shelter there, said the vet was away on a long vacation. Didn't say where. They moving all the animals out … put 'em to sleep if nobody claims 'em?"

"That muthafucka," Duffy spit out angrily. "What about the motel—you get the key to his room?"

Princess said, "Yeah. Ain't nothin' there. Antonio packed up all his shit and put it in the office. I tried to get it like you said but Antonio start talkin' crazy and shit, sayin' I don't need to know what's in it and why I wanna know? I just told him might be some clothes I could sell if he ain't never coming back. Antonio said he wasn't never comin' back an' I shouldn't be worrying about his shit. So I left it alone."

"It still in the office?" Duffy wanted to know.

Princess said it was.

"Will Jimmy give it to you?" Duffy asked. Jimmy was the elderly black man who was the day manager of the *Hardcore*. He had a thing for some of the Figueroa hookers but most of them just shined him on because he was old, ugly and senile.

Princess said, "That old school nigga—? Yeah ... if I suck his dick!"

"Do what you gotta do then, but I need to see his bag. Know what I'm sayin'?"

Princess said, "What's so important about a suitcase I gotta suck a muthafucka's dick?"

"Nigga owes me some money, that's what's so important."

Princess frowned and said, "What about my fifteen hunnert dollars? That's what's important to me! How I get it back?"

Duffy said coldly, "Way you always get yo' money—get yo' blonde, wig-wearing gold tooth black ass out on the street and turn some tricks! Now stop all this drama and get me that punk-ass nigga's bag!"

An hour later Duffy was going through Crane's bag in the penthouse. Princess sat on the edge of the bed smoking a *primo*, watching TV, Oprah interviewing a woman who was psychic, predicting the next terrorist attack on America would be with nuclear weapons, Princess hoping she'd predict something about Oprah and Steadman.

Nothing in the bag but clothes, a brown manila envelope with photographs of the Duchess, Crane's hand-drawn sketches of the interior and a dog-eared paperback copy of Jim Thompson's *The Getaway*. No plane or bus tickets, no address book, no business cards, no scraps of paper with dates, times or scribbled phone numbers. No clue to Crane's plan or where he was. Nothing. Absolutely nothing. Just a brochure about Washington Memorial Cemetery ...

◆◆◆◆

It was ten o'clock Monday night when Trixie's cab pulled off the 405 Freeway at Sunset and pulled to a stop in front of Brentwood's Holiday Inn. She paid the driver, found the ladies room on the 4th floor and settled in for a makeup session. She swiped on lipstick, blusher and eyeliner, flicked lint off Guess hotpants and stood erect to check her cleavage under the DKNY tanktop. She sprayed on Fendi perfume and carefully adjusted the wig of flaming red hair whose curls fell to her shoulders. Once satisfied with her look, she sucked up the last lines of cocaine from her compact mirror, picked up the SONY boombox and left for the elevators and the performance of her life … literally.

She knocked on the door to 1412 and when it opened stepped into the second Mexican revolution that suddenly fell silent. Sporting tattoos and cold hard stares, some seven to ten soldiers of the Mexican Mafia and half as many blacks were either seated or standing around the suite. She stopped when she reached the center of the room.

"Who's Moffett?" she asked.

A bedroom door suddenly opened and a tall, robust, impeccably dressed white man in his late fifties Trixie instinctively knew was Moffett strode in like he was a king. He was followed closely by a grossly overweight, slightly younger white man. That would be the guard Needham Crane said might come. Moffett stuck out his hand and said, "Miss Lee … yes? I'm Warden Moffett."

The booming baritone voice startled her. It was like injecting cyanide into a nest of rats it was so commanding and lethal. Still holding her hand he led her to a nearby couch that quickly emptied without request.

"So. You know our Mister Crane," Moffett said sitting down first, waiting for Trixie to join him and appraising her look but not seemingly too overwhelmed. "May I ask how?"

Trixie dropped down next to Moffett, crossed her legs and leaned back in the comfort of the couch. She pulled out a joint from her purse, lit it, offered Moffett a hit. He declined with a nod.

"Friend of a friend," said Trixie, exhaling, voice tweaking high from the *stress.* "I'm here for the reward ... get myself paid—" She reached back in her purse, pulled out the 'wanted' flyer with Crane's picture on it and handed it to Moffett. "—just like it says here."

Moffett said suspiciously, "And why should I believe you?"

Trixie reached in her purse for the third time in as many minutes, pulled out a folded sheet of paper with names, dates and cities Crane had copied from the money stacks.

"This proof enough?" she asked handing it to Moffett.

Moffett stared at the list in amazement, trying not to look concerned. But he was. He said, "Just names. Anyone could've written these ... school children practicing their penmanship—?"

Poker time. Trixie said, "Let's see if the Justice Department agrees with you, why don't we—?"

Moffett was five years from retirement, decided his best move was to fold. He glanced around the room, shrugged his shoulders and said, "All right, Miss Lee—it's your call ... for now. If you know where our Mister Crane is, suppose you take us to him? Of course if you can't—?" Moffett didn't have to make the threat.

As he started to get up Trixie grabbed his arm, pulled him back down.

"What about my money?" Trixie said.

Moffett smiled. He snapped his fingers. A Mexican, who looked more white than Mexican, with perfectly straight teeth produced an attaché case he placed in Moffett's hands. Moffett snapped the locks, opened it, spun it around to Trixie like a *lazy susan*.

"There's two point five million in cash here," Moffett said. "You get the other half when we find Crane." It wasn't an offer open to negotiation.

"There's something else," Trixie said, sliding the attaché case from Moffett's lap to hers.

Moffett frowned. He said, "And that is?"

She explained her demand in detail and when she finished Moffett's frown faded to a smile and said, "How could I refuse?"

"Someone else once told me that."

Trixie closed the attaché case and stood. She said, "Gotta stop by the Front Desk first," she said holding up the attaché case. "Put this in the safe. No sense dragging this along where we're going."

Moffett said, "Is it far, where we're going?"

Trixie said, "Not as far as Marion."

Moffett's caravan included the Lincoln Town Car limousine in which he was seated with Trixie and Needham. The driver was Mexican. Loaded with M & M soldiers, a Chevy Yukon and Dodge Ram followed a car length apart. From Brentwood they followed a checkerboard of L.A. freeways into Compton's dangerous nighttime streets. In the limo Trixie sat between Moffett and Needham, the SONY boombox on her lap playing a Nirvana CD.

Moffett said, "Do we really have to listen to that?"

Trixie turned off the CD and said, "Tell the driver to exit at Central."

Moffett tapped the glass partition, waited for it to drop, spoke to the driver.

When the glass was up he asked Trixie, "Crane armed?"

"Wouldn't you be if the whole country was looking for you?"

Moffett just grunted. He said to Trixie, "I just don't want any surprises, Miss Lee. I want to be very clear about that!"

Trixie said, "Makes two of us, Mister Moffett. Just make sure you've got the rest of my money when we get back."

Moffett reminded himself she wasn't coming back, list or no list. But then, looking at Trixie's chest, catching a whiff of her perfume, thought bringing her back might be fun for a minute. But only for a minute.

It was midnight when the caravan arrived at Washington Memorial Cemetery, parked and cut off their lights just inside the gates. Several soldiers from the Yukon approached the limo, waited for Moffett to lower the window.

To them Moffett said, "We'll let the girl go in first—" To Trixie he said, "Show and tell, Miss Lee. Needham, let Miss Lee out."

Needham opened the door and got out.

As Trixie started to slide out Moffett grabbed her arm, his booming voice threatening, "No surprises, Miss Lee—?"

Trixie said to Moffett, "I want to live as long as you, Mr. Moffett."

Moffett said, "Just keep that in mind, Miss Lee. Now go."

Trixie placed the boombox on the seat as she slid out saying, "He's in the mausoleum at the far end. Can I leave this here till we get back?"

Moffett cut his eyes and sighed. "It'll be quite safe, Miss Lee. Just go. And remember," he added threatening, "They'll be right behind you every step of the way."

Trixie didn't answer. She just turned and began hiking across the wet grass toward the mausoleum.

"Crane, baby?" Trixie called out as she stepped into the blackness of the mausoleum, feeling her way, knowing several yards behind a small army followed.

A flashlight blinded her. Behind the light Crane's voice said, "That you, Doris?"

"It's me, baby." Trixie followed the light to Crane, embraced him tightly, whispering in his ear. "They're outside. About ten. Moffett. And that Needham guy too—"

Suddenly the mausoleum flooded with beams of light, filled with the sounds of slide action pistols, shuffling of many shoes over the hard stone floor. Their embrace was lit from head to toe. His right hand held the flashlight, his left the .357.

"Drop the gun, miyaté," said the Mexican Trixie recognized as the one who looked more white than Mexican and had pretty teeth. Stepping back from Trixie's embrace, face registering shock and disbelief, he let the .357 fall to the floor. Another Mexican rushed to pick it up. The Mexican with the pretty teeth had a cell phone, punched in a number.

"It's okay. He's alone. You can bring them up." When he clicked off he said to Crane, "Where's our money, miyaté?"

Crane looked at Trixie and said sourly, *"YOU, Doris?"*

The sound of rubber sliding to a stop over gravel, doors slamming, shuffling of more shoes filled the room. But nothing like Moffett's voice.

"Well, well, well … Mister Crane. I was wondering if I'd ever see you again … alive, that is?"

"You double crossed me, Moffett, you faggot muthafucka! I got your trunk just like I said I would. We had a deal!"

"We never had anything, Crane," Moffett said, his face half-lit in shadows of flashlights. "Remember I said *IF* we let you out you no longer existed. I meant that. You had a few weeks of freedom. Even got your dick sucked a few times from what I hear. Fair exchange is no robbery. But did you really think I'd let you walk free knowing what you know? You honestly believed that?"

Crane looked at Trixie. "What kind of deal you cut with this bitch, Moffett—head job and a dime bag of *chronic*?" Crane tried to sound hard and bitter, wondered if he came across that way, if the rehearsals with Trixie had helped.

"Where's the trunk, Crane?"

Crane said, "Fuck you, faggot!"

Needham's meaty fist came out of nowhere, smashing into Crane's face with the force of a sledgehammer, sending Crane back against the stone wall, blood pouring from a split lip. It was all Trixie could do to maintain her composure.

Needham said, "No, Crane. Fuck you," and he hit Crane a second time, and a third, dropping him to the stone floor semi-dazed, spitting up blood and pieces of his new bridge. He tried to cover himself, to protect his shoulder, pulling himself into a tight ball. He'd experienced Needham's fury before, knew what was coming next. Needham's boot plowed into his side, found ribs to crack. Crane cried out in pain but not like he did when

Needham's boot found the shoulder. Crane thought he'd pass out, hoped the wound hadn't begun to bleed again, that the pillow he'd stuffed inside his shirt would protect it, but now wasn't so sure.

Trixie wanted to turn away at the brutality, to run outside screaming. But that wasn't the plan. She couldn't. Crane had warned her it would go down like this and she had to bear it, had to look unconcerned, almost enjoying it. Anything else would give them away, would doom them both.

Needham's boot found more ribs to break. Crane didn't think he could take any more, started vomiting.

"That's enough, Needham," boomed Moffett, walking over to Crane's broken body, kneeling beside him. "That right, Crane—you ready to tell us where the money is?"

Crane nodded yes. Moffett stood up. He said, "Good," motioned with his hand and two Mexicans helped Crane to his feet.

Crane made an attempt to point through the pain of a broken collar bone, throbbing shoulder wound, mumbled through split lips and said, "Money's there … casket—one with my name on it."

Moffett waved his hand again. Several Mexicans began searching the crypt, located Crane's name, began sliding the heavy casket out of its niche and lowering it to the stone floor. The top opened without effort. An unsanctioned burst of laughter erupted in the mausoleum as they saw the money, plowed down to the bottom of the casket to make sure it was all there, lowered the top.

Six soldiers picked the casket up and followed Needham outside. Four remained with Moffett.

"You got your money, Moffett," Crane said as planned. "Get the fuck out and leave me alone, why don't you. I can't hurt you."

"True," Moffett said. "You can't hurt me. But it's the principle, Crane. You know that. It's not really personal at all. In fact, for what it's worth, I always liked you. Still have your model of the prison on display in my office. But I can't let people see me as being soft on crime. You can understand the position I'm in, can't you, Crane?"

Crane could hardly stand. His ribs felt like they were on fire, his shoulder wound throbbed with the kind of pain he'd never experienced before.

"Well go on then," Crane shouted pitifully. "You gonna kill me, kill me! Get it over with!"

"Not me," Moffett said, beginning to laugh. "I'm not going to kill you, Crane. She is—!" and he motioned to Trixie with a nod of his head.

Crane seemed not to understand. He said, "What? What the fuck you talking about—?"

Moffett grabbed a 9mm from one of the Mexicans and offered it to Trixie.

Crane's eyes opened wide in shock. "Doris?" he said in disbelief, hoping his disbelief and shock sounded genuine. "You ...?"

Trixie refused Moffett's gun. Instead she reached in her purse and pulled out a .38, pointed it at Crane. She said, "You dirty motherfucker. After all I've done for you—I didn't deserve that. No one deserves being treated like that, I don't care what you think happened!"

Crane was nearly unconscious. With what little strength he could muster he managed to stay with it, saying, "Wha—? What are you talkin' about, Doris ...?"

"My mother wasn't much," Trixie said the way they'd rehearsed it, drawing on truth. "But she gave me one piece of advice I should've followed—She told me to never get involved with niggers!" she said, again drawing on truth.

Crane looked at Trixie incredulously. He said, "You stupid white bitch. If he double crossed me, what do you think he'll do to you?"

Trixie pulled the trigger five times in rapid succession. The rounds hit Crane's body with such force they spun him around before he slumped to the floor, blood pouring from wounds in his chest and his back. "I told you about calling me a bitch—!"

Trixie stopped firing, threw the .38 on top of Crane's lifeless form, turned to Moffett and the waiting Mexicans. She said, "Can we go now?"

It took a moment for Moffett to recover. When he did he said, "Absolutely. Our business here is finished."

With the casket and it's compliment of soldiers loaded into the Dodge Ram Van, remaining soldiers in the Chevy Yukon in the lead, the caravan moved slowly down the gravel road toward the gate.

In the immediate silence of the limo, Moffett asked Trixie, "If I may ask, what exactly did Crane do to you?"

Trixie picked up the boombox, started the Nirvana CD again.

"You don't want to know," Trixie said as the caravan approached the gate. She suddenly grabbed her crotch, began squirming on the seat between Moffett and Needham. "I gotta go pee," she said with urgency.

"NOW?" Moffett said. "Can't you hold it till the hotel?"

"Got a weak bladder. I don't go now, this limo's a toilet."

Moffett tapped the partition window and when it dropped told the driver to stop just inside the gate. Trixie jumped out and trotted across the grass, disappearing in the blackness of the cemetery. Moffett couldn't wait to turn off the boombox, dialed a number on his cell phone.

"We have the money," he said. "Crane? He's dead. Oh yes, quite sure. The girl's with us, yes." Moffett waited. "All right," he said finally, a sense of regret in his voice. "I'll see to it personally and—"

The C-4 in the boombox suddenly exploded with a deafening roar. It was like a shuttle blastoff. The limousine disintegrated into the sum of its parts—doors, wheels, seats, engine spiraling hundreds of yards into the air as a plume of bright yellow flame billowed up into the night sky. What was left of the limo split in half before it hit the ground amidst a shower of flaming metal.

Five seconds later, triggered by the transmitter in the boombox, the wireless fuse detonated the C-4 in the false bottom of the casket with a force ten times greater than its predecessor, disintegrating the Dodge Ram Van some thirty yards ahead and sending a blinding yellow seventy-five million dollar fireball rocketing even higher into the night than its cousin.

Terrified, the soldiers in the Chevy Yukon suddenly bolted from the van in all directions not knowing if it was next. Once secure behind a row of parked cars, the driver placed a panic call on his cell phone. In rapid Spanish he reported the miyaté must have planted bombs in the limousine and Ram Van. Both were destroyed. No survivors. The money ...? The money was gone. All of it was gone. Everything was gone.

Their soldiers. Only four alive. The others ... Mister Moffett ... Needham ... the miyaté Crane, the girl ... gone. Dead. All dead!

Trixie reached the safety of the mausoleum just as fragments of burning metal rained down on the cemetery. Feeling her way blindly along marble walls, crawling on hands and knees across the cold stone floor the last few feet groping for the flashlight, its beam found Crane sitting up against the stone wall holding his side. The white shirt he was wearing had been ripped off, the bloodbags Trixie purchased from a movie prop house all disintegrated.

"Crane," Trixie cried out, helping him to his feet. "Oh, baby, I know you're hurt. You don't know how hard it was for me to just stand there and watch that fat mother-fucker beat on you like that. But it worked, baby," Trixie said, her voice a mixture of relief and admiration. "Just like you said."

Crane grunted in agreement, struggled into his jacket. He said, "Yeah. Guess it did. Broke the hell out my ribs. Collarbone too. Shoulder hurts like a muthafucka. But I'm alive."

"NOT FOR LONG, you player-hatin' chickenshit muthafucka!"

The beam from Trixie's flashlight spun around in an arc, fell across Duffy's massive plaster cast six feet away, the tiny dread-covered head balanced on top like the movable clown from Jack-In-The-Box. Only this clown was holding a 9mm.

"DUFFY?" Trixie cried out in amazement for the two of them. "We thought you were dead? You never came back? Never called? What happened?" and not appreciating the danger they were in, perhaps because she still cared in some way, walked unafraid behind the flashlight beam over to where he was standing for a closer look at the strange cast that imprisoned half his body. Duffy didn't move as she approached, didn't try to stop her inspection of the cast. He just stood there, slowly weaving back and forth in a stupor of booze and *chronic* ... and vengeance.

"Like you really cared," Duffy spit out angrily, words thick and slow. "That my money out there went up in smoke?"

"Wasn't never yours, Duffy," Crane mumbled painfully through a split lip, pieces of bridge. "Told you that from the get go."

Duffy said, "Nigga, you ain't told me shit! You too muthafuckin' busy goin' behind my back gettin' yo' dick sucked and player-hatin' on my woman here to think anything about me?" Duffy's words may have been thick and slurred, but the hurt of betrayal still clung to their edges.

And with a brain lit up on booze and *chronic*, a 9mm in his hand, he was dangerous. "But I told you what was gonna happen when this was over, didn't I?"

Crane said in desperation, "You don't have to do this, dog—?"

Duffy said, "Shhiit! Nigga, please. You and this white bitch here gonna get what's comin' to you, know what I'm sayin'?"

Still not appreciating Duffy's lethal stance, Trixie abandoned caution a second time. Perhaps still pissed at Crane for having called her that without warning in front of Moffett just so she'd be angry enough to shoot him, angry too because he'd realized she might not be able to go through with it if he didn't.

She shouted at Duffy, *"BITCH?* What did I say about calling me a bitch, motherfucker?" and without thinking she brought the end of the flashlight crashing hard into the side of his head with such force it flew out of her hand, bounced against the wall, fell to the floor and flickered out.

Almost immediately there was the sound of struggling, the loud thud of heavy plaster striking the floor, hands and fists striking flesh, the grunts and groans of pain, coughing and choking sounds and gasping for breaths, scuffling sounds of shoes and the pounding of limbs against the stone floor, scraping of flesh against cement.

The deafening explosions of a 9mm suddenly filled the mausoleum. Burnt orange muzzle blasts flickered in the darkness.

"UGHHH!"

Dead silence. No movement.

Momentarily there was a light tapping of metal against the stone floor. The flashlight beam flickered on weakly through a cracked lens, went off, came back on dimly, moved across the stone floor to Duffy's lifeless form lying on his back, eyes bulging wide in shock, mouth open with the scream still caught in his throat, arm sticking up in the plaster cast like Frankenstein, blood seeping from wounds in the tiny head like holes in a salt shaker.

Trixie stood up slowly, moved the beam past Duffy, saw Crane lying motionless on his side, right arm limp on the stone floor, hand still holding the 9mm, sliver of white smoke drifting up from the barrel. She approached with great apprehension, stood over him for a moment, too afraid to move or speak. She reached down and touched his shoulder.

"That's my bad arm," Crane grunted in pain, exhausted and spent. With great effort he rolled over on his back, tried to sit up, gave it up because of the pain and fell back. "Damn. Everything hurts."

Trixie broke into tears, knelt down beside him, put her arms under his shoulders, helped Crane to his feet.

"That was a stupid thing you did," fussed Crane. "He could've shot you."

Trixie laughed through her tears. She said to Crane, "Just did what I had to do ... protecting my investment. Let's get out of here."

Crane tried to bend down, winced at the pain and stood back up. "You'll have to do it ... go through Duffy's pockets, get his ID."

"What for?"

"Wouldn't want the esé's reading Duffy's name in the obituary column—put two and two together, figure I'm still alive."

"Jesus, Crane, he's ... he's ... " Trixie stammered, struggling with the fading memories of their time together. "I don't know if I can do this, Crane," she said, dreading the task but knowing it was on her, that Crane's reasoning was right, covering their tracks the only chance for them to be together. "Touching his corpse. It's so ... so ... icky." Bracing Crane's battered frame against the wall she bent down and touched

Duffy's body cast with the tips of her fingers, immediately snapped them back as if touching a hot stove, turned away and vomited. "Oh God, Crane ... can't do this. I can't do this ..."

Crane said, "Yes you can. Close your eyes if you have to, but do it."

Trixie didn't close her eyes. What she did was turn off the flashlight, grabbed hold of Duffy's Frankenstein arm and rolled him over on his side. Feeling her way in the dark, Duffy's baggy pants with zipper pockets gave up a big wad of cash, bag of weed, pager, cell phone and his driver's license.

"Got everything?" Crane asked when the flashlight came back on.

"Everything but his soul. Let's get out of here. Place gives me the creeps."

Crane spit out the rest of his bridge and mumbled, "I need me some new teeth."

Trixie said, "Get 'em where ever we're going. Dr. Kruger's Benz is waiting for us at LAX, we've got two and a half million tax free bucks back at the hotel and a ranch to build. I wanna get as far away from this town as I can, as fast as I can."

Crane said, "That two and a half mil has to last us a lifetime, baby—"

Crane couldn't see it behind the dim beam of the flashlight, but Trixie's powder-blue eyes came alive with a flood of tears she made no effort to dry. Her face broke into a wide smile he didn't see, but he heard her say to him, "It had better. They say kids are expensive to raise and we're gonna have a slew of them—"

Crane stumbled out of the mausoleum on Trixie's arm, heard the distant wail of approaching police and fire trucks. They moved through frantic fast gathering crowds, circling around the remnants of flaming wrecks, past others grabbing wildly at flakes of burning money floating to the ground, trying desperately to stamp out flames. You could say they had money to burn.

It hurt to smile but he couldn't help it. For the first time in his life he had the American dream—Freedom. Absolute, unconditional freedom with no strings attached. No one was looking for him because Alonzo Crane no longer existed. A few weeks underground, give the image on the flyer time to fade from public view. Resurface with a new identity and new life. Moffett's words. The offer he never intended to keep.

Money. Big faces. More than he ever dreamed of. In the end he could see that Duffy had been right all along—whatever else there was in life, when it was all said and done, there was only money.

And Trixie.

In all his years he'd never imagined ending up with a white girl. Not after Marjorie's searing memory. He thought of OJ, wondered if Trixie was worth the gamble. Decided she was because she had his back. And if he'd learned nothing else in life he knew a woman who had her man's back was a woman you'd love forever. He finally understood, if he hadn't before, that Marjorie's lifelong hold on him was gone forever, that Trixie was his rib now. Her color shouldn't be an issue of course. But Crane knew it was. Knew that in America color would always be an issue. That even in a supposedly enlightened society, life with a white girl would be infinitely more dangerous than any heist he could ever plan. He would be on his own in uncharted territory. With no script to follow, no movie to guide him, he'd have to create his own roles, play them out very carefully, and avoid the minefields of hatred that lay in wait. Only the labels of whore and criminal made their involvement acceptable to society. And knowing too, if they ever abandoned those labels it would be disastrous for both. And in the way that Duffy had been right about money, so too was Trixie right about who and what they were.

Damaged goods.

THE END

EPILOGUE

The explosions at Washington Memorial Cemetery were reported on *CNN* before daybreak. The official line by the Department of Justice was that combined efforts of all law enforcement agencies had resulted in the breakup of an Al Qaeda terrorist cell in Los Angeles. The explosions were triggered by a firefight between terrorists and government agents who had intercepted the bomb-laden vehicles enroute to their intended target, most likely shipping interests at the Port of Long Beach or the nearby oil refinery. There were no survivors. The fact that a significant amount of money was known to have been destroyed in the inferno was proof, the officials said, that the government's freezing of terrorist's bank accounts was working. Osama bin Laden's terror network was now having to take greater risks in transporting its operating cash in and out of the country by other means.

There it was.

Blame it on the terrorists. Tentacles of the trunk reaching out beyond the criminal justice system. Everybody gets paid.

No mention of Moffett or Needham.

Expendable.

Not a peep about Duffy. A John Doe in the morgue. Fingerprints will eventually give him a name. Burial in potter's field.

Yesterday's news.

For the prison gangs still at Marion, a major setback. Judges, prosecutors, public defenders, wardens and DOJ officials still looking to get paid. No special privileges for prisoners until they do.

They'd send a clone to replace Moffett.

Business as usual. Another trunk. Another offer. Another sucker. Trade in your twenty-five-to-life for a steamer trunk and four weeks of freedom.

Crane who?

Canada. Living on ten acres of land in a ranchhouse he designed. Adjusted to the cold but has trouble with the language. Taking correspondence courses in architecture. Enjoys being a father.

Trixie.

Speaks French like a native. Hosts Tupperware parties. Volunteers at the local orphanage. Sings in the church choir. Waiting for the birth of her second child before taking the high school equivalency exam.

Brady Bunch existence.